WARRIOR

A NOLAN BASTARDS NOVEL

AMY OLLE

Editing: Jessica Snyder Edits
Cover Design: Michele Catalano Creative
Cover Photography: Regina Wamba
Cover Model: Anthony

ISBN: 978-1-944180-12-6

For the warriors.

~

Don't give up. Don't ever give up.

*Cancer can take away all my physical ability. It cannot touch my mind,
it cannot touch my heart, and it cannot touch my soul. And those three
things are going to carry on forever.*
— *Jim Valvano*

CHAPTER 1

MARCH

*I*n the crypt-quiet examination room, Cian Nolan stared straight ahead at the sterile white wall. Like an outlaw dragged finally before a judge, he awaited the final verdict.

A pensive scowl twisted Dr. Hoffman's grizzled features as he swiped his finger across the tablet's screen.

The stark, vivid mixture of terror and dread lashed at Cian, and he dragged in a slow, steadying breath full of dry air and the potent odor of antiseptic. He coughed.

Dr. Hoffman's gaze struck him like a laser beam. "How long have you had that cough?"

If he still experienced ordinary emotions, Cian might've been annoyed. "It was just a cough."

Dr. Hoffman made a sound, then returned his attention to the tablet. "Your labs look good. Great, actually. And you're sure you're feeling okay?"

"I feel fine." Cian hadn't stepped foot in the cage in over a year, but he felt like he'd had his ass kicked.

There was nothing unusual about that, though. Fatigue was his new normal.

"Your MRI was clear. Vitals are strong. Blood work looks good. Your cortisol levels are a little high…"

"I started training again."

"That's probably it." Dr. Hoffman regarded Cian with a frown. "Be careful not to overdo it."

"If I were any more careful, I'd be napping, not fighting."

Dr. Hoffman's rare smile materialized. "You're extremely fit, and I imagine you'll regain your strength quickly. But the chemo caused some slight weakening of the heart muscle, so be sure to take it slow. If you're lightheaded or experience any chest pains, rest immediately and call me."

"Don't worry, Doc. I'm retired." Cian rolled down the sleeve of his gray Henley. "Professional fighting isn't in my future. I have no plans for any marquee matches in Vegas. I'm just trying to get back into a routine."

Dr. Hoffman set aside the tablet. "I look forward to seeing you only when you need your nose reset."

"Ah, the good old days." The corners of Cian's mouth lifted. But he wasn't smiling. He hadn't smiled since this nightmare began.

"You did it. You beat this thing." A brief glimmer flashed in Dr. Hoffman's blue eyes. "You're cancer-free."

The tension that'd tightened every muscle in Cian's body eased from him, but he was too exhausted, too ravaged, to feel anything other than the relief of air filling his lungs.

While he may have won the battle for his life, he hadn't escaped unscathed. Not even close. Cancer had taken everything from him. His career, his fiancée, his peace of mind.

Dr. Hoffman sank down on the stool. "Before you go, we should probably talk about The F-Word."

A host of offensive words beginning with the letter F rattled around in Cian's brain. Fidelity. Faithfulness. Future.

He settled on the one that'd tormented him the most of late. "Family?"

Dr. Hoffman peered over the rim of his glasses and pinned Cian with a look. "Fertility. Your counts are low, which is not uncommon after chemo."

"Is it permanent?"

"Some men regain the ability to produce sperm after treatment, but it might take a year or longer. It may never happen." Dr. Hoffman held out a business card. "They're the best in the business. Give them a call when you're ready."

Cian pinched the card between his fingers and glanced down at the small print.

Chicago Center for Fertility.

He rolled his thumb across the raised lettering.

To make a kid, Cian needed a woman, and he wanted a woman about as much as he wanted another round of chemo.

The protective paper crinkled when he pushed off the exam table. "Just happy to be alive, Doc," he said, shrugging into his wool coat.

Anyone would be.

With the quickness of a pardoned convict, Cian beat a path to the door. "Follow up in six months?"

"You got it." Dr. Hoffman lifted his gaze from the tablet. "If that cough doesn't go away, come back and see me sooner."

Outside, a steady rain pummeled downtown Chicago, and Cian hovered a moment beneath the building's overhang. The business card was still perched between his fingers and, with a soft flick of the wrist, he flung it into the steel trash bin.

A shudder passed through him, and he hiked the collar of his coat to block out the chill spring air.

For a moment, he squinted through the veil of raindrops, then he asked, "What do you want?"

The broad-shouldered man leaning against the building's stone façade kept his gaze conspicuously averted. "Financial security. World peace. To know what the hell color tie I'm supposed to wear with a tweed suit coat."

Cian shoved both hands into his coat pockets. "Ties are for suckers."

A muscle along Kendrick's jawline ticked. "We got a situation."

"We?"

Kendrick risked a sidelong glance at Cian. "It's your brother and sister."

Cian bit down on a curse. "*Step*sister."

"Right. You know where they are?"

"I know." Cian's clipped tone conveyed the fact that he knew, and that there wasn't a chance in hell he would tell anyone.

Kendrick bobbed his head. "Good."

"Are you expecting trouble at the trial today?"

The heavy beat of Kendrick's hesitation thumped inside Cian's chest. "So you haven't heard?"

Beneath Cian's feet, the ground pitched. "Heard what?"

"The judge declared a mistrial."

A nasty curse shot from Cian. "Why the hell did he do that?"

"He didn't have a choice. One juror refused to convict. It was a hung jury."

Dread snaked through Cian, twisting through his gut and around his chest cavity. "One juror?"

"Just the one." Kendrick pulled a cell phone from his pocket. "Held out for four days against the others."

"Did the mob get to him?"

"We're looking into it." After a glance at the phone, Kendrick returned the device to his coat.

The ground rushed at Cian. "They'll try him again, won't they?"

"It's possible. But it'll take months. Years, more like. You know how it is."

Yeah, Cian knew. It'd taken more than a year to get this far, and that was with Cian's brother, Aiden, and his stepsister, Brynn, delivering all but the smoking gun on a silver platter to the DA.

"For now," Kendrick continued, "Moretti is a free man. He'll be back on the street in a matter of hours."

A string of curses fell from Cian's lips.

"That's not even the worst of it."

Cian turned and faced Kendrick directly then. "What's the worst of it?"

"We have reason to believe he'll go after Aiden and Brynn."

The words exploded inside Cian with the devastating irrevocability of a bomb.

"Fucking family," he muttered. "What do you need me to do?"

CIAN'S YOUNGER BROTHER, Rory, lurched to his feet. "You did *what?*"

"I said I would help." Cian slammed his fist into the bright red punching bag.

In front of the wall of windows overlooking the Chicago skyline, Aiden prowled back and forth like a caged animal. "That is the stupidest thing I've ever heard come out of your mouth."

"You were away for a long time." Cian stilled the swinging bag and shot his oldest brother a sly grin. "You missed a lot of the stupid things I've said."

"Why would you agree to do this?" Aiden's long strides chewed up the ground beneath his feet. "We gave the feds a shit ton of evidence and the bastard still walked. What makes you think the next time will be any different?"

Cian glared at the punching bag. But all he saw was his thirteen-year-old kid sister's ashen face when her dad was sentenced to three years in federal prison, and the shadows in both his brothers' eyes.

Then there was Brynn, who Moretti had used to bend her father to his will. Cian's gut wrenched to think about the assault she'd suffered at the hands of one of Moretti's dutiful soldiers. At least that evil bastard was now dead.

But all that pain and darkness. All because of one man.

"It might not be." With a quick sidestep, Cian kicked the bag, smacking his imaginary opponent on the head with the top of his foot.

"Then call Kendrick back." Rory shoved Cian's phone across the coffee table. "Tell him you changed your mind."

Cian hammered the punching bag with a round of furious kicks and blows. When his lungs ached from lack of air and his muscles trembled with fatigue, he twisted away from the swinging bag.

Breathing hard, he snatched his water bottle off the windowsill and squirted a steady stream of the cold liquid into his mouth. With a hard gulp, he swallowed, then gasped for more air.

Yet another workout cut short by exhaustion and weakness. He had no endurance anymore, and his hard will could not bring his broken body into line. He'd spent the past year trying to come to terms with who he was now—not a strong, able man, but a weak one.

Then suddenly, today, Kendrick gave him the chance to be something else. He didn't have to be weak anymore. Though he wouldn't be fit to step foot in an MMA cage anytime soon, he could still fight. He could be more than a burden to his family.

He could fight, and he could help them. Fighting is what he did. It's all he knew how to do.

He could be the one who, finally, brought down Manny Moretti.

Cian lifted the hem of his T-shirt to his forehead and wiped away the beads of sweat. "I'll not be callin' Agent Kendrick."

"So you're going to take on the mob?" Rory collapsed into the sofa cushions. "Miss getting the shit kicked out of you that much, do ya?"

Aiden came to an abrupt stop. "This isn't a professional fight. There are no rules. No refs. If you lose, you don't walk away."

Cian dropped his shirttail. "So I guess I won't lose."

"You have no idea what they're capable of." Rory's dark statement sucked the air out of the room.

"But you do?" Cian said in a low voice.

Dark clouds chased across Rory's sharp features.

Cian and Aiden waited, their silence an invitation.

Aiden pierced the unbroken quiet. "Are you ever going to tell us what happened?"

Rory gained his feet in a flash. "You know what happened. Moretti's goons jumped me. Kicked my ass. Broke my hand." He stalked to the kitchen. "I can't work, have no money, and had to move in with my brother who hates me." With the stiff fingers on his slightly misshapen hand, he grabbed the handle on the refrigerator door and yanked it open. "So I drink my meals and spend my days playing video games." When he kicked the door shut, he cradled a beer in one hand and twisted off the cap with the other. "There's nothing else to tell."

On tired legs, Cian staggered to an armchair and sank into the soft leather. "I don't hate you."

Rory pulled a long drink from the bottle, then he jerked the beer away and swallowed with an audible gulp. "Nothing happened between Corinne and I."

Cian gritted his teeth. "That's what you said."

"Because it's the truth."

"Whatever." Cian picked at the edge of the tape he'd wrapped around his knuckles. "We have bigger issues to discuss right now than my ex."

Aiden dropped into the armchair across from Cian. "What's the plan? How is a retired MMA fighter going to become a mob informant?"

"Actually, I've started training again."

One of Aiden's dark eyebrows lifted. "You're coming out of retirement?"

"I doubt I can get back in shape to make another serious run at the professional circuit." Cian tore away pieces of white tape. "But the gyms are crawling with Moretti's soldiers. He likes to hire the guys for his security and other thuggery. I figure I'll work my way into his inner circle, then blow them up from the inside."

"This is crazy." Rory marched back to the kitchen. "*You're* crazy."

"Moretti will never trust you." Aiden's shoulders were rigid with tension. "Not after Brynn and I ratted him out."

"I'm not just your brother. I'm Alan's stepson too." Cian dropped a curled length of tape onto the coffee table. "Who's to say I'm not as corrupt and mobbed up as dear ol' dad?"

A soft pop of air sounded when Rory opened another beer.

"How can we help?"

At Aiden's question, Rory choked on the swig of beer he'd just swallowed. "We? What makes you think I want anything to do with any of this?"

Cian picked at a corner of the tape roped around his other hand. "Maybe he thought that rather than sitting around here feeling sorry for yourself, you might want to fight back."

Rory's gaze snapped to Cian, his eyes suddenly alight with more fire and fury than at any time in the year since Moretti's goons had broken his hand. "You have no idea what you're talking about."

"You're right." Cian gave the tape a hard tug. "I don't know what I'm talking about because you won't tell me."

Wild rage swept across Rory's features. His body tensed, and for a moment, Cian thought he would explode and the truth would finally come bursting out of him with all the ferocious fury of a hound from hell.

But Rory didn't explode. Instead, the agonizing struggle to reign in his emotions played out on his features, until finally, he turned and walked slowly from the room. After a beat, the sound of his bedroom quietly easing shut reached them.

Into the silence, Cian said, "You need to get Brynn out of town."

"I will."

He gave Aiden a pointed look. "You need to go with her."

"I'm not leaving."

"You said it yourself. Moretti will never trust you. More likely, he'll come after you."

Aiden scowled hard at the coffee table's wood surface.

"There's nothing you can do here." Cian saw Aiden understood this truth.

But his brother was a stubborn ass, so they sat in silence while Aiden grappled unsuccessfully for an alternate ending. "There has to be something I can do…"

"Sorry, brother. This is my fight now."

With a curse, Aiden dropped his head onto the chair's back.

The leather in Cian's chair groaned when he stood. As he passed by on his way to the shower, Aiden's hand shot out and gripped Cian's wrist.

Aiden stared up at Cian for a long moment, his expression plagued by shadows. "Are you sure about this?"

Cian knew the treatment to cure their family of the sickness that was Manny Moretti would be foul. Like swallowing the chemo pill that would make him sick as it tore through his body, everything about it would be unpleasant.

Unpleasant, but necessary.

"I'm sure."

Rather than let go, Aiden's grip on Cian's wrist tightened fractionally.

"Go," Cian said softly. "Be with your family, man."

"You are my family."

Cian glanced down the hallway at Rory's closed bedroom door. "Brynn and the baby need you more than I can do. I got this."

His words hung in the air between them for a beat. Then, with a pained sigh, Aiden's hand fell away.

CHAPTER 2

OCTOBER

Avery Bishop moaned in ecstasy. Pleasure flooded her senses, and she closed her eyes, savoring the delicious bliss.

"I gotta say, watching you eat a cupcake is some kind of experience."

Avery swiped a splotch of frosting from the corner of her mouth and licked the sticky sweetness off the tip of her finger. "This one is so good." She plucked the box from the bakery off her desk and swiveled in her office chair. "Here, I brought you one."

"Yummy. Thank you." Simone's wide brown eyes tracked to the pink box. "It is margarita night, after all. Calories don't count today."

"Oh, I almost forgot to tell you." Avery swiveled back around. "I can't make it tonight."

"What? Why not?" A hint of mischief crept into Simone's tone. "Got a hot date?"

"God, no." Avery shuddered at the thought. "The last thing I need is another man in my life. The one I've got is more than enough."

Simone didn't bother trying to argue that point. "How is your wayward little brother doing these days?"

"Oh, you know, he's...." Avery bit off a large bite of her cupcake.

"He's been quiet lately. Did he finally get his shit together?"

Jamie had *not* gotten his shit together. In fact, he'd stumbled into a bigger, messier pile of poo than he'd ever stumbled into before.

But Avery hadn't shared her brother's latest screwup with her friend. It was too big to share right now. Once she'd gotten things under control, she could tell Simone the whole sordid story. But not yet.

Around the cupcake, Avery made a noncommittal noise.

Simone peeled away her cupcake's wrapper. "Actually, your brother is a real gift, you know?"

"He is?" Her appetite cratering, Avery frowned at the half-eaten sweet treat cupcake cradled between her fingers. "How do you figure?"

"He's like a cheat sheet." Simone dabbed her finger into her cupcake's blue frosting. "All you have to do is look at him to know *exactly* what kind of man you do *not* want to date."

A startled laugh burst from Avery.

Simone licked the frosting off her fingertip. "It's like you've been given the answers to the test. Do you have any idea how much time and disappointment this is going to save you once you get up the courage to date?"

Avery abandoned her cupcake to the paper plate on her desk and whirled in her chair to face her computer screen. "It's not a lack of courage that's stopping me. It's self-preservation."

As a rule, Avery didn't attend parties or go to clubs to meet men. She didn't date, and she'd certainly never invited any man into her bed. Why would she open herself up to that kind of risk?

Drawing in a deep breath, Avery swiveled back around in her chair. "Men are like lottery tickets..."

"Here we go." Simone abandoned her cupcake.

"...there's a brief, magical period filled with hope and promise, but inevitably, you scratch off the shiny coating and discover it's just another loser underneath."

"Some tickets are winners," Simone grumbled.

An inelegant snort escaped Avery. "Yeah, like, one in a billion."

"*Dayum.*" Simone's dark curls shimmied when she shook her head. "Only twenty-four years old and so freaking cynical."

Simone wasn't wrong. At too young an age, Avery had witnessed what a man could do to hurt a woman, and the chaos that'd upended her life in the aftermath would've left the most fanciful dreamer disillusioned.

Was it possible she'd overcompensated by shutting out people, and most especially men?

Maybe.

But probably not.

"Your winning ticket is out there." Simone rescued her cupcake from her desk. "But you'll never find him unless you play the game."

"There is nothing a man can give me that I can't give myself." Hearing her own words spoken out loud, Avery cringed.

Simone's laughter filled the cubicle. "Is that so?"

Avery spun away. "Yes, that's so." She plucked up her cupcake. "I make my own cupcakes."

"There's more to life than sweet treats."

Avery bit into the cupcake, and the flavor flooded her taste buds. "But nothing more pleasurable," she argued around the bite of cupcake.

"Orgasms," Simone snapped. "Orgasms are more pleasurable than cupcakes."

A hunk of cupcake stuck in Avery's throat, and she coughed to dislodge it. "Right. Of course. What I meant was, I can have both. I *do* have both."

"You do?" Doubt drenched Simone's tone.

"You'd be surprised how advanced the technology is these days."

With a hard shove against the desk, Simone wheeled her chair over to Avery's side. "You been holding out on me?"

Avery glanced over her shoulder to make sure no one was within earshot. "Let's just say the self-pleasure industry is…climaxing."

Simone propped her elbows on Avery's desk and plunked her chin in the cradle of her palms. "Spill it. Tell me everything you know."

"I'll send you a website link when I get home tonight."

Simone speared Avery with a look. "Don't forget."

"Promise."

With a satisfied smile, Simone rolled her chair back over to her workspace. "Didn't classes start this week? Is that why you're blowing us off tonight?"

Avery winced. "Oh, uh, I'm taking this semester off."

"What?" Simone twirled around in her chair. "But you're so close to graduating."

Twelve credits. She needed twelve more credits to finish her degree.

"I'll finish next summer. Fall at the latest." Beneath Simone's doubt-filled gaze, Avery squirmed. "I just need to save up a little tuition money, that's all."

Unless she won the lottery, or the academic scholarship her department awarded to one student each year for excellence in their field, Avery's degree was just going to have to wait.

"But without your degree, you can't apply for the promotion."

"I know." The knife of disappointment twisted in Avery's gut. God, she needed that promotion, and the steady paycheck and full benefits that came with it. "There'll be other promotions."

Simone offered Avery a weak smile. "Or better yet, once you have your degree, you can get a job at a real newspaper."

Avery's heart bounced with hope. With a degree, she'd have opportunities, and opportunities meant security.

"The Daily Sun is a real newspaper," Avery said.

The women shared a look, then together, burst out laughing.

Truthfully, working at the tabloid writing stories that ranged from the scandalous to the ridiculous wasn't Avery's dream job. But creating gossip and making up works of fiction wasn't the worst job she'd ever had, either. It was steady work, and it paid the bills. Barely, but it did. That was good enough for her. For now.

"So, why aren't you coming out with us tonight, then?" Simone asked.

Avery spun toward her computer screen. "I need to follow up on a story about the Darlings," she lied. "The public needs their Darling family gossip, or they get restless."

"Well, I happen to be a member of the restless public, so I'll let you off the hook this week. But next week, I'm dragging your butt to the bar with us."

"Got it."

"What's this story about?" Simone turned toward her computer monitor. "Is it gonna be a juicy one?"

Avery wasn't working the gossip rag beat that night. Rather, she'd be working to clean up her brother's latest mess.

She gave her friend the only kernel of the truth she could risk sharing. "Let's just say I'm hoping for a happy ending."

Unfortunately, her happily ever after ending depended on some guy named Mikey "Barbecue Sauce" Ross.

She'd found Hog Heaven BBQ easily enough, then followed the stench of desperation and corruption around to the unmarked black door behind the business.

With a flood of lies and fast-talking, she'd convinced the

doorman to let her inside the backroom that'd been converted into a makeshift casino.

Poker tables with ten or more people crowded around them packed the room. On the sterile white walls, TVs hung every few feet and displayed a variety of games and sporting events, while a pop-up bar and a row of flashing slot machines lined the far wall.

The smells of cigarette smoke, alcohol, and nervous sweat hung thick in the air and saturated Avery's nostrils as she wound her way through the tables.

Mikey "BBQ Sauce" Ross held his office hours in one corner of the room and when she finally got in front of him, she didn't waste any time telling him why she'd come to see him.

"I can give you the money next week." Her promise sounded empty, even to her own ears. "I know that's what everyone says. But I mean it. I swear."

With his overly whitened teeth, Mikey tore off another hunk of his barbecue sandwich. "I already gave your brother two weeks." The mashed-up food filling his mouth garbled his words. "I'm not running a charity here."

At the display before her, she wrinkled her nose. At least now she knew where Mikey got his ridiculous nickname.

What she didn't understand was how in the hell her brother, who'd grown up on the side of an unlucky coin flip, had racked up a massive gambling debt. When she was done saving his neck, she was going to wring it so hard.

"You didn't give *me* two weeks. *I* can get the money." She injected as much confidence into her tone as she could manage.

It was a lie, of course. There was no way she could come up with the five thousand dollars Jamie owed. Not in a week or a month. At most, a week bought her time to come up with a plan.

And right now, she'd kill for a plan that amounted to more than begging a two-bit mobster for mercy.

Mikey pondered her for a moment. Or maybe he was just chewing.

"Oh, c'mon." She blasted him with a bright smile. "What's a few more days?"

He swallowed, then the hard set of his features softened slightly, and just when she thought she'd won him over, his attention bounced to something over her shoulder.

His rigid scowl returned.

Avery glanced behind her, but just then Mikey delivered his verdict.

"Can't do it. It's not my money."

Her head snapped back around. "But—"

"You gotta pay up. You don't pay up, Moretti's not gonna be happy."

The words struck her with the devastating force of a sledgehammer.

"Moretti?" She nearly choked on the name. "*Manny* Moretti?"

"He's not as patient as I am." Mikey lifted his sandwich, but paused before taking a bite. "He's already given you two weeks and not one cent to show for it. That's a real problem."

The creep of terror climbed up her spine, freezing her in place.

Manny Moretti? Jamie was in debt to one of Chicago's most notorious mobsters, and the man that'd destroyed her families' once-peaceful lives? It was not an insignificant amount of money, either. She'd heard of Moretti ordering hits for far less.

Oh, Jamie, what have you done?

CHAPTER 3

"Two days." The stench of desperation was coming from her now. "I'll have the money in two days."

Looking past her, Mikey pushed to his feet. "If you're here for the drop, I'm taking it to Moretti now." He dragged his gaze back to Avery and flicked his wrist at the man behind her. "Take your charity case up with him."

Avery whipped around and came face to face with a tall, broad-shouldered man wearing a scowl as dark as his hair.

Whoa.

The raised collar of his black wool coat grazed the black scruff peppering his severe jawline and a feral light gleamed in his green eyes. His frame was long and lean but with a raw, relaxed power that reminded her of a fierce predator momentarily satiated from a recent feeding.

Gooseflesh broke out across her skin, lifting the hairs on her arms and neck.

For a moment, the strikingly gorgeous man made her forget how truly dangerous her situation had just become. I mean, she was scared, and totally screwed, but she wasn't dead. Yet.

Mikey brushed past her, bumping her shoulder as he slipped by and jolting her from her stupor.

"Wait," she called after him. "I wasn't finished…."

Mikey disappeared through a door behind the bar, slamming it shut behind him.

"You should not have offered two days." The hint of a smile ghosted the stranger's wide mouth. "I tink you coulda got three, maybe four, outta him if ye'd kept at him."

She blinked, surprised by his thick, lilting accent, which she might've considered charming under different circumstances.

Instinct had her reeling. "I don't really care what you *tink*."

"Course not. Why would ya listen to me?" With his hands tucked inside his coat pockets, he gestured widely. "You obviously have everything under control."

She glared at him.

"You should not be upset." He seemed to be fighting back laughter. "Ya did great. I was really rooting for ya."

"Who the hell are you?"

His expression hardened, as though he hid a warehouse full of secrets on the far side of his stony features. "I'm nobody you want to know."

"Well, at least we can agree on that." The words were out before she could bite them back.

The truth was, if she were going to get Jamie out of this mess, she needed this man's cooperation. No matter how annoying he was.

She gave herself a firm mental shake. "Is it true you work for Moretti?"

"I work for no one."

"A freelancer, huh?" Sarcasm rode the edge of her tone.

If he was freelancing for the mob, he was essentially a mercenary. Fantastic.

His gaze fixed on her face. "Something like that."

No, not fixed. *Fixated.*

He studied her intently, his fierce green eyes moving over her features with thorough, even obsessive, attention to detail.

Unnerved, she rushed ahead with her practiced plan. "Tell your boss I'll have his money next week."

His eyes crinkled at the corners and his lips curled to reveal a flash of white teeth, but he wasn't smiling. "Yeah, it doesn't work like that."

"You'll have your money in a week, or not at all." She hitched one shoulder. "It's your choice."

"None of this is my choice, and while I take your point, Manny is not nearly as rational as you and I."

Her heart slammed painfully against her breastbone. "If you're trying to scare me, it won't work," she lied. "I'm not afraid of Manny Moretti."

"No, of course not." His eyes traveled down her body, all the way to her feet, and then back up. A spark of humor twinkled in their green irises. "I can see you're a very tough lass."

She clenched her teeth. "I'll get you your money."

"It's not my money."

"Let me guess. You're only doing Moretti's dirty work for him?" Each word dripped with her loathing. "I hope it's worth it."

A spot on his sharp jawline twitched.

The sound of her frantic heartbeat thrummed in her ears. "Fine. If you won't deliver my message, then I'll tell him myself. Where is he?"

At that, the man laughed. "Why should he, or anyone, believe anything you say?"

"Excuse me?"

"You've gambled away more money than you possess, with no means of repaying it. Your word means nothing."

"You don't know anything about me."

He curled his upper lip. "I know enough."

She folded her arms in front of her. "Is that so?"

"You're impulsive, reckless, and right now, you're desperate, which makes you dangerous."

Fury rushed through her veins, fiery and frantic. Everyone who knew her knew she was the dependable one. As reliable as the CTA.

"You're wrong about me," she bit out.

"Oh yeah? Why don't you prove it? You can start by owning up to your debts."

"It's not *my* debt—" She pressed her lips together, wishing she could pull back the information. "Look, are you going to tell Moretti I'll have the money next week or not?"

For several heartbeats, he studied her with thoughtful intensity. Then something that looked like genuine regret flickered across his features. "Sorry. I don't handle his negotiations."

A brutal anguish pierced her chest. Maybe it was the cruelty of running up against another roadblock, or maybe it was the soft hitch in his voice that did it, but tears closed the back of her throat. Silly, stupid tears.

She would not cry. She never cried. Crying wouldn't help anything. She had to think. There had to be a way out of this mess.

She refused—absolutely *refused*—to lose Jamie, too.

Except she couldn't think with Moretti's man watching her with those probing eyes, feasting on her despair like a parasite. She needed to get away from the towering grump so she could figure out what to do next.

She stepped past him on her way to the exit. "Have a nice life as Moretti's lapdog."

A tunnel of noise nipped at her heels as she passed between the poker tables. Panic squeezed her lungs when she pushed through the door and stepped into the dark alley behind Hog Heaven.

The cold, dark night air engulfed her, and she shivered.

What was she going to do now? What would Moretti do to

Jamie? His goons had beaten Jamie once already when he'd failed to meet the deadline. They'd sent him running with his tail between his legs and promises of repayment by the end of the week, or else....

Even with her and Jamie both working to come up with the money, there was no way they were going to make it happen.

She sagged against the brick wall and dragged a deep, ragged breath into her tightening chest cavity. Her deep breaths became gulps, but her lungs were too tight and wouldn't expand to fill.

She would not panic. She didn't have time to panic.

No panic and no tears.

She had to think.

But the harder she thought, the tighter her chest squeezed.

Get a grip. Think.

No matter what, she would find a way to save Jamie. He was all she had left in this crappy world, and she wouldn't give up on him.

It was no use. She was going to puke.

Bending over, she heaved.

Behind her, the door swung open, and a flurry of sound spilled out into the alleyway with the shadowy figure of a man.

Straightening, she pressed her back against the hard brick. If she didn't move or breathe, he might not notice her. She tried to blend into the wall while she waited for him to leave.

Without a word, he moved to stand beside her.

Having been detected, the breath she'd been holding leaked from her lungs as a hiss of air.

In the distance, an ambulance siren wailed. She focused on the sound, trying to distract her mind from her panicked thoughts.

"Will you have the money in a week?" he asked quietly.

For some reason, she couldn't lie to him. Not even to save her brother's life. She remained silent.

"How much are we talking?"

"Too much." Her voice was a hoarse whisper.

Just then, a sudden racket of noise punctured the quiet, and a garage door slowly raised further down the alley.

Light seeped out from inside the garage into the dim corridor, and she shrank away from the smattering.

She bumped into his solid chest, then flung a scowl over her shoulder. "Do you mind?"

"Not at all," he murmured, his mouth next to her ear.

The butt of a Cadillac appeared, and they watched as the full length of the car emerged, inch by inch.

Suddenly, the brake lights lit up, and the car rocked to a jerky stop. The driver's side door swung open and Mikey bounded out of the vehicle. He hustled back inside the garage while the car engine continued to run.

"Now what do you tink he's doing?"

The question might've been her own thoughts, except she didn't think with an accent.

By slow increments, she crept from the shadows and craned her neck to peek around the corner of the garage where Mikey had disappeared.

There was no sign of him or anyone else.

She spotted the door that led inside the building. It'd been left open, just a crack.

"He went back inside," she whispered into the dark. "Maybe he forgot something?"

Then the memory struck her. He said he was on his way to see Moretti. That's what he'd told the man who was breathing down her neck, literally, at this moment.

She eyed the running vehicle, and the sloppy pieces of a new plan began to crash and churn through her mind. Her head swiveled between the running car and the door Mikey had disappeared through, presumably to retrieve something he'd forgotten. He could be back at any second.

"What are ya tinking?"

The man's question jolted her. She didn't have time to *tink*. Mikey could reappear at any moment.

Besides, what was there to think about? She needed to buy more time for her and Jamie to come up with the money, and the only way to get that time was to go straight to the man at the top.

Before her mind had fully formed a plan, her feet were moving under her.

She darted up the alley with as much stealth as she could manage in her ankle boots. When she reached Mikey's vehicle, she crept around the backend and ran her fingers lightly along the trunk's edge until she found the latch.

She popped the lid, then raised it a fraction, and another. With a deep breath, she ducked her head and swung one leg over the trunk lip. Then she slipped inside the black interior.

Immediately, a hardness pressed against her back, but her gasp of surprise was cut short when Moretti's man shoved her the rest of the way into the trunk and slid in behind her.

What in the—?

The trunk lid came down with a hard thud, locking them together in the darkness.

CHAPTER 4

"What are you doing?" she hissed.

He wedged his big body tight against her back. "I'm comin' with you."

Avery's heart battered inside her chest. "What? Why?" She wriggled against him, but her effort to budge his hefty weight proved useless. "Get. Out."

"I cannot." He fitted his body tight around hers, spooning her as though they were lovers in bed. "The trunk's closed."

"Are you kidding me?" Shockwaves rippled through her. "What in the hell is wrong with you?"

"What the hell is wrong with me? You're the one that jumped inside the trunk of a gangster's Toyota Camry." His accent seemed to thicken with his exasperation. "What are you? A danger junkie?"

She felt him everywhere. His chest pressed against her shoulders. His torso fit tight to her back. His large, powerful thighs cradled her bottom.

"If I wanted danger, I'd have taken the Red Line." She scooted closer to the trunk wall.

"It might be days before he opens his trunk and lets you out." His warm breath brushed a feathery trail across the side of her neck. "Or he might find you in the next five minutes. Then what?"

Again, she wiggled, trying to gain even a smidgeon of space between their bodies, but it was no use. Both tall and broad, he took up most of the room inside the cramped trunk.

"You don't have a plan, do ya?"

Avery squeezed her eyes shut. The feel of his hard body pressed against hers, along with his deep voice and lilting accent, sent warm swirls spiraling through her. She needed to get out of this trunk.

With an aggrieved sigh, she reached back and ran her fingers over the trunk's scratchy lining, searching for the small telltale slit in the liner. "Mikey said he was going to see Moretti. I was just hitching a ride."

He craned his neck and peered at her hands, fumbling in the dark. "What are you doing?"

"Trying to find the emergency release." She winced when she stretched to search farther behind her. "Every car trunk has one."

"Do I even want to know how you know that?"

The way she stretched caused the stubble along his jawline to scrape the side of her cheek. "Everyone knows that," she muttered.

"I assure you, not everyone has the experience that'd impart such knowledge." He bent his neck to avoid her elbow. "So the question remains, how do you?"

"I had to write a book report about it once," she lied.

Suddenly, the car jostled, then a car door shut with a muted bang. She stilled her hand.

When the vehicle started to move, she pulled her hand to her chest, abandoning her search for the emergency latch. It was too late now.

They rolled down the alley, over the curb, and into the street. As the vehicle gained speed, their bodies gently rocked to the car's soft swaying.

"Now might be a good time to come up with a plan." His breath tickled her ear.

A soft fluttering sensation brushed low in her belly. "I'm just going to wing it."

"Why am I not surprised to hear you say that?" His tone was more delicious grumble than biting anger. "So, you're just going to crash Moretti's evening and beg him for more time to come up with the money?"

"Yes." When the car hit a bump in the road, the top of her head caught his jaw. "Sorry."

While he rubbed his jaw, she tried once more to inch closer to the wall, but her movements only had the effect of rubbing her backside against him.

In her ear, his breathing hitched, and his large hand clamped down on her hip. "Stop...," he rasped. "...squirming."

Rigid tension infused every muscle in his body, and his short, choppy breaths rushed across her cheek.

For a time, they rode in silence while the car rambled through the city streets, slowing on occasion before rolling to a stop, idling, then accelerating once more. The pattern repeated several times, and she assumed they'd caught the wave of traffic lights.

They increased speed rapidly, and the noise inside the trunk swelled before the vehicle topped out at a steady pace. She concluded they must've merged onto the interstate.

Moretti owned several homes in and around the city, but she didn't know how far they'd need to travel to reach him tonight.

A spasm of fear gripped her.

"Are ye scared?" Despite the hum of noise inside the trunk, she had no trouble hearing him with his mouth so near to her ear.

"Of you?" She swallowed thickly, then tilted her chin toward the roof of the trunk. "Should I be?"

On her hip, his hand shifted, a small, nearly imperceptible twitch of his fingers that sent a jolt ricocheting through her body. "You're locked in a pitch-black trunk with a total stranger. You have no idea how long it'll be before Mikey 'The Gobshite' Ross lets you out of here, or whether you'll even be able to walk away from this. You owe money to the one man in this town you should never, under any circumstances, owe money to, and you're about to show up on his doorstep, unexpected and uninvited, to bear witness to the multitude of crimes and deceits he's likely carryin' out tonight."

"Well, when you put it like that…."

If she didn't know it to be impossible, she'd swear she could feel his smile. It was faint and fleeting, but even so, a soft smile teased her lips in answer. "I guess I'm a little uneasy, under the circumstances."

It was all she'd admit to, anyway.

"Most women would be close to tears by now."

She made a noise in the back of her throat. "I never cry."

"You never cry, and you put your neck on the line trying to cover someone else's arse."

Her spine stiffened with a sudden spike of trepidation.

"Whose debt is it then?" he asked softly.

Instinct screamed at her not to give this man any information about herself or Jamie. Surely, he'd find a way to use it against them.

"Out with it." His voice was low and even. "I'm going to find out anyhow."

"My brother's."

"And where is he? Home with the sitter?"

She rolled her eyes. "He's twenty-two."

"Apologies. I assumed he was a child, seeing as how he lets his sister fight his battles for him."

"He doesn't know I'm here. If he knew, he'd have told me not to come."

"I suspect this is one of the few times I'd be inclined to agree with yer *eejit*, brother. You need to let him handle this."

She scoffed with her annoyance. "Typical."

"What's typical?"

"Men." She half-twisted around. "You think you're the only ones who are tough. That physical strength equates to power."

"Many times, it does."

"And just as often, it doesn't." Twisting back, she grumbled. "You're just like my brother."

"How's that?" His sardonic tone mocked her.

"You think you know what's best. That just because the thought popped into your head, it's the best and only option."

"You've known me, what? Thirty minutes now? Got me all figured out, do you?"

"I know you have no idea what it's like to put your neck out there for someone you care about. To be willing to give your whole life for them because that's how much you need them to stay around." Her voice cracked over the last few words. "Not because it'll bring you more wealth or power, or because you believe it will position you better in whatever ridiculous game you think you're playing, but because you love them, and you'd do anything to see them safe."

After a beat, he said, simply, "You got me."

At the hitch in his voice, she frowned. Did he sound…sad?

With a scowl, she pushed aside the thought. He worked for Moretti. He didn't have feelings. She couldn't let herself forget that.

"What about you? What's your plan?" She scrambled to restore her barriers. "Or are you just winging it?"

"Maybe I'm just hitching a ride home."

"I doubt that. I think we're headed for the suburbs."

"And?"

"And you don't look like you're from the suburbs."

"Where do I look like I'm from?"

Someplace hard and dangerous. Like prison. "You have city boy written all over you."

"You say that like it's a bad ting."

"Just an observation."

"Is it my jacket?" He lifted his hand off her hip and smoothed his palm down the front of his black wool coat. "I never know what to wear to the underground gambling den. It's too much, isn't it?"

She dragged her bottom lip between her teeth to smother her smile. "Yeah, it's the jacket."

His hand found her hip once more. With his cheek near her temple, he inhaled. That breath, deeper than all the others and just a touch shaky, licked like warm fingers low in her belly.

"Actually, it's your accent." She half-turned her head, as though she might be able to see his face in the dark. "Where are you from?"

"Where do you think I'm from?

"I don't know. That's why I'm asking."

"South Chicago."

A snort escaped her. "I've never stepped foot outside of this city. You are not from Chicago. Fine, don't tell me." She returned her gaze to the trunk wall. "I don't care."

"It's Irish. I grew up in Ireland." His knee nudged the back of her thigh. "City girl."

Her smile broke loose.

Followed immediately by a stab of disappointment. How was it that one of Moretti's goons could make her smile like this? Here, of all places? Now? He was no friend or ally to her, and she had no idea how or why she kept letting herself be charmed by the enemy.

As the last slivers of her insanity induced enchantment faded, the car shifted to a lower gear and began its exit from the highway.

After executing a turn, the vehicle moved at a slow crawl interrupted by brief stops, until finally, they halted, and the engine died. The vehicle jostled, then a car door slammed.

Quiet engulfed them, and they waited.

Had Mikey left the vehicle? Had they arrived at Moretti's home? Someplace else? Her heartbeat sounded in her own ears. Was it safe to escape the trunk, or would she be discovered the moment she popped the trunk latch?

"Your move, boss," the man murmured in a low voice next to her ear.

She chewed her bottom lip while she pondered her next steps.

Rather than take the riskier route out of the car's backend, she reached out in the dark and ran her fingertips across the trunk wall in front of her. When her fingers brushed over the raised fabric, she fumbled with it until she managed to hook her index finger through the looped latch. She tugged.

With a dull pop, a portion of the wall fell away. She rolled onto her stomach, and scooched forward, pushing the seatback down so she could peak through the opening.

The car's interior was dark and empty. She spotted no one outside the vehicle, so she pushed to her knees.

Aware that her ass was now directly in the man's face, she scrambled through the opening and tumbled into the backseat.

She hunched on the floor behind the driver's seat and peered through the sea of parked vehicles littering the driveway and yard at the opulent estate. It didn't look like a house, but more closely resembled a medieval castle. The dark stone mansion had a massive arched wooden front door, several steep turrets, and an array of stone balconies.

Cars clogged the driveway and littered the yard, and the soft driving bass of loud music filtered across the sprawling front lawn.

The man poked his head through the opening. A curse slipped from him.

"What's wrong?" she asked, panic rising in her throat. "Where are we?"

"Looks like Manny's throwin' a house party."

CHAPTER 5

Cian stared through the dark night at the castle-like structure while fingers of alarm clawed at him.

Moretti had built a reputation as a playboy businessman and financier, but it was all smoke and mirrors, a front he used to both bolster and conceal his illegal activities. As part of his façade, he lived an extravagant lifestyle and frequently hosted parties filled with drugs and sex, where he invited local celebrities, tycoons, and politicians to indulge. It appeared they'd stumbled onto one of his notorious bashes.

He glanced over at the woman's huddled form. "You cannot go in there."

"I have to."

"You absolutely do not."

"That's the difference between you and me." Her voice wavered. "I'll do whatever it takes to save my family from people like you and your…associates."

Once, during a fight, Cian was knocked on the nose and stunned for a moment. In a daze, he'd stumbled around, waving his arms in front of him to ward off the next blow.

Now, watching her fling open the car door and scurry toward

Manny Moretti's house, he experienced a strikingly similar sensation.

With a ribbon of sharp curses, he squeezed the rest of the way through the opening into the backseat. He tripped out of the car and, slamming the door shut behind him, stalked up the drive after her.

The chill night air licked at his skin, and he tucked his chin inside the collar of his coat.

The home's long driveway allowed him time to gain some ground on her, but her long, full strides forced him to a near jog.

Her dark hair, cut blunt beneath her jawline, caught strands of moonlight that shimmered with her movement.

As he tracked her, his breath came harder. Or maybe it was the way her brown leather jacket hugged her small waist and jeans molded around her lush ass. She was incredibly generously proportioned, and when she moved, her assets jiggled like a bowl full of Jell-O.

He was no fan of Jell-O, but suddenly, he was starved for a taste.

A pang of surprise struck him at the sudden rush of blood down below. His cock thickened with his arousal, and he marveled at the velvety ripple of lust sloping through his body. He hadn't experienced anything so human in months.

But damn, it felt good, and he took a moment to savor the sensation.

She reached the house ahead of him, and as he moved up the walkway to the front door, noise from the party inside grew louder. People littered the area, smoking cigarettes and catching a break from the chaos indoors, and he followed her winding path between them.

A man blocked the door, allowing entrance only after collecting invitations from the partygoers in trendy suits and flirty dresses. Seeing him, the woman reared back.

She bumped hard into Cian. With her backside pressed

against him once more, a rumble of satisfaction vibrated in his chest.

Her scent, strongest in the secret hollow behind her ear, teased his nostrils.

On a gasp, she whipped around, sputtering apologies.

Until she realized it was him.

Her startled shock fizzled like bubbles in a soda glass. "Oh. It's you."

"You sound disappointed."

Actually, she sounded as though she'd just discovered a wad of chewed gum on the bottom of her shoe.

When she opened her mouth to respond, a smile formed on his lips in delicious anticipation of the tongue lashing she was about to deliver.

"Hey," the doorman barked. "Hey, you. You the new girl?"

The woman glanced over her shoulder.

"Yeah, I'm talking to you." The man pointed directly at her. "You're supposed to use the back door."

"I'm supposed to…? Oooohhhh, *right*, the back door. Of course. Because I'm the new girl." Turning back, she smiled up at him. "Yep, that's me. The new girl."

As she stepped around him, he turned with her. "This is a bad idea."

She offered him a regretful shrug as she backed away. "I gotta try."

Then she whirled on her heel and scurried down the walkway. Before she ducked around the side of the house, she risked one last glance over her shoulder, and their gazes collided, like magnets affixing to one another.

With a frown, he watched her disappear around the corner.

A flash of anger sparked in his chest. Who the hell was this woman? He didn't know her. He didn't *want* to know her. But what in the hell was she doing walking in the backdoor of one of

Moretti's depraved house parties? And why, for the sake of all that was holy, couldn't he stop himself from following her?

For the past six months, Cian had been working his way into Moretti's circle as part of the plan he and Agent Kendrick had cooked up. It hadn't been particularly hard. All he'd had to do was rejoin the gym where he used to train and within weeks, the opportunity had landed in his lap to take on side gigs working "security" for Moretti, who liked to use MMA fighters for protection, as well as for intimidation.

But it'd been six months now, and so far, all Cian had earned was the right to bully a few losers like Mikey to give Moretti the money they owed. While roughing up thugs and mob goons was a lot more enjoyable than he'd expected, he remained locked out of Manny's inner circle.

It wasn't a surprise, given that Cian's brother had snitched to the feds. But the longer this thing dragged on, the more restless Cian grew. Somehow, he needed to convince Moretti he was more like his corrupt stepdad than his saintly brother.

Now, unbelievably, he may have a chance to do just that.

Cian clenched his jaw and twisted toward the front door. He bounced up the porch steps and landed on the stoop.

A wide grin spread across Terence's face when he recognized Cian. "Holy shit, if it isn't One-Punch Nolan." He used the nickname Cian had earned based on his knack for delivering knockout punches. "How you doing, man? You look good."

"I feel good," Cian lied.

"Don't see you at these things too often. You in the mood to have a little fun tonight?"

Cian bared his teeth. "Damn right."

At least, the thought of finding the woman and wrapping his fingers around her slender, reckless little neck held some small appeal.

Terence's deep chuckle rumbled in his chest. "Well, then let's get you to it."

When Terence swung open the door, a stream of shitty techno music and too-loud voices gushed out. Cian crossed into the barrage of noise, but just as he stepped over the threshold, a big, beefy hand smacked him on the chest.

He looked down, then slowly back up to the man's bulky arm and bulbous face. Even before Cian set his sights on Derek DeMarco, he knew who dared to touch him. Only one man was that stupid.

When Derek had hit the MMA circuit a couple of years ago, he and Cian had trained at the same gym and Cian remembered well the little shit with an arrogant strut and the most ridiculous nickname he'd ever heard.

"The Baby Assassin?" Cian had repeated. "What, like, you kill babies?"

Derek's oversized brow had wrinkled with his frown. "I'm an assassin in the ring and I'm young. Like a baby."

Cian couldn't help it. He'd laughed. "Sounds fearsome," he'd quipped.

The Baby Assassin had had it in for Cian ever since, even publicly celebrating Cian's early retirement when he'd gotten too sick to fight. Which hadn't hurt Cian's feelings any.

In fact, he'd taken it as a badge of honor to be enemies with someone like Derek DeMarco who, within months of joining the circuit, had flocked to the dirty mob money being thrown around and was fixing matches and cheating the game in any and every way that paid. By the time he'd faced charges for beating up his girlfriend, Cian well and truly loathed the little prick.

"Where's your invite?" Derek asked now.

Cian patted his pecks, though he knew full well there was no invitation tucked inside his coat pockets. Moretti didn't trust him enough for that. Yet.

He held up his hands. "Aw shucks, I grabbed the wrong coat. Must've left my invitation in the other one."

With a huff of annoyance, Terence flicked Derek's hand away. "Go on in, man. You're all good."

The smirk lingered on Cian's face as he pushed deeper inside the house, until the noise and chaos had completely swallowed him. Bodies packed the grand foyer and the large adjoining rooms. As he wound his way through the crowd, drugs and alcohol flowed freely.

Cian had heard the rumors about Moretti's little get-togethers, where women and drugs were passed around like party favors to powerful men. But he'd known without ever having set foot inside the faux-castle fortress that these parties weren't merely lavish affairs catering to every rich and semi-famous dirtbag in town. The true purpose of Moretti's debauched soirees was not to indulge extravagant appetites.

Rather, it was a trap, and drugs and sex were just the bait. Moretti used the electric glow of such vices to lure in his VIP guests, and like insects attracted to the blue-light bug zapper, the idiots happily swarmed to their own demise.

But while the clueless prey indulged, Moretti, with his fondness for surveillance, was watching and listening through the bugs and cameras planted around the estate and taking notes. Because every good mob boss understood information was power. Power was control, and to men like Manny Moretti, control was everything.

Cian kept his feet moving, afraid if he stood still too long, he'd become prey, too.

He worked his way toward the wall at the back of the most crowded room and claimed a spot where he had the best view of the space. There was no sign of the woman anywhere.

He grabbed a drink from the bar, then resumed his search, until a man stuck a candy dish full of little white pills under his nose.

Cian waved off the drugs, but rather than retreat, the man leaned close.

"They're downstairs," he shouted over the music.

With a small headshake, Cian shrugged. "Who?"

"You're looking for a girl?"

After a beat of surprise, Cian managed a curt nod.

"They're downstairs." The man slapped him on the back. "Have fun."

CHAPTER 6

$\mathcal{A}$very stumbled along the darkened path until she found a door near the back of the house. Her nerves coiled tight when she slipped quietly inside the house before anyone could stop her.

A long staircase unfolded at her feet, and she followed the sounds of music and voices drifting up to her.

When she stepped off the bottom stair, she squinted into the large, dimly lit room, trying to make out what lurked in the shadows.

But a big-shouldered brute blocked her path. He held out his huge hand. "Cell phone."

"What? Why?"

"No phones past this point."

Unease slithered down Avery's spine. She wanted to ask him why the hell not, but she understood the rule wasn't negotiable. If she wanted in, she'd need to comply.

Waves of dread swamped her as she handed over her device.

Feeling suddenly naked and unprotected, she took a few tentative steps into the murky dimness. Women crowded a makeshift dance floor in the center of the room, dipping and swaying to the blaring music. Other partygoers lounged on over-stuffed couches and chairs, watching.

As she moved through the room, Avery felt their gazes watching her, tracking her every movement.

Though she was still wearing her cropped, faux-leather jacket, she shivered. What the hell kind of party was this?

The sudden memory of walking into high school in her cheap, tattered clothes arose to disturb her. She wasn't wearing those old rags anymore, but she felt more out of place than ever.

The instinct to hide nearly overwhelmed her, and she scurried over to the bar. Maybe they needed help serving the drinks and she could seek refuge behind the wooden barrier.

As she approached, the bartender greeted her with a half-nod.

She leaned close. "Do you need any help?"

Confusion flickered across the man's face.

"I don't know what I'm supposed to be doing." She made another cursory glance around the room, and seeing no waitstaff or servers, turned back to the bartender. "I'm the new girl. Do you know what I'm supposed to be doing?"

A stiff smile cleared away his confused frown. "Here, have a drink."

He set a glass of white wine in front of her, then moved away to take another order.

Desperate to quiet her screaming nerves, she snatched up the wineglass and swallowed a large gulp. She only needed a little liquid courage to help her blend in, then she'd find Moretti and plead her case. That bastard had to be lurking somewhere in the shadows of this creepy place, didn't he?

But even as she scanned the room for Moretti, her eyes searched for a huge Irishman with a jawline hard enough to cut diamonds and covered with pleasantly ticklish scruff.

Next to her, a young woman with dark blond hair slipped onto the barstool.

Avery offered her a smile. "Hi."

"Hey."

"Cool party, huh?" God, she was such a dork.

The woman gave her a strange look. "Yeah, I guess."

So much for blending in. Avery hid her face behind her wineglass.

"I haven't seen you here before." The woman's expression was both curious and cautious. "First night?"

Avery choked down the slug of wine. "I'm…Natasha."

When the girl smiled, she appeared rather young and pretty. "Sasha."

Avery leaned in. "I do not know what I'm supposed to be doing," she confessed.

"There's really not much to do." Sasha accepted a glass of wine from the bartender. "Party. Dance. Talk to people."

"That's it?"

"That's it. Eventually, one of the guys will approach you."

Avery suppressed a groan. On the long list of things she did not need, a man interfering with her plans was high up there. Tonight, she was interested in only one man.

The image of penetrating green eyes floated through her mind.

Not that one.

What the hell was wrong with her?

Moretti. She needed to find Moretti and convince him to give her more time to come up with the money.

A shot of fear sliced through her. Would he recognize her? She was only a child the last time she'd seen him, but she bore a passing resemblance to her mother.

Fear coiled and twisted into a sickening knot in her stomach.

"…and if you like each other, he'll offer for you."

Sasha's statement knocked into Avery, jerking her from her thoughts. "I'm sorry? He'll offer for me?"

"Mr. Moretti handles all the negotiations and stuff, so you

don't have to worry about any of that. We get paid at the end of the night."

Avery wrestled with Sasha's words, trying to twist them into some sensible shape.

"Don't worry." Sasha misunderstood Avery's silence. "Even after Moretti takes his cut, it's still good money."

"The men…," Avery gulped, "…pay you?" Understanding slithered through her with a slow, devastating creep. "How much?" Her question squeaked out.

Sasha leaned back on her stool and looked Avery over. "If I were you, I wouldn't take less than five hundred."

"Five hundred? For…? To…?" She couldn't say the words. *To have sex with them?*

Why hadn't she realized it sooner? It should've been obvious the moment the guy at the front door had picked her out of a crowd of rich people as the new girl. Of course it was a sex party.

Moretti's dirty fingerprints were all over every disgusting thing that went on in this city. Drugs, gambling, scams, and cons. She should've realized he'd find a way to monetize sex, too.

But she wouldn't accept all the blame for her ignorance. Moretti and his ilk were good at keeping secrets. Secrecy gave them their power.

One of Sasha's small shoulders lifted. "Some girls make enough money in a night to buy a car. Staci was able to quit her job waiting tables."

"Quit her job? To work here?" Avery's thoughts were spiraling. "For how long?

"However long she wants."

"Can she leave?"

Sasha's giggle carried a youthful ring. "Sure. But why would she want to?"

"Well…what if she meets someone she likes? Can she just… stop…working?"

"Of course." Sasha scooped up her wineglass. "That's the whole point. We're all looking for a Sugar Daddy to set us up."

Avery glanced around the room, taking in the women filling the dance floor and the men watching from the shadows with a fresh perspective.

A bead of moisture broke out on Avery's forehead. "Doesn't it creep you out? The thought of depending on these men?"

Sasha made a sound like a snort. "Beats living in shelters."

The words crashed over Avery. Of course. It wasn't about the men, or even the money. For Sasha and the others like her, it was about security. Safety. They might need a place to stay or have bills that needed to be paid. And they needed it so badly, they were willing to pay with their bodies to get it.

Avery hated this place. She hated that Sasha was here, and that she felt offering herself to a stranger was her best, or only, option.

Wishing to hide her reaction, Avery stared into her wineglass. "The shelter on Lake isn't that bad."

"It's probably the best one. That, or Fullerton."

"Have you tried the new one out on Division?"

Sasha shook her head. "My friend stayed there once and said it wasn't good."

"No security guards?"

Sasha sliced Avery with a meaningful look. "The security guards were the problem."

With a change in the music, lights fanned out across the dance floor and the momentary brightness allowed Avery her first real look at Sasha's face.

Struck by the girl's youthfulness, she tipped her head to one side. "How old are you?"

Sasha's chin took on a defiant set. "Twenty."

It was a lie, Avery knew, but there seemed no point in pressing the subject. Besides, two men had appeared at the opposite end of the bar and one of them pointed at Avery, then said something to his friend, who immediately looked her up and down.

The slow smile that curled his thin lips roiled her stomach.

"These men? Who are they?" she asked Sasha. "Have you met any of them?"

"They're rich guys. Businessmen, mostly. But Katrina met an actor last week, and I heard some NFL players hang out here sometimes."

"Oh, yeah?" Avery gulped down more wine.

"Yeah. One of the girls said some fighters are here tonight."

"Fighters? Like boxers?"

"Yep. MFA boxers, or whatever it's called. You know, like that Colin Maguire guy?"

"Uh… Conor McGregor?"

Sasha snapped her fingers. "That's him. He's kind of yummy, don't you think?"

Distracted by her reeling thoughts, Avery muttered her agreement. How young were the other girls? Were they all twenty or under?

Were they all poor too?

Young, pretty, and poor. The prey of the rich and powerful. To them, girls like Sasha and Avery were mere playthings. They were to be bought and discarded, nothing more.

Something like fury, except with a lot of fear mixed in, surged through Avery, and she began to shake.

There was a time she could've been just like Sasha, desperate and forced to make scary choices. But her brothers had protected her. They'd protected each other. Ever since Manny Moretti set out to destroy her parents' lives when Avery was ten years old, it'd been the three of them against the world, with the world mostly kicking their asses. They'd lost a lot of battles, and now that Logan was gone, only Avery and Jamie remained to fight this war.

The men at the end of the bar leered at her again, and a kick of adrenaline banged around inside her. Would one of them offer her money for sex? How much? Sasha said it might be enough to buy a car. New or used? Would the money be enough to pay back some of Jamie's debt? Enough to pay this month's overdue rent?

If the whole setup wasn't so vomit-inducing, she'd be tempted to find out.

The thought caused her stomach to heave.

No. Uh-uh. No way.

She tossed back the rest of her drink. She could barely hide her disdain for most men in a normal setting. No way could she act civil toward one who was considering paying her to have sex with him.

She needed to find Moretti, buy her and Jamie some more time, then get the hell out of here. That was the plan.

The only plan.

She wished Sasha good luck, then slid off her barstool.

But she'd made it only a few steps when the two men from the bar stepped in front of her, blocking her path.

Her gaze bounced between them, and the looks on their faces made her stomach clench.

With a tight smile, she attempted to move around them.

"Hold on." One of the men grasped her arm, clasping his fingers tight above her elbow. "Where you headed so fast, darling?"

Their sinister expressions and the man's too-firm touch turned her blood to ice in her veins.

CHAPTER 7

*C*ian stared down the long, dimly lit stairwell. A creeping dread snaked through his gut as he descended the stairs.

The basement had a completely different vibe than the party upstairs. While a few pairs and small groups clustered in corners, mostly, the men down here didn't mingle. They stood apart, alone, observing the action on the dance floor, which was crowded with young women.

Only young women.

In scant clothing, they bopped and swayed to rhythmic pop tunes like the ones he'd expect to hear drifting from his thirteen-year-old kid sister's bedroom. The entire scene was bizarre and creepy.

He ignored the perv-fest and probed the shadows, searching for the woman.

It didn't take him long to spot her. She stood apart from the others. With her short, natural hair and sparse makeup, she was less flashy than the women swarming the dance floor, and her clothing covered more skin than it revealed. But the skintight jeans and brown leather jacket she wore couldn't conceal her long, shapely legs and the incredible swells of her generous hips and breasts.

Remembering the feel of her hip beneath his palm, he curled his hand into a fist.

The other men noticed her too. Male eyes prowled over her, greedy and predatory, and jealousy snarled through him.

A kick of self-disgust swiftly followed, dousing his lust like a bucket of ice water dumped on his head. He was no better than the rest of these men.

She scanned the room, presumably looking for Moretti so she could throw herself at his non-existent mercy. When her sight line danced close to where he stood, his body tensed in anticipation. He wanted her notice. Longed for it, really.

Just then, a presence appeared at his elbow.

Without turning, Cian knew who'd approached him. His body stiffened with tension.

Manny Moretti had black hair, dyed unnaturally dark to hide the peppering that'd begun to occur now that he'd reached his sixties, and olive skin. His features were well-formed, but small scars pitted his skin, evidence of an acne-filled adolescence.

As an uninvited guest, Cian wondered what Manny would do. Would he toss Cian out? Make a scene?

"Didn't expect to see you here." Manny swirled the tumbler in his hand and the golden-amber liquid danced in the glass. "I thought you thought you were too good for us."

"I've been training a lot, trying to get back into shape." Cian feigned great interest in the activity churning around them. "Thought I'd take a night off."

Manny sipped his drink while he openly assessed Cian over the rim. Then he slowly lowered the glass. "How is your brother?"

The muscles in Cian's back rippled with the tightening of his shoulders. The brother who'd talked to the feds and provided evidence that, if not for one stubborn juror, should've put

Moretti in prison for a very long time? That brother? Or the one Moretti had tortured and badly broken his hand?

Along with his work to infiltrate Moretti's inner circle, Cian had spent the past six months constructing a wall between himself and his family. With Aiden and Brynn hiding from Moretti, and his mom and thirteen-year-old kid sister back in Ireland to escape the bad press and humiliation brought about by Alan's indictment and trial, all he'd had to do was avoid Rory.

To any outside observer, Cian was a loner. He had no family. No friends. No lovers. That's the way it needed to be until this mess with Moretti was over, once and for all.

"I have no idea what me brother is doin'." Cian banished all traces of emotion from his voice. "We are not close."

Manny studied Cian through heavy eyelids. Just when Cian thought he would push it, a young woman sauntered by and ensnared his attention. A slimy smile curled his lips.

She was young enough to be his daughter. Possibly even his granddaughter.

Cian sipped from his tumbler and pretended a calmness he didn't feel. It took everything in him not to end the man right then. The leering light in Moretti's eyes turned Cian's stomach. To him, these women were nothing more than expendable pawns in a game of power and corruption.

Like Brynn, who Moretti had sent his thug after as retribution against her dad when Alan had dared defy Moretti. Moretti's goon had used a knife when he'd attacked and violated her. He'd hurt her for no other reason than to punish her father and control him with the threat of another assault.

The soulless smile that'd slithered across Manny's face lingered. "You picked a good night. I have several new girls joining us this evening."

To drown out a curse, Cian sucked down another swallow of his whiskey. The alcohol burned his throat, and he grimaced.

Manny's bleary gaze kept a steady hold on Cian now. "If you

see something you like, let me know. I can arrange a meeting for you."

Disgust lashed at Cian. So the women were for sale. Did his woman from the trunk know that? Had she known that when she'd carelessly thrown herself into this situation?

Cian's gut clenched, and his gaze snapped back to her.

He hadn't come to this hellish place to chase after attractive women, and even if he felt so inclined, no woman was worth the inevitable misery.

Not even one so pretty.

Where a moment ago he'd longed for her notice, now he willed her not to see them.

"You're too good to me." As Cian watched, the woman took a small step backwards and two men from the bar moved with her, effectively pinning her in the corner. Her fake-ass smile couldn't hide her growing uneasiness.

"There are a lot of beautiful girls here tonight." Moretti raised his bourbon to his lips. "I'm sure you can find one to your tastes."

Of course, Cian could say no. He had a choice. Moretti always gave his marks a choice. How did they prefer to be controlled? Through sex? Drugs? Money? How about all three?

Cian got to pick which puppet strings he wanted to dance to.

For a man who hadn't felt anything but fear, pain, and emptiness for the better part of a year now, drugs were way too tempting a vice, and he wasn't stupid enough to gamble at one of Moretti's rigged poker tables.

In the corner, the woman's mouth moved as frantically as her hands.

And that's when it hit him. He could let Manny think women were his weakness.

As they had once been.

It was too good an opportunity to pass up. If he wanted to run with Moretti, he had to prove he was as depraved as the rest of them, and here was his chance to do just that.

He should welcome the moment. Indeed, he'd been waiting six long months for such an opening to prove himself. But his stomach heaved with the gross scenario unfurling in front of him.

One of the men touched the woman's elbow, and she jerked her arm away, then laughed to hide her unease. She slipped between the two men and out from the shadowy corner.

As one, the men turned with her.

With her back to Cian, the woman slowly inched away while her hands continued moving in wide, wild circles.

The men followed her, their expressions dark and leering.

"A meeting would be nice." Cian set his drink on a nearby table. "I've found the woman I want."

CHAPTER 8

$\mathcal{A}$very distracted the men with frivolous chatter long enough to escape Creep One's unwelcome touch.

She took a step back, and another. "Well, it was nice meeting you both. I gotta go…meet…someone…"

Would they stop her if she tried to leave? What if they offered to pay her for sex? Was saying no really an option? Despite what Sasha had said, Avery honestly did not know what the rules were in a place like this.

By slow increments, the men inched closer, carefully corralling her into the darkest of the room's dark corners.

"C'mon, you can't leave now." Creep One, the taller of the two men, drew nearer still.

Creep Two angled close enough that his body blocked her view of the room behind him. "We were just getting to know each other."

Fear sparked a pyre of panic in her chest. "Oh, well, you know how it is…being the new girl…I gotta…work…and stuff."

"The boss won't mind." Creep One's gaze crawled down her body. "We're good friends."

Tiny beads of sweat broke out across her forehead. "I really should go."

Instinct screamed at her to run for the door and never look back. No matter if it'd blow her one last shot to help her brother.

Creep Two slithered closer and instinct triumphed. She sprang forward, and in one fluid motion, darted between the two men.

She'd nearly drawn her first full breath of freedom when a large, beefy hand clamped around her wrist.

With a groan of frustration, she whirled on Creep One and gave her arm a hard tug. But his grip held firm, and a slow, dark smile touched his mouth.

Panic beat a hollow drum in her chest.

She felt a presence at her back a fraction of a second before a deep voice with a lilting accent spoke near her ear. "Sorry, fellas. This one's mine."

A rush of air left her body.

Creep Two puffed up his chest. "Look, man, we've been talking to her for a while now." His conviction fizzled as the man from Mikey's trunk moved to stand beside her.

With glittering green eyes, he peered down into her face with an intensity that caused her stomach to flutter. Then his gaze dropped to Creep One's hand, still caging her wrist.

The creep released her immediately.

She rubbed away the feel of his touch while her rescuer leveled his severe glare at the other men. Beneath the force of his regard, the creeps seemed to shrink several inches.

He let them squirm for a long moment, like worms on a fishhook, then he simply gave them his back.

One corner of his mouth pinched with the ghost of a smile. "Would you like to have a drink with me?"

Words jammed in her throat, and she could only nod.

He crooked his arm. She looped her hand under his elbow, and she resisted the urge to sag against his solid strength.

Though merely steps away, he led her to the bar, and she slipped onto a vacant stool. A pang of regret squeezed in her chest at the loss of his muscled forearm beneath her palm.

While he signaled to the bartender, she scrambled to recapture her composure. When he passed a wineglass to her, she snatched it up and chugged down half the rosy liquid in two large gulps.

"Thanks." She tipped her glass. "For the drink, but also…" Her throat constricted, and she sucked down another swig of wine. "Those guys were getting annoying. I didn't need your help or anything, but wow, they would not shut up, you know?" She pushed a hard puff of breath from her lungs. "It's nice to get away from all their yammering."

"You're welcome." Casually, he sipped his drink while bodies crowded in around them, clamoring for the bartender's attention.

She hardly noticed the commotion swirling around them as she stared into his eyes and tried to put a name to their fascinating color. They reminded her of a spring lawn as the golden brown of winter faded and the first lush green blades appeared.

He held her gaze comfortably. "Have you found Moretti?"

A guilty flush heated her skin. "Not yet, no. I was, uh, distracted by Mo and Larry over there." She tossed back the last swallow of her wine, then set the empty goblet on the bar and slid off her stool.

"Wait." His hand touched hers.

The shiver that chased through her had nothing to do with the icy chill inside Moretti's house. She stared at his long fingers and large palm covering her smaller hand. His size and warmth at once comforted and unsettled her. Her thoughts careened toward all the things he could do with those hands. So far, he'd used them more to protect than to harm. What if he used them for pleasure?

Slowly, he pulled his hand away. "What is your name?"

It was a simple question, but the heat in his voice made her belly squeeze deliciously.

Barriers. She needed barriers. Quick.

He'd already breached her outer walls and if she wasn't careful, he'd be deep inside her keep within moments. She grasped wildly for obstacles to throw in his path. Any barriers at all that might form a blockade between them.

"Natasha." The lie stuck in her throat, and she swallowed thickly.

There was a slight movement at the corners of his eyes where his long eyelashes tangled, but he didn't challenge her.

From behind, a hard body knocked into her, and she pitched forward. When she crashed against her rescuer's chest, he steadied her with both of his large, warm hands.

The guilty party was halfway through an apology when he cut off abruptly. The color seeped from his complexion, then he stammered out another apology and fled.

Confused, she glanced back at her rescuer, only to find the same lethal scowl on his face that'd sent Creep One and Two scurrying on their way as well.

What was it with his guy? Did everyone else here know him? Had he built a reputation for himself working for Moretti?

The disturbing thought struck a chord of fear in her chest. Did they have good reason to be afraid of him? Or was it simply that nasty scowl that so intimidated them?

She studied his striking face for a moment. He did look a little mean, she supposed. He was also taller than most and well-muscled.

When another body bumped against her in the crowded space, she witnessed the dangerous flash in his eyes, and suddenly, it all made sense. He looked like a man that wanted to fight. Like he was dying for a reason to plant his fist in someone's face if they'd only give him one little reason to do so. Any reason at all.

She recalled then how Sasha mentioned some of Moretti's clientele were professional athletes, football players and MMA fighters.

Realization dawned. "I know you."

One of his dark eyebrows quirked.

"You're that fighter. Cian something…Norris? Noles?"

He grimaced as though in pain, then gestured for the bartender to refill her drink.

"Am I right?" She resettled on her barstool.

"*Kee*-an."

"What?"

He sipped his drink. "My name. It's pronounced *Kee*-an."

"What did I say?"

"*See*-an. It's a hard C, not soft."

She shot him a thoughtful frown. "Are you sure about that? Isn't it the Boston *Sel*-tics?"

"The Boston…" His grimace deepened at his obvious pain. "They say it wrong."

"I'm pretty sure they don't. I mean, it's their name."

"They bastardized it. It is pronounced *Kel*-tic." Exasperation threaded through his words. "They're an ancient people—you know what, never mind. Forget it."

The sound of her throaty laughter filled the space between them. "I'm just messing with you."

His smile, reluctant at first, broke wide, and she nearly tipped off her barstool.

Wow. He had a great smile.

It bothered her how much she liked his smile. Indeed, she wasn't sure which she liked more. His smile? Or getting a reaction out of him?

"It's *Kee*-an, not *See*-an. *Kel*-tic, not *Sel*-tic. Hard, not soft." Her eyes took a leisurely stroll over him. "Got it."

Her gaze lingered a little too long on his body.

One corner of his mouth hooked up, letting her know he'd noticed.

"You're about what? 6'3? 190?" She scooped her wineglass up and pretended her interest in his body was merely professional. "Are you a middleweight?"

Someone bumped her shoulder.

With his drink in hand, Cian straightened to his full height and positioned himself so that he stood between her and everyone else in the bar area. "Light heavyweight when I was active. I've dropped weight since I retired. You know fighting?"

His body didn't touch hers, but his heat stretched out like tendrils of warm ribbons wrapping around her, and for the first time since arriving in this strange place, she didn't feel cold.

She swiveled on her barstool so she could see his face. "I've covered a few matches for the paper where I work."

He stiffened beside her. "You're a reporter?"

The air crackled with the danger she'd walked into. "Uh, no. I'm at a tabloid now. I started as a sportswriter at a small paper. They only gave me the stories no one else wanted to write."

"Like MMA fights?"

She winced. "And Motocross…. Sorry…."

He appeared more amused than offended.

With each exchange, she grew more intrigued by him. "Is that why you came to Chicago? For your career?"

"I moved here when I was sixteen and my mom remarried."

As someone who'd never set foot outside the city where she was born, Avery couldn't fathom leaving the only home she'd ever known and moving to the other side of the world. "That's a big move for a teenager."

He hitched one of his broad shoulders. "It wasn't so bad. I had my brothers with me."

At the unmistakable softness in his voice, she smiled. "How many brothers do you have?"

"Two." Then he sighed, and it was a weighty, burdensome sound. "I have two brothers."

Wondering about that sigh, she propped her elbow on the bar and rested her cheek against her knuckles.

"And…" He trailed off.

"And…?"

"Five half brothers."

Her arm dropped heavily. "Seriously?"

"Seriously."

"You have seven brothers? You're not joking?"

"I am not joking." He stared into his glass, giving it a little shake to knock the ice loose.

"Wow." It was all she could think to say, so she said it again.

So freaking fascinating.

The spot between his eyebrows crinkled, and she wished he'd look up so she could study his expression. "Sounds like an interesting story."

"It's not interesting at all. Our Da was a piece of shit philandering arsehole, and here we are."

"Do you ever think about going back to Ireland?"

He shot her a glittering glance. "All the time. I probably will one day."

"What are you waiting for?"

He rattled his ice again. "I need to settle a few things here first."

She wanted to dig deeper and ask him more questions. The reporter in her was dying to know every detail about his life. The reporter, and not the woman who was so enamored with his eye color and the way he watched everything that was happening around them, but also making her feel like she was the only person who mattered to him. Definitely not her.

With a start she realized, of all the dark, deranged things going on in this room, this man was by far the most dangerous to her, for reasons that had nothing to do with the mob or Moretti.

An odd twinge tightened her chest. "Well, I should probably go find Moretti…"

He shifted his weight. "Don't go."

She gave her head a defiant shake. "I know you think it's hopeless, but I can't give up on my brother. No matter how small the chance that I might be able to help him." Her heart pounded its pain. With ruthless resolve, she shoved down her emotions and met Cian's gaze. "He's my brother. I've got to try, right?"

Several heartbeats passed. To anyone watching, it might've appeared as though they were engaged in a staring contest. But she and Cian weren't competing. They were connecting, seeing in each other something of themselves.

He blinked first. "I have a proposition for you."

"A proposition?"

"I think I can help you with your situation."

"You want to help me?" Dread spilled through her like icy water. "And why would you do that?"

"Don't you want to know how first?"

Cold dismay filled her chest. "First, I want to know why."

He took a moment, as though considering his next words carefully. "You need money to help your dipshit brother…"

Oh no.

"I have money…."

Oh no oh no oh no.

"It seems there is an obvious solution here. A way we can help each other out."

Ohnoohnoohnoohnoohno.

"You don't even know me." Her sheer disappointment dampened the edge in her tone. "Why would you help me help my brother?"

"I know you. We spent twenty minutes locked together inside a car trunk." His too-sexy smile flashed on his tanned face. "You don't walk away as strangers after something like that."

Her lips longed to answer his smile with one of their own, so she pressed them tight together, smothering the traitorous urge.

"How?" Her throat constricted and reduced her voice to a pained whisper. "What exactly are you proposing?"

"I want to buy you for the night."

CHAPTER 9

"*B*uy me? You're kidding, right?"

"Isn't that what we're all doing here tonight?" A touch of displeasure floated across his expression like a phantom. "As the new girl, I thought you knew that."

She shouldn't feel so hurt. But the lash of pain was undeniable. She didn't know what she hated more—that he turned out to be the vile sleaze she presumed he was, or that he thought so little of her to make such a disgusting proposition. Her throat squeezed tighter.

She'd grown up poor white trash, and no matter how hard she'd fought, she could not escape other people's opinion of her. Not fully. Maybe she never would, and she'd forever be the type of woman a rich guy assumed he could purchase at a debauched sex party.

Unable to look at him, she stared over his shoulder. "Why didn't you make your move in Mikey's trunk?"

"I don't know what kind of guys you've been dating, but this is not me making a move."

She shifted her gaze to his face. "Then what is it?"

His eyes captured hers and wouldn't let go. "It's a mutually beneficial arrangement."

An inelegant sound escaped her. "Is that what the kids are calling it these days?"

He leaned close, and the fresh scent of laundry detergent and warm skin teased her senses. "I want Moretti to see me buying a woman for my pleasure. But I don't much care to deal with any women tonight."

Despite herself, she inhaled. "I'm a woman."

He drew a slow breath in through his nose. "I am well aware."

Why did this delicious smelling man have to be a scumbag? Why, for once in her life, couldn't she lust after a decent, boring guy?

"Why would you want Moretti to know that about you?" She turned her head slightly, which brought her mouth a mere whisper from his. "He'll only use it against you."

"I have my reasons," he murmured.

"What reasons?" A thought struck her. "Are you a cop? Is this whole thing a setup?"

He cursed, as though she'd placed a hex on him. "I am not a cop." A growl reverberated in the back of his throat, and he returned to his barstool, putting some space between them. "Look, you need money, and I need…to keep up appearances."

Like the masochist she apparently was, she missed his heat, and his scent.

"This way, you can pay off your brother's debt, and I get what I need."

Surprise nearly knocked her off her barstool. "You're actually going to pay me?" She repositioned on the stool to keep from sliding off, and her knee knocked lightly against his. "Like, real money?"

"Yes."

"So, you'll pay me, and then we'll…?"

"Fuck?"

Her cheeks on fire, she gave a curt nod. "Yes."

"I will not pay you to have sex with me." His reply was instant and forceful.

"Then what will you pay me to do, exactly?"

"I told you. By letting Moretti know I've chosen a woman here tonight, you'll be helping me."

Her mouth twisted into a cynical smirk. "I'll be helping you… by sleeping with you?"

"My offer doesn't involve sex." He lifted his glass to his lips and sipped the amber liquid.

She leveled him with a disbelieving look. "You're just going to give me the money? For no reason at all?"

"I have my reasons, and while they don't involve sleeping with me, they will cost you."

She frowned. "What do you mean?"

"You'll pay with your reputation. Everyone here will know I've bought you. They'll watch us go upstairs together to a bedroom." The deep timbre of his voice crawled all the way to the pit of her stomach and smoldered. "And they'll assume we followed through on our agreement."

His gaze held hers, and her heart flipped over inside her chest. "Oh, well, my reputation *is* worth an awful lot." Sarcasm saturated her tone. "A small fortune, really."

If she'd ever had a reputation to hold on to, she would've lost it years ago. Besides, these people didn't know her, and she didn't plan on seeing any of them ever again. She couldn't care less what they thought of her.

A lame laugh died on her lips, and she cleared her throat. "You said you're retired from fighting. Do you work? How do you have this kind of money lying around to buy women you don't want to sleep with? Are you just crazy rich? Is this what rich people do with all that cash they're hoarding from the rest of us?"

To her rambling questions, he said, simply, "I have access to money."

She'd barely formulated the thought that having access to money was not the same as being personally rich when he hit her with his next words.

"But I never said I don't want to sleep with you." His gaze on her face was as soft as a caress.

"Yes, you did." She sounded weird, like she was out of breath. "You were very clear."

"I said my offer does not involve sex. Not that I don't want to have sex with you."

"No, you said we won't be having sex. Period."

Lust hardened his eyes to brilliant green chips. "Do you want to have sex with me?"

"That's not what I—" Her sputtering teased up the corners of his mouth. "Whatever, just…never mind."

"If you want to further negotiate the terms of our agreement, I'm willing to hear you out." He hid a grin behind his glass.

She ate her smile. "I do not."

Then the moment of shared humor changed, and a light passed between them, soft and seductive. The smoldering flame that flickered in his eyes lit a spark in her veins.

She stared, held by his intense gaze, so she watched the fire in his eyes dampen, then be replaced slowly by a gentle, aching worry.

"You do not want to be in debt to a man like Moretti. Not for one day. Not for three weeks." Dark shadows crowded his features. "You do not want him to know who you are. Please believe me. Take the money. Pay off your debt and be done with it. Never come back to this place again."

His desperation seemed to seep through her skin and sink into her bones.

Since this fiasco with her brother had started, she hadn't felt safe or at ease for even one minute. Her appetite had fluctuated between nonexistent and overactive. She wasn't sleeping well at night, and during the day, she experienced maddening mood swings, from anger to despair to fear and helplessness.

It all came crashing back down on her now, and she started to shake. "My brother owes Moretti five thousand dollars. You got that kind of money lying around?"

"I've got it."

The tremors in her body became a seismic quake. "I don't see how this could work. One of the girls said Moretti pays us our cut at the end of the night." She licked her lips nervously. "I mean, I'm not exactly on his payroll. He doesn't even know who I am." At least, she prayed he didn't. "Isn't he going to ask questions? What if he tries to pay me and discovers I don't belong here? What happens then?"

He dragged one fingertip through the condensation on his glass. "I've already settled things with Moretti."

She yanked her gaze away from his finger. "You did?" She peered closely at his face, pondering his words, then her eyes went wide. "You already paid him for me?"

His head dipped in a small nod. "I'll pay you your money directly."

Sudden fury recoiled through her. They treated these women like trinkets to be passed around for their enjoyment. It was disgusting and infuriating and she wanted to scream with the righteous anger welling up inside her.

With his eyes, he implored her. Or maybe it was a look of warning.

She strangled her rage. "How? You have five thousand in cash on you right now?"

While he sipped his drink, his expression remained impenetrable as a Supermax prison cell. "Do you have a digital wallet I can send it to? I will make the transfer by the end of the night."

Her heart thrummed in her ears. This was crazy. *She* was crazy for even considering it. But the mere thought of all that money in her possession within hours tempted her more than she liked to admit.

She had no reason to trust this man. None. Not one. And she had several thousand reasons she should not believe a single thing he said or did.

"So what do you say, Natasha?" He put a fine point on her name. "Do we have a deal?"

Hysteria climbed up her spine and threatened to steal her composure. On a soft curse, she squeezed her eyes shut.

It was so much money. Money she had not yet been able to find and, despite what she'd been telling herself and anyone that would listen, would not be able to come up with in a few days or even weeks.

This money would solve all her problems. Jamie would be safe, for now at least. She could sleep again. All she had to do was hang out with Cian a little while longer?

It was too attractive an offer to pass up.

She lifted her chin but couldn't quite meet his gaze when she stuck out her hand. "Deal."

CHAPTER 10

When he wrapped his hand around hers, it surprised him to find that it trembled. Something in his chest sparked, a brief flash that quickly flickered and died out.

Reluctantly, he released her.

She rubbed her freed hand up her forearm. "What do we do now? I have no idea how this works."

When he'd learned of Cian's interest, Moretti had appointed him a private room for his use on the home's second floor.

He held up the key Moretti had given him. "We have a room upstairs."

"So that's it? Now I'm...," she licked her lips, "...yours?"

Her words landed with the force of a punch in the gut. The blood in his veins heated with the whoosh of fire that flared inside him.

I'm yours.

He signaled for the bartender, then ordered a fresh bottle of the wine she was drinking.

With the freshly corked bottle, he slipped off his barstool. "Shall we?"

A flare of panic glittered in her eyes. "What if someone stops us? What if they know I don't belong here?"

"I'll tell them you're with me."

She frowned and her gaze darted around the room, as though she feared someone might jump out at any moment and snatch her. "No one will believe that," she muttered. "We're going to get found out."

"If anyone stops us, I'll tell them I'm infatuated with you and to leave us the hell alone."

She crinkled her nose, which was small and straight, and turned up slightly near the tip. "Infatuated? With me?" She shook her head and her silver hoop earrings danced, peaking through the glossy strands of her hair. "Don't say that. Then they'll *know* we're lying."

A lock of her dark hair had fallen across her forehead, and he itched to push it back. "Okay, how about this? If anyone questions us, which they won't be, we'll say I have unique tastes and you've agreed to accommodate them."

"Unique tastes?" Her wide-set brown eyes filled with curiosity. "What, like, you're kinky?"

He lifted one shoulder.

She arched a dark eyebrow. "Are you?"

He gave her a secret smile. "No one will doubt it."

"That might work…" With her small white teeth, she chewed on her bottom lip for a moment. Then heaved a heavy sigh into the air. "But let's be honest, everyone here is probably hella kinky. I mean, it's a freaking sex party. Where you pay a stranger to have sex with you." She brightened as though cheered by a new thought. "What if I had something special that none of the other girls had?"

She had flawless olive skin, full peach-colored lips, and a way of looking at him, her head tilted to one side and her gaze level, that was both a warning he'd entered the no bullshit zone and a soft plea not to break her heart.

Every time he thought he'd finally scared her into abandoning her irrational plan and fleeing this place, she came right back at him with another swing from a new angle. Every single time.

She was a firecracker, a colorful ribbon screaming across the sky. By comparison, the other women were mere sparklers.

"What do you have in mind?" he asked, desperate to hear what she thought she'd come up with.

"I don't know..." Distractedly, her fingers fluttered to her neck. "What do guys like?"

"You don't honestly want me to answer that, do you?"

She snapped her fingers. "Oh, I got it. Let's say I'm a virgin."

His eyebrows climbed. "Are you?"

She mimicked his secret smile. "Would anyone dare doubt me?"

"Only a fool." He held out his hand. "Shall we?"

She eyed his outstretched hand as though he offered her poison, but then she lifted her chin and met his eyes. Though she appeared calm and composed, he could see the fear that shimmered in her toffee brown irises.

Regret nipped at him. "If I wanted to hurt you, I could have done so in the trunk of that car."

Her saucy smile tugged at his groin. "You could've tried."

The ripple of his laughter still rumbled in his chest when she placed her hand inside his. Her icy fingers trembled, and he squeezed.

With his other hand, he pinched the bottle's neck and the stem of an empty wineglass between his fingers, then he led her away from the bar.

Curious onlookers tracked their movements as they wove their way across the room, but no one stopped them. Still, he gripped her hand tight, more tightly than was necessary, and noted every too-long stare.

Upstairs, loud music pumped through the house. Bodies packed the sprawling space, so he placed his hand at the small of her back and stayed close at her side, maybe a touch closer than he needed, as they picked their way through the crowd toward the foyer.

A grand, open staircase led to the second floor, and as they climbed the steps, her hand in his, a roomful of strangers observed them.

Together, they moved down the long hallway. Her jaw slack, she stared at each of the closed bedroom doors as they passed by, as though she could see what was happening on the other side.

Noise from the party downstairs faded the further they delved into the home's massive interior, and by the time they reached the door at the end of the hall, the sounds were barely discernible.

He used the key to release the lock. Then, with a soft shove, the last barrier to their private room fell away.

Soft lighting from a lamp on the bedside table cast a dim glow over the large bedroom. He flipped the switch beside the door and light cascaded down from a crystal chandelier to reveal an excessively elegant room with soaring ceilings, brocade wallpaper, and a huge king-sized bed submersed in luxurious bedding.

She stepped over the threshold ahead of him and he followed her, closing the door behind them.

The lock clicked when he turned it over, and she spun around.

He showed her both of his palms. "You don't have to be afraid."

"I'm not afraid." She tipped her chin with a defiant tilt, but at his look, her shoulders sagged with acknowledgement. "Maybe you should be afraid, too."

"Of you?"

"M-Maybe I lured you here."

"For what purpose?" He narrowed his eyes at her. "Are you planning to fuck me to death?"

A smile might've quirked her mouth, but she turned away

before he could confirm its appearance. "Well, when you say it like that…"

"I'm not gonna lie." His gaze roamed over the walls, searching the shadowy corners of the room for signs of any cameras. "That'd be a pretty cool way to die."

Her soft laughter coaxed a smile to his lips.

He meandered over to the nightstand beside the bed and inspected the drawers and the lamp for recording devices.

Her shoulders rigid, she walked along the end of the bed. Creamy velvet drapery blanketed the far wall, presumably blocking out the view through the windows. When she reached the lush curtains, she stared at the heavy mantle for one long, agonizing moment.

Then she pulled in a prolonged, shaking breath and turned slowly to face him. "Now what?"

The slight tremor of panic in her voice screwed his insides into a tight fist.

He moved to the two plush chairs by the window and deposited the wine bottle and glass on the small round table positioned between them. Then he shook out the heavy drapes and searched behind them.

When he found no evidence of any surveillance, he turned to her. "Now we wait."

CHAPTER 11

ncertainty crowded out the fear on her pretty features. "For how long?"

He settled in a chair. "Long enough to be believable."

She folded her arms over her abdomen. "So what? Like, two minutes?"

A smile tugged at the corners of his mouth. For more than a year, he had found little to make him laugh. With her, he'd smiled more in one night than he had in a very long time.

"I thought you were a virgin." He tipped the wine bottle and liquid flowed into his glass. "What do you know about male stamina?"

"You can learn a lot from books."

"Books?" He raised the wine bottle, an offer.

She moved to the table and plunked down her empty glass. "The public library has a treasure trove of books on the subject."

"The public library, huh?" Filling her glass, he slanted a quick look at her. "Damn, and I let my card expire."

"It's free to renew." She accepted the glass he handed to her.

"They have a lot of books about sex?"

"They have books on every subject." She took a hearty swallow from her glass. "You should see their collection of Irish works. They even have a replica of the Book of Kells."

Surprised interest rose within him. "I didn't know that. Do you like to read?"

Her face brightened. "Oh, yes."

"What do you like to read?" He lifted his glass to his lips.

"Everything. Anything. I used to spend hours at the library every day. I've probably spent more hours inside the Chicago public library than any other place in my whole life."

He sipped his wine, using the glass to hide his fascination with her sudden animation.

"I've still only read a tiny fraction of the books on their shelves." She sank into the other chair. "Even if they'd stayed open 24 hours a day, I probably wouldn't have been able to read them all."

"Why didn't you check the books out and take them home?"

With one hand, she swirled her glass and watched the blush-colored liquid slosh around. "I didn't have a library card."

"Why not?" He studied her profile. "You said they're free."

"They are if you're a resident."

He propped one elbow on the chair's arm and rested his chin on the cradle of his palm. "You said you were born and raised in Chicago."

"I was." She shook her hair away from her face, then glanced over at him. "I didn't have a home address."

Slowly, he lowered his hand. "You didn't have a home?"

"Not all the time, no."

Another long pause stretched out while his mind grappled with the information. "You were homeless?"

"We were in and out of housing."

"How long?" His chest tight, the words leaked out of him.

"I'm not sure how much it adds up to… probably a few years."

Wine turned to cement in his mouth. "Years?"

"Probably. From the time I was ten and my dad lost his job. Then my mom got sick, and we stayed in shelters, or sleep in the car, or wherever. Last year, my brother and I finally got our own place."

Since she was ten? That was most of her life.

"I spent as much time as I could at the library." A whimsical smile touched her lips. "For a while, I'd hide in the bathroom until the staff closed up and left for the night. But they found me out eventually and that was that."

He chewed the wine-flavored cement.

"Books were my escape. Still are." The light in her eyes turned shrewd. "I remember thinking the world had already written me off as poor white trash, but I'd be damned if I was going to be poor and stupid." She laughed alone. "It worked out. My public library education saved me from becoming my parents."

"How's that?"

Her soft sigh was heavy with weariness. "Unable to find steady work. Homeless, hungry, sick, eventually." She shot him an impish grin. "With three ungrateful, mouthy kids."

"You're one of three? I'm the middle of three." He'd grown a little lost in her and forgotten himself. He hadn't meant to share more details about his family.

She ducked her chin, and her hair fell forward to block his view of her profile. "I was in the middle too."

"Was?"

"My older brother died."

He closed his eyes against the slash of his regret. "I'm sorry."

She tucked her hair behind her ear. "Me too."

"What happened?"

Huge, sad eyes found his face. "I couldn't save him."

"I'm sorry," he said again because he truly hated loss and death and grief. Fuck all of that. "I didn't mean to upset you."

"It's okay." Her sincere smile brightened her eyes. "I couldn't save my big brother, but now, thanks to you, I can save my little brother."

He pulled out his phone. "Let me send you the money right now."

She straightened in her chair. "They let you keep your phone?"

He glanced over at her while he waited for the website to load. "Yeah, why?"

"Never mind."

He logged into his account, then asked, "What's your handle?"

When she gave it to him, he arched one eyebrow, but typed in the digital address. He read it back to her, then finished the transaction and hit Send.

He returned his phone to his coat pocket. "I don't know how long it will take to go through. In a few minutes, why don't you check your account?"

"I wish I could." She held out her empty wineglass. "But they took my phone when I came in."

Ah. So that's what had perturbed her. He leaned forward and plucked the wine bottle off the table.

With all the illegal activity taking place at this party, it made sense that they'd confiscate any devices capable of video or voice recording at the door. Now that he thought about it, he wondered why Terrence hadn't asked him to turn over his phone. Maybe Derek's attempt to keep Cian out had distracted him from his duties?

As he refilled her wineglass, he considered how he might use the knowledge of this security breach to gain further inroads with Moretti.

He returned the bottle to the table. "We'll check that it went through before we go our separate ways tonight." Worry marred her features, so he added, "I made you a promise and I won't back out."

"Thank you." A swoop of her hair fell across one eye.

He dipped his head, trying to peer behind the curtain of the silky curtain. "Do you believe me?"

"I do."

"But you're upset."

"I'm not upset. I'm super happy right now." She sniffled.

Baffled, he scratched his jawline. "Super happy, huh?"

"Yes." The word was a watery whisper. "I'm really happy you're not a pervert."

"Then why are you crying?"

"I'm not crying. I never cry. It's just..." The column of her throat worked when she swallowed. "I really needed that money."

Her watery words struck him in the center of his chest. "And now you have it. You don't have to be afraid anymore."

"I'm not afraid." She ran a hand through her dark hair, pushing it off her face. "I'm tired."

Her expression, a mix of determination and devastation, tweaked a chord of familiarity in him. He'd seen that look before many times when he gazed in the mirror.

"That's a hard place to be," he said softly.

She eyed him warily. "Are you making fun of me?"

"Not at all. I know exactly how you feel."

"You do?" Doubt riddled her words.

"I've been where you are. You've lived with the fear so long, and felt it so intensely, that you can no longer fight against it. You can't keep throwing punches and hitting nothing but air. You're too exhausted to go on, so you surrender to your fate."

"Yes," she whispered.

"Damn if the battle didn't nearly kill you, but it didn't, and it's over now. You won." A smile nudged up one corner of his mouth. "Now you're invincible."

He expected her to laugh with him, but she only regarded him with somber eyes. "I don't feel invincible."

"Fear cannot touch you anymore."

A disbelieving frown touched her features. "Nothing scares you?"

"I didn't say that."

"What are you afraid of?"

He didn't hesitate. "Mirrors. Calendars."

Her startled laugh rang out. "Fine, joke if you want to."

It was the truth.

But he shouldn't have told her so much, so he laughed with her. "We superheroes can't reveal all our weaknesses."

"Superhero? You?" She considered him. "Nah. Superheroes are pretty boys from Hollywood. You're not a pretty boy."

"Thank you."

She shifted in her chair. "Oh, I didn't mean it as an insult."

"I didn't take it as one."

"I just meant you aren't classically handsome."

"Now I'm insulted." Smiling, he drank.

"No! I mean, you're hot. Like, totally hot. But you're hot in a 'that guy is totally out of my league' kind of way." Her hands flitted through the air as she spoke. "It's insanely sexy, but definitely not superhero-y. You know?"

He marveled at her. "I have no idea."

"Okay, forget it."

"I don't think I want to forget it. Explain it to me again."

Laughing, she gave her head a shake. "I'm dropping it."

"This out of your league thing. What does that mean?"

Her smile faded, taking with it a piece of his heart. "I'm me, this normal, dorky, still-a-virgin-at-twenty-four-years-old girl, and you're you, this mysterious, dangerous, unafraid guy with crazy sexy charisma." The faintest hint of sorrow colored her tone. "You're out of my league because we're not even on the same playing field. Guys like you and girls like me, we're not even playing the same game."

He wanted to ask her what game she thought they were playing, but he suspected he wouldn't like her answer. "When you say a guy like me, do you mean a guy with dark hair?"

"No, of course not."

"A guy with tattoos?"

That killer smile reappeared. "No."

"Then what?"

With a thoughtful, slightly playful expression, she studied him for a moment. The way her gaze roved over him, naked and assessing, smoldered in his veins.

"I mean, it's all of it." Her eyes softened. "Taken together, it adds up to… something… different. I can't describe it, but it's as subtle as a freight train."

Rattled by her assessment, he pulled a smug smile into place and stretched his legs out in front of him, crossing them at the ankles. "It's the superhero thing."

Her husky laugh set fire to his blood. "It is *not* the superhero thing."

"It is." With a cocky grin, he drank his fruity wine. "I know it is."

The lightheartedness of the moment expanded between them like a beam of warm sunlight. On a soft sigh, her laughter died out, and he grieved its absence.

Into the quiet, she said, "I feel like I owe you for doing this for me."

"You do *not* owe me."

"But it's so much money… It feels like I should give you something in return."

"If it feels like you should, you most definitely should not give me another damn thing." He gentled his tone. "We were clear about the terms of this arrangement from the start. You've already fulfilled your end of the bargain."

She deflated in her chair, dropping her head onto the seatback. For a moment, she stared at the ceiling, then she rolled her head lazily to the side. "I have a coupon for that new pizza place downtown."

"I like pizza."

She perked up. "Or how about a massage? I know a masseuse at a ritzy spa. I might be able to hook you up with a freebie."

"I do not want a massage. But there is one thing I want from you."

CHAPTER 12

*H*er heart thrummed a warning tune in her ears.

"Okay." She dragged out the word. "What is it?"

"Tell me your name." His thick lilt was even more disarming when also under his direct gaze. "Your *real* name."

Dammit. She didn't know how he knew she'd lied. Clever man. Had he observed something in her behavior that gave her away? She used to have a decent poker face, but somehow, this guy had slipped past her usual defenses.

The twinge of her begrudging respect almost made her forget he was a dangerous man.

"Avery," she said. "Avery Bishop."

A light came into his eyes, and for a moment, chased away the shadows. "Notapawn," he muttered the address she'd picked for her online account. "A bishop. I get it now."

His appreciation of her little joke shouldn't have pleased her so much. The warmth that touched her cheeks quickly spread through the rest of her body.

She shouldn't feel this way. Warm and pleased. She was locked in a bedroom at Manny Moretti's house with a man she'd only just met, who'd *bought her* for the night, and she couldn't be sure whether her taut nerves were because of the danger she was in or the irascible charm of the man sitting beside her. What the hell was wrong with her?

He set down his half-consumed drink. "I think we've been in here long enough. Do you want to go home now?"

"God, yes." She lurched to her feet. "Please, let's get out of here."

The hallway was quiet when they left their private sanctuary. Iron sconces threw soft shadows across the corridor as they journeyed.

Suddenly, up ahead, one of the bedroom doors wrenched open and a woman burst out into the hall, slamming the door shut behind.

Cian placed his body between Avery and the woman.

Avery rose on her tiptoes and peered over his shoulder. "Sasha?"

Sasha's top had fallen open, and she tugged it back into place.

Alarm shot through Avery, and she stepped around Cian. "What are you—?"

The door flung open with enough force to bang against the wall, and a giant man with a menacing scowl loomed in the doorway.

"Where are you go—?" The beefy man cut off his question when he noticed Cian and Avery.

Cian moved to stand beside Avery, and the two men exchanged a look. Dark tension filled the space between them.

Avery's gaze bounced from Sasha's pale face to the man. "Hey, Jos, are you okay?"

"She's fine." The man stared hard at Cian when he grasped Sasha's arm. "Aren't you?"

Sasha rolled her eyes, then nodded. "Yeah, I'm okay."

As the man pulled her into the bedroom, Sasha glanced back at Avery over her shoulder, and her expression set off another ripple of worry inside Avery.

She took a step forward. "Sasha, wait—"

The door slammed shut.

Avery stared at the white door, her stomach twisting into knots. Should she pound on it? Or should she believe Sasha when she said she was all right?

Riddled by doubt, she turned away from the door. With every step she and Cian took toward the main party spaces, the compulsion to get out of Moretti's house intensified.

Her heart raced when she scrambled down the foyer stairs and plunged through the crowd. A bottleneck of partiers slowed her mad dash for the basement where her cell phone awaited rescue, and panic rose in her throat.

Then Cian moved to stand close at her back, and her rapidly disintegrating composure stabilized. Though she knew it was impossible, it felt as though he'd loaned her some of his solid strength.

They made their way downstairs, where the party's vibe had changed. Or maybe it was only the contrast with their quiet moments upstairs that made the party now seem more frenzied. The music was louder, and the dance floor overflowed with gyrating bodies. Couples engaged in overt sexual acts didn't bother seeking seclusion in the shadows.

As they moved through the dimly lit room, a darker reality played out before her. An angry bruise marred one woman's arm. Behind another woman's fake, overly exuberant smile was a bleak, empty stare.

The stench of desperation and fear turned Avery's stomach. Her skin flushed hot.

Panic rising, she twisted around, needing proof Cian was still there with her. Immediately, his eyes captured hers, and she could breathe again.

Then, over his shoulder, she spotted Sasha rushing towards them.

Relief loosened the knot in the pit of her stomach.

"Is everything all right?" she asked the moment Sasha reached them.

"I just want to get out of here." On her tiptoes, Sasha scanned the room. "I can't find my friends."

Over Sasha's head, Avery looked at Cian. She hadn't et formulated her question when he nodded his answer.

The strange surge of affection she felt for him frightened her.

"We're heading out now," she told Sasha. "Do you want a ride?"

With a relieved huff, Sasha landed hard on her heels. "That'd be great. Thanks."

They reached the place where Avery had left her phone, and while she searched the heap of confiscated devices, Cian pressed his own phone to his ear. Unable to make out his words over the noise, she could only wonder about his call.

After a lengthy hunt, she plucked her phone from the pile. But Sasha's quest to find her device continued, so Avery kept a lookout in case the hulking man last seen with Sasha thought to bother her some more.

During her patrol, she spotted a local politician, who she recognized from his TV ads with his smiling wife and three cheery children. Now, he ground against a woman on the dance floor who was most definitely not his wife.

Her phone in her hand, Avery fought the urge to flip it on and capture a photo or quick video of how this public servant spent his free time. She searched the other faces nearby. How many other lawmakers were in attendance tonight? Was infidelity the worst of their transgressions?

She wasn't morally opposed to sex parties. If consenting adults wanted to kick back and get kinky, more power to them. But she couldn't shake the bad vibes of this particular sex party, where the girls seemed a tad too young and vulnerable and the men *a lot* too predatory.

Would it break her heart if she caught something on tape that put an end to Moretti's depraved shindigs? Not even a little.

The idea struck her like a bolt of lightning. Her heart galloped along with her racing thoughts. If she could sneak a few photos, what would she do with them? Turn them over to the police?

But she immediately discarded the notion. Even if she managed to catch someone in the act of committing a crime, her efforts would be futile. Moretti was buddies with the city's police chief, and she had no doubt her eyewitness account, even combined with photographic evidence, would amount to little. There might be a week of inconvenient questions, then it would all die down and everything would go back to corruption as usual.

She'd seen it enough times to know that's how it'd go. They'd gotten Moretti himself all the way to a trial, and still, he'd somehow walked away a free man.

Just then, the newly appointed chairman of the Liquor Control Commission sauntered by, and Avery's thumb grazed over her phone's sleek surface.

While it was true she'd likely not be able to convince law enforcement to do their jobs, what if the local media got a whiff of Moretti's salacious parties? Big names doing big scandals equaled big news after all. All she needed was proof, evidence.

She was only one click away from snagging it.

If she captured a few photos and got them into the right newspapers, if enough Chicagoans saw them and were outraged by them, there's no telling how things might snowball. With enough outcry, arrests and resignations might be possible.

A story that big could topple Moretti's entire empire. It might expose all his dirty dealings and the criminal ring of bribery and blackmail he used to protect himself from prosecution.

There'd be no going back to normal after that.

All she had to do was take a few pictures.

A bead of sweat broke out on her forehead.

It would be so easy, and so very dangerous.

Her dad had tried to stand up to Moretti once, and for his insolence, he'd lost his job, their home in a nice neighborhood, and ultimately, his life.

But Avery wouldn't dare challenge Moretti directly. She'd do it secretly. Sneakily.

She pressed the button to switch on her phone, and with a few stealthy swipes across the screen, readied her camera.

She raised the device a fraction, and just when she was about to snap her first photo, a large body stepped in front of her.

Avery tipped her head back and looked up, and up, into the scowling face of Sasha's giant.

"Hey." He ejected a sharp whistle between his teeth, and when he'd caught Sasha's attention, he jerked this thumb over his shoulder. "Let's go."

Sasha shook her head. "I'm taking off. Maybe next time."

Anger crowded his expression. "You're not leaving."

His arm shot out.

Avery slid between him and Sasha, thwarting his attempt to grab her. "She said she has to go."

Vicious fury contorted his features. "Bitch, mind your own business."

Avery didn't fully register the extreme danger she was in until the man's beefy fist was coming at her.

CHAPTER 13

There was a time, when Cian was young and full of piss and vinegar, before cancer, that he'd start fights just to finish them. He always finished them, no matter how bloodied or dazed the battle had rendered him.

Now, he only wanted to go home.

Then the goddamn Baby Assassin had to go and put his hands on Avery.

He watched Derek's meaty paws clamp around her upper arms, then he shoved her aside. When she stumbled and crashed into Cian's chest, he caught and steadied her.

With the jarring impact, a flash of memory hit him like a thunderbolt of a man, who he'd later learn was his biological father, striking Cian's mother hard enough to knock her to the ground. At four or five years old, Cian had been too young to fight back, but the sharp bite of terror and helplessness had stayed with him since that day. He recalled standing there, watching his father hurt his mother, his chest heaving with fury and terror.

And helplessness.

He couldn't protect them. Not his ma. Not Rory. Not that day.

Right then and there, he'd vowed he'd never be helpless again. When he grew up, no one would dare fight him.

Then the mob came after his family.

It was Cian's first memory, and the last time he stood by and watched while some piece of shit tough guy manhandled a woman.

Avery's doe-eyed gaze struck him in the solar plexus. "I can't leave without her."

He spared a quick glance for the other woman. The unmistakable shadow of fear touched her youthful features.

She was young. Too young.

Derek curled his hands into fists at his sides and stepped up to Cian. "She's coming with me. You want a piece of ass, go find your own."

Cian lost the battle over his patience and rolled his eyes. To the woman, he asked, "Do you want to stay here with him?"

She gave her head a firm shake. "No."

A resigned sigh dragged from Cian. "She's coming with me."

Through clenched teeth, Derek seethed. "If you weren't such a lightweight now, I'd kick the shit out of you."

Around them, the heads within earshot turned in their direction.

Cian lifted his shoulders and dropped them heavily. "You could try."

Like the petulant man-baby he was, Derek yanked off his T-shirt, and he threw it to the ground with a roar of anger that sent people backpedaling to get out of the way.

Unhurried, Cian shrugged out of his coat. Slowly, he dragged the hem of his Henley up his torso and tugged the shirt off over his head.

When he turned, he found Avery staring at his torso. Her lips parted, and her dark eyes huge in her small face, she made a thorough, intense inspection of his upper body.

Beneath her appreciative gaze, his muscles rippled.

He was still putting on weight and had lost some of his definition, but she didn't seem to notice.

He held out his shirt and coat. "Do you mind holding these for me?"

She hugged his clothing tight against her chest. "You don't have to do this. We can make a run for it."

Her tender concern teased a smile to his lips, and he winked. "I won't be long."

When he faced Derek again, the crowd had formed a tight circle around them, and the two fighters stalked around the perimeter, sizing each other up, assessing.

The tension between them infected the small audience and reminded Cian of his early fights, which were nothing more than fight clubs in basements, garages, and abandoned warehouses where the spectators were as much a part of the action as the fighters.

But he wasn't at an amateur fight club. He was on the mob's playground now.

He hadn't planned to come here tonight, and he certainly never wished to be the main attraction, but it'd been a gift, of sorts. *She* had been a gift.

Getting to kick the shit out of the Baby Assassin, just this once, was a bonus.

By now, the two MMA fighters, current and former, held the room's rapt attention, so when Derek lunged at Cian with a wild swing, a collective gasp of surprise erupted from the onlookers.

But Derek, ever a shitty fighter, telegraphed his move, and Cian spotted his attack before it'd even begun. During Derek's strike, Cian reached out and flicked his wrist, smacking the tip of Derek's blunted nose with his knuckles.

It was nothing more than a soft tap, but the shock and precise placement of the strike would sting enough to make the eyes water. It was a warning shot. One a better fighter would've been able to dodge easily.

"You're still leaving yourself open for that shit." Cian tsked. "You're not a baby anymore. Time to man up and learn how to block."

Cian's taunts enraged the little prick, as he knew they would. He wanted the bastard's anger directed at him and not at the girl.

"Fuck you, Nolan."

Cian chuckled, enjoying Derek's flustered frustration. "If you say so."

Derek came at Cian again, cranking his arm back behind his head before throwing another wild swing.

He'd never learn.

Cian ducked to avoid Derek's flying fist, but his follow up strike connected. Cian's head snapped back with the force of the blow.

Blood seeped from the corner of his mouth, and he stuck his tongue out to taste it. A slow smile pulled back his lips. It felt good to get hit.

Adrenaline lit and crackled in his veins, and his mind focused like a laser.

He used to love this. Fighting had been his life, and he'd loved everything about it. The power, the strategy, the justice. He'd loved the hours spent training his body, pushing his physical endurance to the limits, and honing his weapons. He'd craved the competitiveness among the other fighters, the taunting, the drama, the drive to get better, stronger. He'd loved it all.

Until he got sick.

Slowly, his strength had faded. His speed slowed. His endurance dwindled. Mental toughness became a weakness. By the end, the cancer had beaten the drive and determination out of him, and he was on his knees, clutching the stuffed animal his kid sister had given him and begging whatever gods had forsaken him for mercy.

In that moment, he would've done anything just to end it and be done with it.

He could never be the fighter he once was. That part of him had died, claimed by that fucking illness that'd tried to take everything from him.

But for a moment, while Derek pranced around like a strutting peacock, Cian was enjoying himself once again. With a smile on his face, he circled the tight ring the crowd had formed.

Derek lunged, and Cian dodged. Derek danced and probed while Cian ducked and darted out of the way. To the onlookers, it might've appeared as though Cian lacked the will to fight or was postponing his inevitable beat down.

But he was not avoiding Derek.

He was waiting, studying his opponent's speed and tendencies. Once he'd gathered enough information, he'd make his move. Until then, he'd watch, much the way a cat stalks its prey before striking.

The crowd continued to grow, and as their numbers swelled, they pushed in closer, trying to see the action.

From the corner of his vision, Avery shouldered her way past a couple of guys that had blocked her view. One man, not noticing her beside him, used his bigger body to create more space and his shoulder knocked against her chin.

Cian's adrenaline lit like a fuse.

He planted his feet into the ground and drew up to his full height. His muscles rippled with barely restrained fury as he raised his clenched fists.

Derek lunged with a speed so swift and powerful it startled a collective response from the crowd.

But Cian was ready for him. With his left arm, he deflected Derek's attack, and immediately followed up with his right fist, crashing into Derek's jaw with a bone-crunching blow.

The Baby Assassin stumbled back two steps, weaved, then dropped like a stone.

One punch.

That quick, lethal strike had earned Cian the nickname.

In the moments it took the stunned crowd to realize the fight had ended, Cian strode toward Avery. When he reached her, he didn't stop, but grabbed his clothes and her hand and kept right on walking toward the exit.

He laced his fingers with hers. "We gotta get out of here. Now."

When he tugged her away from the scene, she craned her neck and stared down at Derek's unconscious face. At the last moment, she snatched her friend's hand.

"I thought you said you retired." She scrambled to keep up with his ground eating strides.

"I did."

"It didn't look like it back there." Her breath came in quick puffs.

He pressed his phone to his ear. "How close are you?"

"Ten minutes out." Rory's severe curse walloped Cian's eardrum. "I told you I wanted nothing to do with this shit."

"Sorry. I'm in a tight spot or I wouldn't have called you."

"Forget it. I don't want to know." Rory cursed again. "Be there in ten."

Cian disconnected the call and redoubled their steps. "This way."

They had to get out of there before Moretti learned Cian had taken out his prized show pony.

They burst from Moretti's house like thieves caught mid-heist and sprinted down the driveway packed with vehicles.

A voice rang out behind them, and a kick of fear spurred Avery's pounding steps.

Another yell sounded, and Avery twisted around as Sasha's footsteps slowed, then halted. She peered through the dark night.

Avery slid to a stop without releasing Cian's hand, jerking him back in his tracks.

The voice pierced the quiet night once more.

"That's my friend." Sasha gave Avery a half-wave as she back away. "I gotta go."

"Wait." Avery took a step toward her. "Let me give you my number. In case you ever need a place to crash or want to hang out...."

A light smile teased Sasha's mouth. "Are you sure?"

"Yeah, I'm sure." Avery read off the digits.

When Sasha finished entering them into her phone, she walked backwards toward her friend's voice. "I'll, uh, see ya around." Then she set off across the lawn.

When the darkness swallowed Sasha, Cian tugged on Avery's hand. "We should go."

She let him lead her to the end of the driveway.

In the street, they slowed their pace but still moved quickly through the quiet, upscale suburb. While her breaths came in sharp pants, he appeared unaffected by the exertion.

At the first crossroad, he turned, and she scurried to keep up as he moved between the shadows cast by the streetlamps.

When they reached a black sedan parked in front of a vast estate, he cast a quick glance over his shoulders, then yanked open the back door and motioned for her to get inside the vehicle.

Without a moment's hesitation, she moved to duck inside the car's dark interior, but at the last second, she pulled up. For the second time in one night, she was about to jump into a car with strange men.

The Avery of two weeks ago would never have been so reckless.

But *this* Avery needed to get away from Manny Moretti and anything that might be credibly described as a sex den.

She climbed inside the car, and Cian slammed the door shut behind her, then slid into the passenger's seat.

Another dark-haired man sat behind the steering wheel, and she glimpsed his profile when he turned to Cian. He didn't speak, but the aggravated tilt of his head spoke volumes.

Without a word to the driver, Cian turned to Avery. "Where to?"

Since she didn't know where they were, she said, "You can just drop me at the closest L station."

"It's a little late to be riding the L." Facing front, she couldn't see Cian's face, but his voice reflected the scowl she imagined on his face.

"Maybe she doesn't want you to have her home address."

Their driver also spoke with a thick Irish accent. "Hadn't thought of that, had ya?"

She could hear Cian's scowl deepen.

But the man made a good point. One she should've considered when she'd agreed to let Cian take her home. Man, she was having an off day.

"I'm in Lake View." After tonight, no more risk-taking, she thought as she dragged the seatbelt over her shoulder and clicked it into place "Broadway and Addison."

The driver steered the car through the quiet, upscale neighborhood. When they reached the highway junction, she discovered Mikey's trunk ride had taken them at least thirty minutes north of the city.

She supposed it wasn't de rigueur to host a sex party in town. Such events needed to take place farther outside the city, where the properties were not only huge but also secluded and private.

On the interstate, they aimed for the Chicago skyline.

No one spoke inside the vehicle, but the two men carried out an entire conversation with subtle glances and muted grunts and sighs. The tension between them was a thick, palpable thing.

Avery didn't have to wonder about their relationship for long. Even in profile, she recognized the similarities of their features.

Rather than poke the tension-filled balloon, she pulled out her phone and logged into her digital wallet. When the data loaded, her mouth dropped open. She stared at her phone while shock and joy, and a big fat wave of relief, whipped through her. The money had arrived in her account.

The rest of the ride flew by, and the heavy friction inside the vehicle could've ignited a fire and she wouldn't have noticed. Nothing could bring her down.

They exited the highway and traversed the darkened city streets in her north Chicago neighborhood. She'd lucked out when she found an affordable apartment in the charming vintage walkup that'd been converted from an old hotel.

But what she'd gained in the building's location, she'd sacrificed in square footage. Her apartment was a four hundred square foot, one bedroom dwelling on the top floor, that she could afford all on her own if she had to, since Jamie wasn't the most reliable when it came to paying his share of the rent.

She was damn proud of her tiny apartment. One day, she hoped to have a house all her own.

When the car rolled up to the stop sign at the end of her street, she unfastened her seatbelt. "This is me."

The car slowed to a stop.

"Wait for me," Cian said to the driver as he reached for his door handle. "I'll be right back."

Avery popped her door's latch. "I'll just jump out here."

Cian swung his door open wide. "I'll walk you up."

"You don't have to—"

But he was already out of the car.

When he headed up the front walkway, she stopped him with a hand on his arm, then tipped her head to the side. "This way."

They bypassed the building's front gate and slipped down the narrow alley. At the last set of iron stairs mounted to the brick building, she started to climb.

"Is there a reason we're using the fire escape and not the front door?" He drew up the collar of his coat against the chilly breeze. "Afraid of waking up your boyfriend?"

She shushed him, and they scaled the rest of the stairs in silence. On the platform at the top, she crouched before the lone window.

"Tell me the truth." His feet landed in the line of her sight. "Are we robbing this place?"

A low chuckle tickled her chest as she fumbled with the latch. "It's my bedroom window."

"Your bedroom doesn't have a door?"

She stood as she hauled the window open. "Rent was due last week."

"Can't you pay your rent?" His voice was suddenly soft and full of concern.

Her heart flipped over at the sound. "I can now. But I don't want to deal with my landbastard tonight."

He shuffled closer until the toes of his shoes nearly touched the tip of hers. "So you'll be all right?"

"Me?" She slipped her hands inside her coat pockets. "I'll be fine."

"Why don't I give you my number?" Light from the building cut shadows across his face. "In case you run into any more trouble."

"I never run into trouble. I'm a sweet, innocent virgin, remember?"

His smile set her pulse racing. "Of course. It's your brother I should be worried about. Any chance he's around?" He peered through her bedroom window. "I'd like to meet him."

"Okay, fine." Clumsily, she fumbled for her phone and switched it on. "What's your number?"

He relayed the digits to her, and she saved the information.

She stared at his name on her contact list while a struggle played out inside her heart. For her, the best-case scenario would be that they never saw or talked to each other again after tonight. But the thought triggered an odd pang inside her chest.

In a crazy night, in a crazy world, he'd been the singular point of sanity. More than once, it'd been not only reassuring, but comforting to have him by her side.

With a sinking in the pit of her stomach, she realized she was going to miss that.

She lifted her chin but didn't dare seek his gaze. "Well, I' not going to call you."

"I wish you would," he said softly. "If you need me."

"If I need to swindle some poor fool out of a big old wad of cash, you'll be the first one I call." He was smiling when she laid her palm on his chest and gave him a playful shove. "Man, you are such a sucker."

He snagged her hand.

In the split second when she thought he would tug her close, her heart took flight. She imagined melting against him and lifting her face up to his.

Oh, you want to kiss me now? Go right ahead.

Wish to steal my heart? Take it, it's yours.

Wanna watch me to fall for a mobster and criminal? Weeeeeeee!!

Want to ruin my life? Have at it. I won't be able to stop you.

Luckily, he didn't pull her close.

What he did was far, far worse.

CHAPTER 15

*W*ith the lightest of touches, he dragged the pad of his thumb across her knuckles, and a ripple of sensation shot up her arm to her heart where it zinged through her veins faster than she could say *please love me.*

She turned her palm and let her fingers dance over his warm skin. When she brushed a spot on his knuckles, he winced.

With a frown, she lifted his hand and angled it to catch the light. A soft gasp eased from her. "You're bleeding."

"It's nothing."

Still holding his hand, she dabbed the damaged skin.

A sudden wind blew a tendril of hair across her forehead, and he uncurled his fingers so that the tips toyed with the wayward strands.

Then he dipped his head, bringing his eyes level with hers.

Her breath caught in her throat, and for a long, suspended moment, she was frozen, until his mouth brushed over her lips. Heat sparked and smoldered and spread through her.

She had kissed boys before, but not many, and none recently, so she had a small sample size to go by. But this kiss… it was the most incredible kiss she'd ever experienced.

He tasted like a cupcake, all sugary goodness and velvety softness, with decadent bursts of saccharine sprinkles. He lured her in with his vibrant colors, then over-delivered on the promise of his scrumptious flavor. She had to have another bite, and another.

"Wow," she breathed.

He gasped for air, as though he'd been held under water too long. He blinked at her, shocked and startled.

A jolt of self-consciousness rushed through her. "I'm sorry, I—"

With a soft growl, he swooped in and claimed her mouth with his. Hot and hungry and so intensely good.

From inside the apartment, a loud noise sounded.

On a gasp, she broke away. "I gotta go."

She scrambled through the window and reached up to haul it shut, but at the sight of him on her fire escape, his eyes ablaze with lustful secrets, she couldn't resist grabbing him by the coat collar and pulling his head down for one more kiss.

His lips were soft and his chest solid, and she melted against him as molten fire raged through her veins.

Another thump behind her threw cold water over her head, and she jerked back.

"Thank you." She snatched one last taste of his sweet lips. "For everything."

Then, with a hard shove against his chest, she pushed him out of the way and slammed the window shut.

She yanked the curtains closed and spun around a split second before Jamie stuck his head through her bedroom door.

"Oh, hey." He glanced around her tiny bedroom. "I didn't know you were here."

"Yep." She clasped her hands in front of her. "Here I am."

"Who were you talking to? Did Dale catch you on your way up?"

"What? No. I wasn't talking to anyone. It was nobody. I mean, there's nobody here." She tugged back the curtain, giving him a brief peek, then yanked it closed again. "See?"

He quirked his eyebrow. "You okay?"

"I'm fine. Good. Real good." Her cheeks burned.

Why was it so hot in here?

His sharp gaze shifted from her face to the window over her shoulder.

"Did you know you were in debt to Manny Moretti?" she blurted out. "You told me owe Mikey that money."

Jamie's gaze snapped back to hers, and the color slowly drained from his face. But his expression held no traces of shock or surprise. Only guilt.

He knew.

Fear punctured a hole in her heart. "Moretti has destroyed people's lives for less than what you owe him." A drum beat of terror thrummed in her chest. "He could've killed you."

"You think I don't know that?" He bit off his anger with a curse, then shoved a hand through his dark hair.

Beneath the crushing weight of fear, hers and his, fury bubbled and frothed in Avery's chest. "What were you thinking? Why were you gambling at Moretti's tables? Why were you gambling at all?"

"Because I'm tired." The words erupted from him. "I'm tired of working three jobs and still having to crash on my sister's couch. I'm sick and tired of fighting for scraps while everyone else lives like kings. I'm sick of it, Ave."

Her heartbeat echoed in her ears with a chaotic rhythm.

As if through a tunnel, she heard herself say, "I got the money."

Shock filled his expression. "What? Where? How?"

She waved away his questions. "It doesn't matter. I'll send it to you tonight."

"How did you come up with that kind of money so fast? Did

you steal it?" His gaze cut to the window and back. "Where were you tonight?"

"I didn't steal it." She wriggled out of her coat and flung it across the bed. "Just shut up and take the money, okay? Pay Moretti back and be done with this. And no more gambling."

He screwed his mouth into a stubborn line, and she knew he wanted to argue with her. But he also knew he'd fucked up, and he had no choice but to take the money and pay off Moretti.

His head bobbed with his curt nod. "Okay."

When he left, she closed her bedroom door and sagged against it. Her bones ached for rest, so she grabbed a shower and brushed her teeth, then crawled into bed.

She snuggled under the covers, desperate for her first peaceful slumber since this whole crisis had started.

But she couldn't sleep.

She couldn't forget all she had seen at Moretti's home that night, and all that she'd learned. Jamie. The young girls. The fear and desperation.

Cian.

Memories of that kiss lived in her veins like an erotic hum. A delicious tension built in her stomach to recall the feel of his hot mouth on hers and the decadent taste of his arousal.

Then she remembered who he was, and the sensual river sloping through her body ran dry.

He was a mobster. Moretti's man, no less.

She'd likely never see him again, and even if she did, she certainly could not kiss him.

He was dangerous. Totally off limits. He was part of Moretti's ugly world, and no matter how yummy he tasted, he'd only ever leave her with a nasty sugar crash and torment her with an extra hour on some demonic contraption at the gym.

A soft despair pulled at her heart. She expelled a huff of air at the ceiling, trying to dislodge the heaviness weighing on her.

Where was Sasha tonight? Was she some place safe, or in a

shelter? What happened to her harasser after Cian knocked him out? What about the other girls? What about the next party? Or the next sucker to lose at Moretti's rigged gambling tables?

Fear and fury sat like rocks in her stomach, and she rolled to her side.

She was so tired of watching this story play out again and again. She'd seen it with her parents, with Logan, and now Jamie had barely escaped his brush with the devil. Behind every life she'd watched be ruined, there was Manny Moretti.

For as long as she remembered, he'd terrorized this city as a slumlord, a drug dealer, a runner of illegal gambling rings, and a trafficker of pretty much every other illicit vice. How many more casualties would there be in this corrupt man's unrelenting quest for money and power? How had he been allowed to carry on, unchecked, for so long?

It was as if he were untouchable, and he'd remain so unless, or until, someone did something to stop him.

Gooseflesh prickled across her skin.

Someone should expose Manny Moretti for who and what he really was. Someone should shine a light on his dark schemes and shady operations. If they did it right, they could expose the politicians and law enforcement authorities who helped prop him up and protect him.

Just one good investigative journalist could bring down the entire racket.

But no journalists worked the mob beat anymore. The last one that tried, Moretti had threatened and destroyed their career. Then he bought the paper they worked for and killed the story. Now, there was no one.

Except her.

The thought shot through her like an electric jolt, and she sat up in bed.

Could she do it?

No, she couldn't.

She shouldn't.

It would take too much time to research Moretti's vast and tangled web of criminal activity. It was too much work for her to pull together all by herself. Moretti knew how to hide his crimes and it'd be impossible to find all the proof she'd need. It'd require a lot of digging, a lot of sneaking into dark, ugly places.

It would be dangerous.

Still…she'd gotten deep inside his personal residence in one night. It hadn't even been all that hard.

What might she accomplish if she applied a little effort? If she gave it some forethought and planning?

Besides, there was no one else who would do it.

Terror struck like an icy dagger in her heart. She ignored it.

She was a professional, or she wanted to be, one day. When she could afford the rest of her tuition, she would be.

Professional journalists went into war zones. They looked dictators and cruel tyrants in the eyes and demanded they answer for their crimes. Journalists bore witness to the truth in the face of a hundred thousand lies, demanding honesty and righteousness so that wrongs might be made right. Surely, she could flirt her way through a few sex parties to gather the evidence she needed.

Bile rose in her throat, and she swallowed thickly.

If she wrote this story and got it published, it might be the kind of work that'd win her the competition for her department's scholarship. If she won, she'd finish her degree and get the promotion at the Daily Sun.

She could do this.

For Sasha and all the girls who had to stand in front of the mirror and agonize whether they should allow a rich man to pay them for sex, and for the others, like her brother, who were young and beaten down, and so desperate for a future they believed they'd never have, that they placed that one last bet, hoping to strike gold.

For her parents, and for Logan.

For them, she'd turn her fear into fuel, and, with enough luck, she'd take down Moretti's entire criminal enterprise, once and for all.

She flipped to her other side and stared at the window where she'd kissed Cian only an hour before.

If she was going to take them all down, she'd most likely have to take him down with the rest of them.

CHAPTER 16

*I*n the aftermath of that kiss, Cian stood on her fire escape, paralyzed while the veil of his numbness burned away, singed by the feel of her warm mouth against his and the whisper-soft strands of her hair tickling his fingers.

The numb detachment surrounding him for months gave way, and suddenly, his senses flooded with sights and sounds and smells.

Of her.

Her color, her taste, her scent, her softness. Everything collided and overwhelmed him. Like a shock to his non-beating heart, he gasped for breath, slamming back to life. After the long sleep of creeping death, he was awake.

Alive.

On weak legs, he started down the fire escape stairs, and nearly stumbled. He gripped the cold metal railings and held on while emotions pummeled him.

So much emotion.

All he'd thought destroyed by the disease and the death that had stalked him came rushing back.

Memories of the last time he'd been overcome menaced him.

His feet moved under him, slow at first, then faster, until he was taking the steps two, then three, at a time.

He remembered the night when he feared he was losing his fight against the cancer, the most formidable opponent he'd yet faced. The grief had overwhelmed him as he'd laid awake in the dark, hugging the stuffed animal his kid sister had given him after one of his worst chemo treatments.

Tears burned a path down his cheeks, but he didn't wipe them away. He didn't push down the pain. He let it sear him. Because the pain was proof that he was still alive.

But he'd cried. He'd cried because of the pain. He'd cried because he'd never be the man he'd dreamed he'd become. He'd cried because he'd never be someone's husband or dad. He'd cried because a bleak, pain-riddled future stretched out before him, and there was no hope in the dark.

At that moment, he'd wished he was already dead. He'd wished to set himself and his family free from their pain of witnessing him die. He was a burden to them, not only because of the illness, but because the inevitability of loss was so fucking painful.

Watching his mother cope with his diagnosis and treatment had been the hardest. No one should have to watch their child suffer. It was the cruelest fate, and he hated that he caused her that pain.

That night, crying in the dark, he'd vowed to never be the reason someone lost their entire world.

He jumped over the last several stairs, trying to outrun the memories, and landed with a jarring thud on solid earth.

His feet back on the ground, reality slowly settled in his bones. As he strode back to the car where Rory waited for him, he knew he could never see Avery Bishop again, and he damn well could not kiss her. Or let her kiss him.

When he'd agreed to help Kendrick, he'd forfeited a normal life. He couldn't date. He couldn't hang out with friends or family. The more he wanted to be with someone, the further he needed to run in the opposite direction, lest Moretti learn of his weakness and try to use those Cian cared about as a bargaining chip to control him. As he'd done to Brynn.

It. Could. Not. Happen.

Never again.

By the next morning, Cian had reigned in the emotions unleashed by Avery's sweet, somewhat inexperienced but hot as fuck kiss.

Though it was Saturday, he arrived at The Hathaway Group's headquarters downtown a little after nine o'clock.

With Alan in a prison cell, Aiden and Brynn now ran the company. But since Alan had invited the menace Moretti into their lives, a crime that in Cian's opinion warranted thirty years, plus the three he'd already been sentenced to serve, they stayed away from Chicago and, as much as possible, oversaw operations remotely.

While they managed most of the work through email and Zoom meetings, occasionally, they needed Cian to send them physical documents or stop by one of the homes they were renovating to take photos or video some footage. So, once or twice a week, Cian stopped by the office where he checked on things and picked up the mail. Often, he chose the weekends for his visits so that he could avoid the staff and any awkward questions.

When he walked into the main office suite, he expected to find the space empty, but he discovered Brynn at the coffee station.

Fear lashed at him, and he stalked toward her. "What are you doing here?"

"Good morning to you, too." She poured a stream of coffee into her cup.

"Does Aiden know you're here?"

"Of course." She returned the coffeepot to the warming pad.

"We need to stop by the Wabash project and figure out what we're going to do about that nightmare."

"Where is he?" Cian glanced around the office suite, but no one else was there. "Why isn't he with you?"

"He ran to get us some breakfast." She took a sip of the steaming brew, then wrinkled her nose. "Decaf just isn't as good as the real stuff."

Cian tugged on the collar of his coat. "You're not supposed to be anywhere near Chicago."

"You seem to have things under control here." She dumped the contents of her coffee mug out in the sink. "So Aiden checked with Kendrick, and he thought it was safe enough for us to come home for a few days and deal with a couple of things."

He clenched and unclenched his fists at his sides. If Kendrick had given his okay, and Cian also knew of no impending threat against Aiden and Brynn from Moretti, it was probably safe enough for a brief visit. Moretti was a power-hungry and ruthless con man, but he was also a practical fellow, and Aiden and Brynn posed no immediate danger to him or his illegal rackets.

Still, Cian didn't like it. Moretti hadn't forgiven or forgotten the role they'd played in his legal troubles, and if Cian and Kendrick were wrong, the potential consequences were far too great.

The spot between his shoulder blades burned with tension as he entered the vast corner office overlooking the Chicago River.

Brynn appeared at the door and leaned against the doorframe. "You're here early."

"I couldn't sleep." He flung his coat over the desk chair and sank down onto the smooth black leather.

His gaze lingered on her growing belly for a moment before he turned his head away and stabbed the computer's power button with his finger.

While he waited for the machine to power on, he rocked back in the chair. "What's on the agenda for today?"

A soft smile curved her mouth. "You know, you don't have to pretend to care about this kind of work. It's enough what you're doing to help us."

"Oh, that's grand." He reached for the computer mouse. "I'm just going to play solitaire until it's time to go to lunch then."

With her laugh, her pretty face lit up.

She pointed to the small meeting table near the door where she'd left her laptop. "Mind if I work in here?"

"Have at it." Rather than start the game, he opened the browser, then hunted and pecked his way across the keyboard. A-v-e-r-y B-i-s—

"Are you whistling?"

"Was I?" He cracked the knuckles on his right hand. "Sorry."

"It's okay." She bent her head over the laptop, then looked up. "It's just, you never whistle."

"I'm trying some new things." He bit down on his tongue and searched for the P.

"Omigosh," she gasped. "You met someone."

He lifted his hands away from the computer, as though she'd been caught in the act. "I don't kiss and tell."

Her eyes grow huge. "There was a kiss?"

"Hell, yeah, there was a kiss."

She bounded up from her chair. "Who is she? Where did you meet her? When do you see her again?"

"Like I said, I'm not the kind of guy to kiss and tell."

She smacked his desk with both of her palms. "Oh. Em. Gee. You love her."

"What?" He ran a hand over his mouth to hide his smile. "You're crazy."

Cian adored his stepsister, who was not at all crazy, but cool as hell. For years, he'd been constantly disappointed that more women weren't as chill and fun to hang out with as Brynn.

She folded her arms. "Since when are you not that kind of guy? You're totally that kind of guy. If you expect me to believe you're suddenly not that kind of guy, it can only mean one thing."

Cian hadn't been able to help Brynn with all she'd been through, so the least he could do was let her have a few minutes of fun at his expense.

He laced his fingers behind his head. "Oh, yeah, what's that?"

"She's special." Brynn propped her hip on the edge of the desk. "So, who is she?"

"Who is who?" Aiden asked as he stepped through the office door.

Cian pulled his surly scowl into place and stabbed a finger at Brynn. "Will you get her out of here?"

A tantalizing aroma followed Aiden into the room. "What'd she do now?" he asked and a white cardboard box on the table next to Brynn's laptop

"He met a girl." The words burst from Brynn.

Aiden's gaze flickered to Cian. "A new girl? Or did you and Corinne get back together?"

"It's not Corinne." Like one magnet drawn to another, Brynn and Aiden moved together. "He was whistling."

"Whistling?" Aiden pulled her into his arms and dropped a kiss on her forehead. "What song?"

"I didn't recognize it." Brynn laid her head on his chest. "It was a jaunty tune though."

"Uh-oh..." Aiden slipped her arms around her and inhaled deeply, as though smelling her hair, or breathing in her soul. "Did you say jaunty?"

As one, they turned toward Cian, twin expressions of humor and curiosity on their faces.

"Are you two finished?" Cian stretched out his legs under the desk. "We need to talk."

All traces of humor vanished, and they pulled apart.

A pang of regret struck Cian in the ribs. He hated to bring up Moretti and memories of the most painful periods in their lives.

He knew Aiden and Brynn wanted to forget all that had happened, all that Moretti had done to them. But none of them could afford that luxury right now.

With a grimace, he asked, "Have you made a decision about what you want to do?"

They shared a look, then Aiden tipped his head. He slipped his hand inside Brynn's, and she gave him a soft smile.

"We're going to close Hathaway Group and start our own company," she said. "Together."

A long breath leaked out of Cian. He knew it must be hard for Brynn, shutting down the company she'd helped build with her dad, but it was the right decision. With Alan's arrest, the company's founder, a cascade of business-killing events had followed. Asset forfeiture, missed payments, lawsuits, stop work orders, and penalties. Through it all, the publicity had been brutal.

Cian would become the public figurehead at Hathaway Group while Aiden and Brynn worked behind the scenes to shuffle all the company's legit business over to the new venture. Then, when the time was right, Cian would shut down the family business.

He pushed up from his chair. "I'm happy for you."

"We'd love it if you'd join us." Hope and uncertainty braided through Brynn's voice. "If that's something you'd be interested in."

At the table, Cian flipped open the cardboard box crammed with baked goods. He stared down at the tasty-smelling treats and waited for a craving or the desire to consume one of them.

Nothing.

He closed the box. Twisting around, he leaned against the table and regarded his siblings.

His lips twitched as he tried, but failed, to smile. It was no use. There was no way to soften the blow.

"I think it's time to enact Plan B," he said.

CHAPTER 17

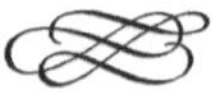

The words dropped like a sledgehammer. Nothing soft about them.

"Who's going to tell Rory?" Brynn's worried gaze darted back and forth between Aiden and Cian. "He's not going to like it."

"He's going to hate it." Aiden shoved a hand through his dark hair, and Cian glimpsed the scar that ran from his temple to his ear. A near-miss from a bullet and another reminder of Moretti's appetite for vengeance. "I'll tell him."

Brynn chewed her bottom lip for a moment while her mind worked through the strategy they'd devised months ago. "I'll contact the tabloid tomorrow and make an anonymous tip."

"Not necessary." Cian flicked the box open again. "I have a contact at the paper."

"Which paper?" Brynn asked at the same time Aiden demanded to know, "Who?"

"Don't worry about it." He picked out a sugary donut. "Focus on making your arrangements."

"It's her, isn't it?" Brynn's tone lightened with her curiosity. "Is she a reporter?"

Cian seized the opportunity to distract from the painful topic. Because that's what Avery was—a distraction. Nothing more.

When Aiden and Brynn had had their fun, they cranked out a few hours of work, then headed out to visit the nightmare house.

He grabbed something to eat at the food truck parked outside the office building, then he hit the gym for a couple of hours. Afterwards, he returned to the Hathaway Group owned penthouse where he'd been staying.

As he strolled around to the skyscraper's side entrance, two men detached from the shadows and blocked the path in front of him.

He made a swift appraisal of both men. The taller man was older and uglier, and the smaller man, though lean, was well-muscled. By the way they'd positioned their bodies, leaving themselves vulnerable on their flanks while trying to intimidate him with puffed up chests and mean glares, it was clear neither man knew how to fight.

Cian expelled a weary sigh. "What's this about then?"

The smaller man stepped close enough that Cian could've reached out and grabbed him by the throat. "Mind if we come upstairs and have a little chat?"

Cian curled his hands into tight fists. "I mind very much."

The kid shot a nervous glance at his partner. With dark hair and eyes, he looked vaguely familiar, but Cian was certain they'd never met.

The kid licked his lips. "It's not a question."

"Who the fuck are you?" Cian snapped.

"I'm n-nobody. Just delivering a message."

The soles of Cian's shoes scraped against the sidewalk as he faced the kid fully. "Well, get to it, why don't ya?"

He swallowed heavily. "We need you to fight."

Surprise rumbled through Cian. "Who's we?"

"Mr. Moretti."

Cian folded his arms over his chest. "Why isn't Mr. Moretti asking me himself?"

"Because he sent us to do it." The pipsqueak's partner shook his head and chuckled, as though Cian said something funny. "He's a very busy man."

Through narrowed eyes, Cian assessed the younger man. Nervous sweat glistened on his upper lip and forehead.

Jesus Christ, what was this? A mobster-in-training program? Had Moretti really sent this little prick here to deliver Cian's orders? It was insulting.

Not to mention, Dr. Hoffman's warnings had scared Cian straight. He didn't want to risk his life for fighting, and he especially didn't care to put his neck on the line fighting for Moretti.

He adjusted the strap of his gym bag across his body. "Tell Moretti I said no thanks."

"It's not an invitation," the sidekick cut in.

"You broke DeMarco's jaw." The young pup shuffled his feet. "He's out six weeks at least."

Shite. The curse vibrated in Cian's throat.

"He's got a fight next weekend and now, because of you, he can't fight in it." The sidekick clapped one hand on Cian's shoulder. "So you'll be doing it in his place."

Cian went unnaturally still. Slowly, he turned his head and stared at the man's hand. In his mind, he counted. Three... Two...

The man withdrew his touch.

"Even if I wanted to help Moretti out, which I fucking don't, I cannot do it. I won't be winning any matches. I retired a year ago." He shouldered his way between the two men and strode toward the building's entrance.

Both men hounded his steps. "You don't gotta win. You just gotta stay on your feet for two rounds."

Cian's pace slowed. He stopped, then twisted around. "You want me to throw the match?"

An uneasy dread snaked through his gut. Rigging fights

sounded innocent enough, but he knew plenty of decent, hard-working fools who put down a lot of their scant money on these bouts. He'd hate to swindle them.

But it was a fast and easy way to get inside Moretti's criminal circle. Maybe his little gambit with Avery had paid off and Moretti now believed in Cian's corruptibility. What would Agent Kendrick say? Would match fixing be enough to put Moretti away for real this time? Cian couldn't imagine the crime commanded a lengthy jail sentence.

But would it be long enough for them to keep building the case against him while he was behind bars? The man had a seemingly endless rap sheet of other crimes.

Dammit, but he hated to cheat the game. It'd been the one pure thing in his life, and he loathed corrupting it.

Before he agreed to do anything, he needed to talk to Kendrick. To do that, he needed a little time. And chances were, Kendrick would tell him he needed to get the orders directly from Moretti if they were going to make the charges stick.

With a mean scowl, Cian stared venom-tipped daggers at the men. Like gnats buzzing around his head, he longed to swat at them. "I want to talk to Moretti."

While the sidekick shook his head, the pup whimpered. "You're not setting the conditions. Mr. Moretti is."

"Yeah, well, if he wants a fighter in the ring next weekend, he needs to make it worth my while."

The kid scoffed, and the ugly one grumbled, but neither argued with him.

Cian bared his teeth. "If he wants me to dance, he needs to ask me nicely."

CHAPTER 18

*A*very tugged on her floppy wool hat, pulling it snug over her blond wig. She opened her notebook and pretended great interest in the writings on the page while, secretly she watched the action unfold in the corner booth at Moretti's favorite casual dining restaurant.

Her small table for two was far enough away that Moretti wouldn't catch her, but too far away to eavesdrop on his conversations. While the frenzy of the dinner rush hour swirled around her, she noted who he hosted at his table, how long they talked, and the general mood of the meeting.

The waitress appeared at her table with a drink that Avery didn't order. She tipped her head towards the bar. "From the gentlemen at the end."

Avery glanced over to find a trio of men in business suits wearing an assortment of slimy, sleazy, and goofy grins.

"No, thanks. I'm driving," she said, though she didn't own a car. "Thank them for me, anyway?"

"Sure will."

For the moment, Moretti was alone, so Avery returned to her notebook. After only six days tailing Moretti, she'd taken several pages of notes and compiled a long list of business dealings and associations she intended to follow up on to unravel his web of criminal activity.

She frowned at her notebook, pondering Moretti's connection to a drug dealer named Sanchez, when a shadow fell over her table.

"Excuse me." Sleazy placed one hand on his hip and hit her with his toothy grin. "My friends and I would like to buy you a drink."

She offered him a tight smile. "I'm sorry, but I'm working tonight."

"That's fine. I totally get it." His smile collapsed, and he shifted his stance to his other foot, but he didn't leave. "But, uh, we were trying to be nice."

The smile froze on her face. "And I'm not trying to be rude. I just want to do my work and go home."

"Fine." Palms up, he backed away. "Have a nice night."

Across the room, the man Moretti paid to drive him around town approached the boss. She'd learned that his driver doubled as a secretary of sorts to Moretti, bringing him information and delivering his messages to others.

Beneath the brim of her hat, she watched them talk for a few moments, then as the driver left the restaurant, she scribbled down the event in her notebook.

From the corner of her eye, she detected Slimy working his way toward her. She kept her head down and pretended not to notice him.

But he came to stand at the edge of her table anyway. "Hi. I'm Gary. Can you help me out? My friends and I have a bet."

With a sigh, she leaned back in her chair.

"My friend thinks you're single." Gary's chuckle was as greasy as his hair. "But I say there's no way a woman as gorgeous as you isn't already taken."

She folded her arms over her abdomen and opened her

mouth to tell him what she thought of his stupid bet. But the retort died on her lips when she spotted Cian across the room.

She couldn't deny the spark of excitement that swept through her with his sudden presence.

"Get lost, Gary."

After a beat of shocked silence, Gary shook his head and slinked away.

Unable to take her eyes off Cian, she watched him weave through the tables, his movements light and swift, almost graceful. His taut leanness and sinewy strength captured a trail of gazes as he moved toward Moretti's corner booth.

As he approached, Moretti waved his hand, granting Cian permission to sit, and he lowered his big body into a seat at the edge of the booth.

A sudden stab of disappointment pierced her.

Since the weekend, her heart had tried crafting a tale around Cian where he was a good guy stuck in a bad situation, much like Avery herself. Because surely, a guy who'd give her all that money, who helped her dodge all the landmines at Moretti's party, and protected Sasha, a woman he likely didn't know, then risked his body in a brawl, had to be good, didn't he?

But she knew better than to trust her heart, so she'd researched him online and found out he'd retired from fighting because of an unspecified illness. Reading that, she couldn't help but wonder if that was what caused the sadness in his eyes.

She also learned that his stepdad was serving a three-year sentence in a low security prison for laundering Manny Moretti's dirty money, and that his brother, Aiden, had escaped a similar fate by turning over evidence to the feds and testifying against his stepdad and Moretti.

Pictures from the trial showed Cian's mom and a young girl with sad eyes like his, but she could find nothing more about the family.

For a few days, she'd spun a story in her mind, where Cian

was like his brother, standing against Moretti. But now, here he was, having dinner in public with the well-known mobster his stepdad had taken the fall for, and that his brother had betrayed. Did that mean Cian was a mobster too, like his stepdad?

As Cian and Moretti met, for once, she wished she weren't so close to the action. She didn't want to observe and take notes about Cian's conversation with Moretti. If they were scheming to destroy another family like hers, she didn't want to discover evidence of his corruption.

She didn't want to feel the tiny cracks of disillusion forming in her heart.

She didn't want proof he wasn't just a man in a tough spot trying to do the right thing.

The rush of early evening diners dwindled, and the noise-level in the room dampened to the soft drone of patrons talking and the occasional clink of silverware.

Soon, the intense chat at the mob boss's table ended, and Cian stood. He waited while Moretti slid to the end of the booth and climbed to his feet. The men exchanged a few more words. Then Moretti brushed by Cian and headed for the exit.

With Moretti gone, Cian pulled out his wallet and dropped several bills onto the table. When he turned, she expected him to travel the same path Moretti had taken out of the restaurant.

Instead, he looked directly at her.

The shock of being seen by him ran through her body. His eyes never left her face as he moved toward her.

The prolonged anticipation of his arrival was excruciating.

By the time he stood at the edge of her table, a gnarly ball of lust and longing had tightened her belly.

She forced a pull of air through her lungs. "Hey."

"Hey."

With only one word, his voice reached inside her and brushed between her legs.

"How are you?" A heart-rending tenderness flickered in his eyes. "Are you okay?"

"I'm okay." She closed her notebook and slid into the bag hanging on the back of her chair. "Do you want to sit down?"

His steady gaze bore into her. "I want to buy you a drink."

"I'd love a drink."

Cian signaled to the waitress standing behind the trio at the bar. Avery ignored the men gawking at her and Cian. She didn't care if it made her a liar or a hypocrite. She wanted nothing from those men.

She couldn't say the same about Cian.

He dragged the other chair around the table and sat beside her, so close she could feel the heat from his body and smell his clean, manly scent. She drank in the comfort of his nearness, even as it overwhelmed her.

His gaze, cool and gemstone bright, revealed nothing. But he had to feel the peculiar, eager tension building between them, didn't he?

The waitress delivered their drinks, a wine for her, the same type she'd been drinking the other night, and a tumbler of whiskey for him.

He lifted his drink to his mouth. His lips parted and the tip of his tongue pressed against the glass.

Her senses spun. She should say something, but words tripped and tumbled on her tongue. In every way possible, he disturbed her.

"Should I go?" He returned the tumbler to the table. "I'm making you nervous."

"Not nervous, no." She touched his hand, and with the light contact, a jolt ricocheted through her body. "Stay."

CHAPTER 19

*H*is gaze dropped to her hand on his, then bounced back to her face.

She curled her fingers into a fist and pulled her hand away. "I should ask you what you're doing here."

"Why don't you?"

She tried to decipher his unreadable features. "Because I'm afraid of what the answer will be."

"I suppose I could ask you what you're doing here instead."

"Yeah…" She drew an imaginary line on the tablecloth around the foot of her wineglass. "I'm not going to tell you that."

"I didn't think so."

"Are you mad?"

"I'm not mad. I'm not going to tell you what I'm doing here, either."

"So I guess that makes us even."

"Even?" A husky rasp came into his voice. "Or at odds?"

His eyes touched hers, and her pulse skittered. "If we don't tell each other anything, we won't know for sure where each other stands, and if we don't know, we don't have to be...enemies."

"I don't want to be your enemy." His gaze fell to the spot

where her neck and shoulder met.

Her fingers flitted there and brushed over her throbbing pulse. "So, we're just two people sharing a drink, not talking about the things we're afraid of talking about?"

"Who said we're afraid?" The flicker of his smile devastated her. "Speak for yourself."

"Sorry. Not afraid of anything. Just calendars, right?"

His shoulders shook when he shuddered. "Absolutely."

She leaned with both her elbows on the table. "Okay, I have to ask. What's with the calendars?"

"Calendars are damn bullies, is what they are. Always reminding you that time is running out. That your plans are a joke." The sudden, silent sadness on his face entranced her. "That dreams of who and what you can become may be for other people, but they're sure as shit not for you. Do you even know if you'll be here when the page needs to be flipped next? In fact, you do not."

"I never thought of it that way before." She laced her fingers and propped her chin on her knuckles. "Great, now I'm afraid of calendars, too. Any other terrors you wish to share with me?"

Something dark and serious flashed in his eyes. "I'm afraid whatever you're doing here is dangerous."

She sucked in a breath that rolled into a groan. "I'm only trying to protect my family."

"You mean your brother?"

"I mean my family. My home. My city."

The light in his eyes became a smoldering flame. "That's a lot of responsibility."

She dropped her chin, as though she might hide from him.

"I want what you want." He spoke in a low voice.

From beneath the sweep of her eyelashes, she risked a peek at him.

Every time their eyes collided, the pull between them seemed to grow stronger. Was she the only one that felt the charge in the air surrounding them? WDid only she feel electrified by the delicate, sensual thread coiling between them?

With everything in her, she wanted to believe he felt it, too.

More than that, she wanted to believe him when he said he wanted the same things she wanted.

"Really?" She slid one finger through the moisture on her glass.

He shifted his grip on his whiskey, and his knuckles brushed her hand. "Really."

At the light touch, her whole body filled with wanting.

What was this thing between them? Their connection was cosmic. Chemical. It thrilled and devastated her at once, because of course she'd have a cosmic, chemical connection with him, one of a handful of men in this town she absolutely could not get involved with.

With his index finger, he stroked her thumb. "I want to protect my family, too."

She stared at their hands, riveted by the way his large, scarred fingers delicately fondled hers. "Define family."

"My two brothers, my kid sister and stepsister, and me Ma."

"What about your dad?"

"He's dead."

With a soft gasp, she looked up to find his gaze still clamped on her face. "I'm so sorry."

"Don't be."

Impulsively, she squeezed his hand. "You said your mom remarried. What about your stepdad?"

"He's on his own. I'd only help him if there was no other way to help the others."

Her heart lightened. Despite all the evidence, he stood with his brother and against their stepfather. He was a good guy. She knew he was.

"Thank you for telling me that."

"You're welcome." He turned his palm and laced his fingers

between hers.

The gentle pressure and heat of his touch sent currents of desire swooping to her belly.

She'd never felt this way before. She'd never wanted to be with a man so much. Her attraction to other guys had never outweighed the downsides of being intimate with any of them. The risks of letting them see her completely for who and what she was, of giving them the power to accept or reject her, to deem her worthy, or not, of their affection, had always been too great.

But right now, she didn't care about any of that. She wasn't under any illusions that someone like Cian would want to be with someone like her forever. Empty promises weren't what she wanted from him. She wanted to touch him some more and taste him again.

"I wish we hadn't met like this." A hot ache formed in her throat. "I wish…"

He leaned close. "What do you wish?"

"I wish we were different people."

His gaze caressed hers, and the sensual thread of their attraction tightened. "I like you the way you are. Though I prefer brunettes."

Heat warmed her cheeks that he might find her desirable. "Well, I wish you were you and I was me, and everything else was different."

"Me too," he said softly.

The sensual web spun ever tighter.

On impulse, she held out her hand. "Hi, I'm Sadie. I'm from Minnesota, but I'm attending school in Chicago."

Slowly, he reclined back in his chair. He regarded her for a moment, then one corner of his mouth tilted slightly upward.

He wrapped his hand around hers. "Nice to meet you, Sadie. What are you studying?"

"Uh…psychology. And you are…?"

With the pad of his thumb, he stroked the back of her hand.

"Todd."

"You don't sound like you're from around here, Todd."

"I'm in town for a work conference."

"What do you do?" His nearness was like a drug, and she inhaled lightly, craving another hit of his scent.

"I work in IT."

"That sounds fascinating."

Crinkles appeared around his eyes when he smiled. "How far are we going to take this?"

Disappointment crashed over her, and she groaned and dropped her head. After a moment, she stole a look at his face. "All the way?"

His dark eyebrows climbed higher.

When he didn't outright reject her, hope raced through her bloodstream. "If I were just a college student and you a tourist, what would happen between us tonight?"

"Well, when we finish our drinks, I'd ask you to show me your favorite place in the city." They'd never fully broken contact after their handshake and his fingers toyed with hers, exploring and learning. "What would you say?"

"I'd say let me show you."

Something flared in his eyes. "And when we left here, where would we be going then?"

The gentle glide of his fingers stoked the fire in her belly. "There's this old, abandoned house on Kenwood near campus. Most of the windows are broken out, and it's a total wreck, but it's kind of gothic and so regal, and every time I walk by it, I have to stop. I don't know what it is. I love that house."

"Is that Sadie's favorite place?" he asked in a low voice. "Or Avery's?"

She cringed. "You got me. Sadie loves the beach. We're definitely going to go check out the beach."

One corner of his mouth hooked up. "I like the beach."

Her gaze lingered on his lips. "While we were there, I'd

wonder what it'd be like to kiss you."

"You wouldn't have to wonder. I'd show you."

The slow, seductive lick of his words sent a delicious shudder through her. "After we kissed, I'd invite you back to my place for another drink."

"I'd like another drink."

"My place is small—I'm a college student after all and the cost of living in Chicago is ridiculous—but it's clean and safe, and there's a teeny-tiny sliver of a view of the lake from my bedroom." She bit down on her bottom lip. "Would you like to see it?"

"I'd love to see your view." A husky rasp infected his tone.

Her mouth went dry at the sound. "If we were different people, I'd ask if you wanted to get out of here?"

For the first time since he looked at her across the room, his gaze left her face.

She experienced the loss like a kick of grief. "Can't we keep pretending? Just for tonight?"

His Adam's apple bobbed. "I need to know that when the pretending stops, we're not in a lot deeper than either of us can afford to be."

"Meaning?"

"Meaning, in the morning, we'd have to go our separate ways. It'd be just this once."

"Just one night together?"

With the promise of those words, the delicious tension between them became unbearable.

The sadness in his eyes reached his voice. "I'm sorry, but that's all I can offer right now."

Their gazes locked.

She sipped her wine.

He sipped his whiskey.

"In that case, what do you say, Todd? Want to be the mistake I'll regret in the morning?"

CHAPTER 20

*L*ies. So many lies. So many words he wanted to say, but could not.

He couldn't tell her the truth about his meeting with Manny Moretti, or that he'd soon be throwing fights as part of a plan to take down the mob boss for rigging matches. He couldn't tell her he hasn't craved a woman in months and has never wanted one the way he wants her now.

But finally, he could give her one truth. "I cannot think of anything I want more."

At the soft catch of her breath and the darkening of her pupils, a cannon of lust fired through him.

For too long, he'd felt nothing but dead inside. No feelings. No interests. Certainly, no arousal. He hadn't had sex in so long he wasn't even sure he still knew how to do it. But he wanted to try. For her.

He leaned close, trying to catch another whiff of her sweet scent. "Do you want to get out of here?"

Her lips parted when her breathing quickened. She nodded, then reached for the coat and bag slung across her chair back.

He pushed to his feet and held his hand out to her. When she laid her slim fingers in his palm, a sensual charge pulsed up his arm to his chest. Then, when she stood, her body brushed against his and the punch of his lust nearly drove him to his knees. He closed his eyes for a moment, savoring it and the tease of her scent across his senses.

His hand moved to her waist, and she lifted her chin, bringing her mouth a whisper from his lips.

"Tell me you feel it too." Soulful brown eyes searched his face. "Tell me I'm not the only one."

"You're not the only one," he said, though it pained him to admit it.

He dropped enough cash on the table to pay for their drinks and a healthy tip. As they moved toward the exit, he glimpsed the bitter scowls from a couple of tools at the bar, watching them leave.

In the good old days, Cian might've tossed them a smug smirk to get under their skin, but their obvious interest in Avery's curves pissed him off too badly, and he didn't want to play stupid games. He wanted to snarl at them, then drag her into his arms and whisk her away.

Outside, big fluffy snowflakes dropped from the night sky and tumbled lazily to the wet pavement. The ramp where he'd parked his car was two blocks away, so they set off in that direction, but he made it only as far as the first recessed doorway before his possessive urges won out.

With a quick sidestep, he ducked inside the alcove and tugged her with him. When their bodies collided, he came alive with the contact.

She blinked up at him with wide, shocked eyes. Then her surprise changed to hunger. She gripped the collar of his coat and raised up on her tiptoes as she yanked him down to her.

The feel of her lips on his mouth sang in his veins. She nibbled and tasted, and the warrior inside him gloried in his triumph.

When she started to pull back, he intended to let her go, but at the last, he snatched her hand in his, then slipped his arm around her waist and spun her so that her back pressed against the building's brick wall.

He flattened his palm beside her head to steady himself, then he eased close until her abundant curves molded to the contours of his body.

She stared up at him with wide eyes.

His heart thumped wildly as, slowly, he lowered his head and stole another kiss.

The luscious pressure of her mouth worked through him like a spell, enchanting him. He lifted their clasped hands over her head, holding her while he explored her with his mouth. At the spot where their wrists touched, their pulses throbbed hard together.

When he lifted his head, the sensation of her lips against his remained.

Her short, rapid breaths came as quickly as his own. "Do you kiss all the women you're with that way?"

"How's that?" he asked, his chest rising and falling steadily.

"So..." She pressed her fist to her chest, above her heart. "Intense."

"It's different with you." The truth hit him like a kick to the groin. He brushed a kiss across her forehead. "What about you? Do you kiss all your boyfriends like this?"

"I've never kissed any guy like *this*. With tongue and hands and licking..." A shiver chased through her body. "I think that kiss the other night was my first real kiss."

"I wish I'd known. I would've put my all into it."

"That wasn't your all?"

He stared into her eyes, their mouths barely touching. "Not by far."

She made a sound, like a whimper.

Satisfaction curled his lips. "I'm glad I'm the first man to give you a proper kiss."

"There was nothing proper about that kiss."

Their breaths mingled as puffs of air between them.

"That kiss was proper as fuck." He rasped for air.

"I must be forgetting. Maybe you should show me again, to remind me." Her eyes fluttered shut, and she tipped her face upward.

Damn, but she was a treat.

He slid his fingers along her jawline and gently gripped her chin. First, he dropped a kiss on the tip of her nose, then her eyes, and last, her lush mouth. He licked and ate, and her soft moans fed his arousal. Just when he'd nearly grown lost in her taste and her heat, a thought niggled.

He broke the kiss. "If you've never been proper kissed before, does that mean…?"

She blinked several times. When the passion finally cleared from her eyes, a rush of pink stained her cheeks. "That I've never been proper fucked either?"

He inclined his head.

"That's what that means." Uncertainty touched the edges of her features. "Does that surprise you?"

"It does."

She watched him closely. "Does it bother you?"

"Not at all." Something in his chest squeezed tight. "You've waited a long time for this."

Her small shoulders lifted. "I've been busy."

"No one is *that* busy."

The bright flash of her smile quickly flamed out. "I guess…I don't trust easily."

He studied her through narrowed eyes. "Why now? Why me?"

She pondered his question for a moment. Then, with the tip of her finger, she touched the corner of his mouth. "It's your smile. It's crooked."

"Crooked?" At the brush of her skin against his, his voice constricted with want. "Like a criminal?"

She laughed.

He loved that she laughed, so he said, "Like, it's in the middle of a heist?"

"Yes, exactly. It's trying to steal the heart of every woman who sees it."

He only cared about one woman's heart.

"I've never been told my smile is illegal before." He tried to frown, but his soft chuckle ruined the effect. "I haven't received a ticket or a citation."

With a huff of impatience, she rolled her eyes. "Fine. It's not crooked."

He wanted to kiss her again.

The dimple in her cheek appeared when she fought her smile. "It's lopsided."

A rumble of surprised laughter vibrated in his chest. His gaze riveted to her mouth. It was as though the generous proportions of her figure extended to her full, pouty lips. She was gorgeous, and smart, and fun, and… she deserved better than him.

"You could have any of those guys at the bar tonight. They're not dangerous to you." The sudden somberness knocked him in the ribcage. "They don't have to keep things from you. You should pick one of them."

"Yeah, I know." She scrunched her nose adorably. "Problem is, I don't want any of those guys."

"You want me."

"I want you."

"Even though you believe I'm Moretti's man."

He felt her stiffen, and he wished he could claw back the words. An invisible force seemed to wedge between them, separating their bodies.

"Aren't you?" Her eyes pleaded with him for an answer he couldn't give her.

He wanted her to know the truth, and not for some sentimental devotion to honesty, but because he cared what she thought about him.

In his silence, soft heartbreak painted her expression. "You're not denying it."

"Nor am I confirming it." He missed her smile, so he nudged her gently with his elbow. "I can't tell you the truth. You might be a cop."

A wisp of hope brightened her features. "Do I look like a cop?"

"Absolutely not."

Her shoulders slumped.

"You're too cunning, and way too crafty. You must be something more."

"More?"

"Much more."

Her dark eyes sparkled. "Like…an FBI agent?"

"Or a spy."

The pure delight that lit up her face arrowed him through the heart. "Really? You're not just saying that?"

"I never joke about law enforcement."

With a playful smirk, she flattened her palm against his chest and shoved. "You're just trying to flirt with me."

He clasped his hand over hers. "I will never lie to you."

She searched his face, her eyes probing deep into his soul. "Won't confirm nor deny? Is that the game?"

"If that's more than you're willing to risk, I'll take you home right now and never bother you again." He lifted her hand and pressed a kiss to her palm. "Just say that's what you want, and it'll be done. No questions asked."

She uncurled her fingers and brushed his cheek. "I don't want that." Her shoulders lifted and dropped back down with a helpless shrug. "I want you."

He sagged with his relief and brought his forehead to rest against hers. "I want you too."

She sucked in a sharp breath of surprise. "You do? Why? I mean, w-why me? Why now?"

"Because you're a fighter. Proud, fierce, pissed off." With one hand, he touched the side of her face. "Because your mind is working on a thousand different puzzles all at once, and it's sexy as hell." The other hand cupped her cheek. "Because you'd sacrifice your own safety to help someone who can't help themselves." Gently, he tipped her head back so he could watch the hunger building in her eyes. "Because I've never liked kissing all that much, and all I want to do is taste you, lick you..." He took a small nip at her mouth. "Because I can't stop craving you."

Her breathing had grown ragged and uneven. "Learned all that in one trunk ride, did ya?"

"That," He nibbled her bottom lip, "And your ass feels incredible pressed against my cock."

Her husky laugh melted a corner of his cold heart.

He wanted to touch. To taste. To take. The yearning was carnal, primal.

A few days ago, he didn't know if he'd ever experience sexual desire again. Now, he wanted this woman with a desperation that bordered on reckless.

He was suddenly, completely, agonizingly desperate to give her the first proper fuck of her life.

CHAPTER 21

The drugging effect of his kisses still pumped through her veins and her legs were heavy as she climbed the dark, narrow steps of her fire escape.

"I thought you said you had the money to pay your rent." Cian reached the top landing behind her.

"I did." She bent down. "I paid it already."

"Then why aren't we using the front door?"

She dragged open the window. "In case my brother is here. I don't want to see him right now."

He squeezed his big body through the small opening and straightened to his full height inside her bedroom. The small space seemed unbearably tiny.

With a soft grunt, she hauled the window closed, shutting out the chilly night air. When she turned, he stood beside her bed.

His chest heaved slightly from their climb and his eyes when he looked at her gleamed like gemstones. "Take it off."

Startled shock flew through her. "Excuse me?"

He pointed at her head. "The wig has to go."

A beat of laughter rattled loose, and with one sweep of her

arm, she pulled off the hat and the wig. She chucked them toward her closet as he closed the distance between them.

Her heart galloped when he reached for her, then pinched when he pushed his fingers through her hair and murmured, "There you are, *mo chailín álainn.*"

She wondered what his words meant, but before she could ask him, both of his large hands cupped the sides of her face and the feel of his touch against her skin set fire to their smoldering need.

They came together with a desperate crashing, and he claimed her mouth with his, as though his life depended on it.

when his tongue slipped inside her mouth, gentle but demanding. Suddenly, she was melting, and she gripped his wrists, holding on to stop from dissolving into the floorboards.

Her heart thumped wildly in her chest, and she feared it might explode, throbbing out its last beat for him. He tasted like hope when she was starving and had none.

Long ago, she'd learned not to hope. Hope was dangerous. She didn't hope for a home, or for their next meal. Hoping never got her anything. Hard work. Determination. Lying, cheating, stealing if need be. Those things might get her what she needed. Wishing for them would not. She never hoped. Not anymore.

Cian's mouth ate at her lips and with the dizzying swoop that flew through her, her knees buckled. With a moan, she tightened her grasp on his large wrists. She wanted to breathe him, drink him, eat him. She wanted to lick him, so she did.

The thrill of his taste and touch zigzagged through her, and for a moment, she nearly forgot he was the most dangerous person she'd ever known. Not only because he was Moretti's man, but because, for him, she wanted to hope. Even though she knew—she *knew* way, way deep down in her bones—she didn't dare.

He trailed his fingers down the sides of her neck until his hands met at the spot where the fabric of her blouse gaped.

When he worked the top button, his skin brushed the upper swells of her breasts and eager longing coiled tight in her belly.

While he undid the rest of her buttons, she slipped her hands beneath the hem of his shirt and touched the smooth, taut skin over his abdomen.

Desire unfurled in her like waves on the ocean, one after another, and she realized she'd never wanted to do anything like this before. She never wanted to get naked with a guy and explore all his hidden hollows and secret spaces.

Now, she lived for the anticipation.

Finally, he freed the last button and spread her blouse open wide, exposing her bra and bare skin. His green eyes flashed.

Suddenly, the fabric felt oppressive against her skin. She shrugged it off her shoulders and, reaching back, unhooked her bra and pulled the scrap of material away from her body.

His fiery gaze clamped on her breasts, and a jolt of sensation shot from her heart to her core.

Slowly, he eased closer. She closed her eyes.

Time seemed to stop.

Then, as if from another dimension, his lips touched her brow above her right eye.

A breath leaked from her lungs.

His mouth brushed her temple and the crest of one cheek. He dropped a trail of featherlight caresses that made her heart pound and gooseflesh tingle across her skin.

Then he tugged his shirt off over his head and her vision filled with lean masculinity, tanned skin, and a small smattering of tattoos—words written in another language on one of his rounded pecks, a crest or shield on his biceps, and a warrior's dagger on the inside of one forearm.

She stared, wishing to memorize him by heart. If she was only going to have one night with him, she wanted to remember everything.

With his deft fingers, he easily popped the button on her jeans, and she wriggled out of them.

When she stood naked in front of him for the first time, a pang of insecurity lanced her. Compared to his lean, muscular body, her healthy curves bordered on chubby. Instantly, she regretted the last two dozen cupcakes she'd consumed.

He laced his fingers with hers, then led her to the bed. Still wearing his pants, he sat on the edge of the mattress and pulled her between his thighs. His height brought his face almost to hers. While he stared into her eyes, he caressed the heavy underside of her breasts with the pads of his thumbs.

Then he skimmed his hands down her torso to her waist. "I want to please you," he said, his eyes glittering with sincerity.

She trailed her fingers down the side of his face.

"I want to touch you, Avery."

The heat in his voice made her belly squeeze deliciously. "It's Sadie, remember?"

He hooked his foot around her ankle and tugged until a little space opened between her thighs.

Her body clenched, aching for his touch.

His hands on her waist tightened, and his thumbs came together above her springy curls. "Avery."

With her name still on his lips, he bent his head and softly suckled one nipple. His hot breath fanned over the kiss of moisture. Her nipple puckered, and he smiled.

"Avery," he whispered.

Inquisitive masculine fingers slipped between her legs and found the heart of her aroused flesh.

She gasped with the first touch.

"Avery," he murmured.

She lifted her knee, placing it on the edge of the bed, and his large hand pushed deeper between her thighs. His fingers teased her entrance, then dipped slightly inside her body, only to retreat again. A raspy moan tore from her throat.

While he stroked her slippery heat in slow, erotic circles, he spoke her name three more times. The words stole inside her chest like phantom fingers curling around her heart and squeezing.

Three times, he chose her.

Not Sadie.

Avery.

No pretending.

Three incantations that worked over her like a spell, or a curse, and with each utterance of her name from his lips, she opened more for him.

He plucked the chords of her body with his gentle fingers until her soul sang. Moans of pleasure piled in her throat with the waves of voluptuous sensation pulsing outward from her center.

She gripped his broad shoulders, trying to steady herself as the pleasure built and built, until the heat between her legs consumed her entire body. The fire raged through her, burning away the fake facade they'd attempted to erect between them, leaving only the essence. The essential.

Only Avery and Cian.

Together.

His clever, tender fingers toyed with her while his hot mouth clamped around one pebbled nipple. Her head fell back, and her hands moved to his nape, holding his head to her breast.

With each soft flick of his fingers, the barrier she'd built around her heart, piece by cruel piece, cracked. And when he pushed one finger fully inside her, years of her hardened determination dissolved in a rush of warmth.

Just one kiss, one whisper, and her cool fortress crumbled to dust.

Luxurious licks of fire lashed her as he pulled her head down to him and captured her mouth in a soft, smoldering kiss.

Emphatically, she kissed him back, thrilled and terrified by the moment. Her knees buckled.

He slipped one arm under her bare bottom and slowly rose to his feet. She tumbled onto her back on the bed. He stood beside her, and she reached for him.

But he didn't come to her. Instead, he remained standing there as he gazed down at her naked body.

Slowly, his hands moved to the front of his pants, where he unfastened the button and dragged down the zipper. The material dropped to the floor, his belt buckle hitting the hardwoods with a heavy thud.

Through his boxer briefs, the outline of his long, hard shaft jumped.

On his knees, he climbed onto the mattress and covered her body with his warmth and delicious strength. He brought his face close to hers and stole a soft kiss from her mouth. Then he lifted his head and peered into her eyes.

The moment stretched out. While they stared, their undeniable connection seemed to tighten and intensify. She swallowed thickly against the lump forming in her throat.

It was too raw. Too real.

She experienced a shimmer of fear. "Just this once, remember?"

"I remember." He placed his palms on the mattress on either side of her head and took a small nibble from her bottom lip.

Then he blazed a trail of hot kisses down the side of her neck, to her clavicle, over the swell of one breast, and over her beaded nipple.

Her soft murmur slid into a moan. "Don't forget."

With his lips, he kissed her ribcage and her navel. The bristle of his scruff stung the sensitive skin of her inner thighs, and his hot breath touched her most intimate place.

She clenched the bedsheets in her fists, desperate with the expectation of his carnal caress. Her body wept for him.

But when he didn't touch her, she lifted her head.

Over the expanse of her naked body, his eyes captured hers.

The look on his face seized her heart. Achingly vulnerable, beautifully fragile, deeply emotional, his longing reached inside her, terrible and tactile. She could feel his desire on her skin like a tattoo.

Want thrummed through her veins, his or hers she didn't know. It gripped and controlled her.

Only then, when he'd taken command of her soul, did he consent to touch her.

Not with his fingers, but with his tongue.

The slow glide tore a groan of her pleasure from her that echoed around her tiny bedroom. She dropped her head onto the pillow and rolled her hips against his decadent kisses.

He ate her with his mouth and stroked her with his fingers, the twin pleasures feeding her need. Desire ignited in her breasts and her stomach, and she rocked against him. Another loud groan escaped, and she slapped a hand over her mouth to stop the sound from passing through the thin walls.

Her name fell from his lips once more, and she felt the low vibration of his voice between her legs.

Passion spilled over and she cried out with the intense pleasure that swept across her flesh from the soles of her feet to the crown of her head. She gripped the pillow above her head and thrust her hips frantically. Her ears rang as her body convulsed around his fingers, sucking him deeper.

When the crashing wave of her orgasm dispersed, he rose between her thighs and laid his palm flat against the soft swell of her abdomen. With the pad of his thumb, he pushed through her moist curls.

"I can't..." Her protests died in her throat when he gently circled her clit.

The devil's smile curled his lips.

Around and around, he dragged his thumb in slow, slippery spheres.

Her knees fell apart.

Her awareness narrowed to the sly teasing of his fingers, where the soft slide in and out was a delicious counterpoint to the soft circling.

He shifted his hand, changing the angle of his touch, and she jerked at the delicate aggression. He drove her higher, rubbing and stroking, then delving deep.

She arched her back and moaned. Her body was no longer hers, but existed only for his torment of pleasure. His name dropped from her tongue, over and over, like a plea.

He answered with a soft flick of his fingers that flung her into the voluptuous waves of another rolling climax. She swelled and crested, dipped, then swelled and crested again. Each time she thought the orgasm had ended, another ripple of sensation shuddered through her.

When finally the beautiful torment ended, he stretched out beside her on the bed.

She rolled to face him. Color sat high on his sharp cheekbones and his green eyes burned with the heat of his desire.

He was all her dreams brought to life. Strength. Security. Comforts and pleasures that had been forbidden to her all her life. Delights she thought she'd never experience.

He was better than cupcakes.

By a lot.

She reached out and pressed her palm to his cheek. "I'm sorry. I wanted to please you, too."

His hand found her hip. "That was only the warmup. The main event is yet to come."

CHAPTER 22

*H*ow could he have doubted if he'd find pleasure with her? He marveled at the frantic throbbing of his blood burning through his veins.

His desire was an exquisite ache.

He wanted more. Like a starving man suddenly presented with a feast, he couldn't get enough.

With an inward groan of regret, he left the bed and crossed to the small desk near the window where he'd tossed the plastic bag with the box of condoms they'd stopped and picked up at the corner store.

He fumbled through the bag and tore open the box. When he returned to her with a string of packets, he paused for a moment beside the bed and gazed down at her body. She was beautifully made, lush and firm, shadowed in the places he yearned to delve.

His questing gaze slid over her breasts, her belly, her thighs. Everywhere his eyes touched, her body flushed pink.

He stretched out beside her, and when she pressed close, the brush of her naked skin against his sent a surge of hunger gripped him. His hands on either side of her head on the bed, he leaned down and pulled one pert nipple into his mouth. Then he blew a warm breath ver her skin, and she shivered, as he'd hoped she would.

"Avery…" Want constricted his throat, reducing his voice to a pained whisper. "Do you still want to do this? It's okay if you've changed your mind."

In answer, she pulled his head down to her and fed him a deep kiss that had him groaning into her mouth.

The kiss left him dazed, dizzy. Damn, but he'd never been this rattled by being with a woman before. He frowned down at her, wondering about his reaction to her.

Her small hands rushed over his torso, and he sucked in a sharp breath.

With her fingertips, she blazed a trail from his naval to the base of his shaft. "That's a yes, in case you were wondering."

His hands shook when he reached between her legs. Gently, he teased and probed until her slick arousal covered his fingers.

When her soft moans became husky groans, he rose over her. She parted her thighs and the pink pussy glistened up at him.

Whatever happened next, there would be no pretending.

While she watched him with huge, round eyes, he dipped one finger into her wet heat, then brought his fingers to his lips and tasted her honeyed sweetness.

Her lips parted with her soft gasp, and her chest rose and fell with her rapid breathing.

He ripped into one of the condom packets, then rolled the sheath over his rigid erection. The next moments rushed past him in a haze of soft sounds and glorious sensation.

The head of his sex poised at her entrance.

Her sweet snug flesh grasping at his hard length.

The small wriggle of her hips and his guttural gasp when sensation shot through him.

He nudged deeper

Her body had difficulty taking all of him inside her. Against the delicious resistance, he eased deeper, and she gasped.

"Do you want me to stop?"

"No!" Her arms flew around his neck. "Don't stop."

"Avery, I don't want to hurt you—"

Her legs tightened around his waist. "Do. Not. Stop."

Over the next moments, they completed the slow, miraculous slide of his cock into her warm, wet depths.

Buried all the way inside her, he gripped her waist with both of his hands and held her still. With even a whisper of friction, he was done.

He didn't want it to end.

Not ever.

When he could manage it, he moved his hips, slowly. So slowly. Each exquisite slide was a special torment that threatened to finish him.

She moved under him, her hips coming up to meet his gentle thrusts.

He let her set the pace, and her eager motions fueled the haste of his expanding need. When she pressed her heels into the mattress and arched upward, pursuing her pleasure, victory roared through him.

A victory far sweeter than any of his wins in the ring. He had a new favorite sport—pleasuring Avery.

He reveled in the lusty pants of her ragged breathing. Every one of her greedy moans stoked the fire in his veins, reviving what he'd thought long dead. Each sensuous sound he wrung from her rekindled the flames of his once-dormant desire.

The moment almost felt too big. Too overwhelming. Too carnal and arousing.

His balls ached, but he clenched his jaw against the force of his lust and determined to use his body to gratify hers. His arousal expanded and deepened until he was so turned on, the pleasure hurt.

The pleasure-pain burned through him, and he was alive once again.

Beneath him, her cheeks flushed, her lips parted, and her breasts swayed with the thrusts of his body into hers. God, what a gift, to get to help her find climax with a man for the first time.

A bomb of suppressed emotions exploded inside his chest, and he gasped against the pain. He would never forget this moment.

Never much of a talker in bed, he found himself muttering soft endearments right along with filthy sex words. He encouraged and praised her and told her all the ways he wanted to fuck her.

He parted her warm flesh over and over, again and again. Her thick, lush moans and hot, wet heat battered his control. Above her, he clenched his jaw against the pain of trying to prolong what his body demanded. His breaths escaped in ragged, needy huffs, but he willed his body to wait for her.

After his diagnosis, a wall had gone up inside him, separating who he once was from who he had become. Being with her, moving inside her, reminded him of what he was before.

Before cancer.

Before weakness.

Before despair.

She reminded him of who he used to be.

Strong. Bold. Confident.

Alive.

Her sex clamped around him, squeezing and sucking him deeper, and his world suddenly narrowed to the place where hard flesh invaded soft.

Barriers breached, all rushed in to overwhelm him. He felt everything—joy, hunger, fear—all at once. She made him feel it all.

A voice in his head argued that he didn't want to feel again, feeling hurt too much, but her greedy moans rattled through him like an earthquake, and he couldn't think about anything other than the tight clenching around his cock.

Holy fuck, but it felt so good.

She felt so good.

When he brushed his fingers along her slit, she cried out his name and he was lost again. Lost in her heat. Lost in her hunger. Lost in her heart. Lost in her.

The pull of her pulsing flesh drew the ecstasy from him in great, luscious surges.

With his orgasm, the last, pitiful shield he scrambled to erect to hold back the emotions gave way, and a guttural groan tore from his chest.

He collapsed on top of her and, dropping his forehead to her shoulder, dragged deep, desperate breaths into his lungs.

When his breathing evened out, he lifted his head and peered down into her face. "Are you okay?"

"I…" Her dark eyes shone in the dim light, and she swallowed thickly.

A pucker of worry formed between her eyebrows, and he suspected the mild shock and confusion touching her pretty features reflected on his own face.

He nibbled on her plump mouth.

She stared into his eyes when she kissed him too, and her fingertips grazed his cheek. "Cian…?"

"What is it, *a cuisle*? Did I hurt you?"

"No, I…." A shimmer of fear disturbed her eyes. "Is it always like that?"

"What? Sex?"

She nodded. "Is it that…" She seemed to flounder for a word to describe what had just happened between them. "Is it like that every time?"

The question struck him in the chest. "Sex has never been like that before."

Her concerned frown deepened. "Was it bad?"

He expelled a sharp huff of air. "Holy fuck, no. Was it bad for you?"

"It was better than cupcakes." A soft devastation tinged her voice.

"Don't you like cupcakes?"

"They're my favorite." Panic filled her eyes. "What does that mean?"

He found her hand buried in the sheets and laced his fingers through hers. "I think it means we're good together."

"Sexually." She held onto his hand as though it were her only anchor. "We're good together sexually."

"Does that freak you out?"

"Yes. It doesn't freak you out?"

"No. It's unexpected, and complicates things, for sure. But I want you too much to give a shit about any of those things." With his defenses momentarily obliterated, the truth came pouring out of him. "I can't stop wanting you. I don't think I'll ever stop wanting you."

He pulled from her slick wetness and pushed up off the bed. On unsteady legs, he staggered toward the tiny trash can in the room's corner.

As he neared the wastebasket, a year and a half's' worth of grief, a tangle of anger and fear and loss, rushed forward and knocked into him with enough force that he stumbled. His arm shot out and his palm smacked the wall to stop himself from falling.

"Cian? Are you okay?"

A spasm closed the back of his throat, and he could only nod.

He heard her bare feet hit the wood floors, then pad over to him. From behind, she smoothed her hands across his back.

"I'm okay." He glanced at her over his shoulder.

She looked at him with big brown eyes, brimming with concern for him. She spared no worry for her nakedness.

She was so fucking beautiful.

Something in his chest spasmed, the flutter light and fleeting, and utterly foreign.

Her hand squeezed his nape, and she laid her cheek against his back. "I'm glad."

His heart gave another wrench, and he realized the sensation wasn't completely unfamiliar. It was a bit like grief, except lighter.

He reached down to slide off the condom.

A soft curse slipped from him.

She lifted her head. "What is it? What's wrong?"

"I think…the condom broke."

CHAPTER 23

She stumbled back. *"What?!"*

"It's okay," he said, turning.

"When did it break?" Her voice climbed with her growing hysteria.

"I don't know."

"Did it break while you were taking it off?"

"Maybe."

She paced back and forth at the end of the bed. "But you don't know."

"I don't know."

"Oh god." She sucked a deep breath in through her nostrils.

"It's okay."

"Why are you so calm about this?" Even as she asked, her mind played with percentages. What was the chance she'd become pregnant from this one time? Her first time?

Slim.

Unlikely.

Improbable.

But not impossible.

What in the hell had she done? She'd hooked up with a man

she knew far too little about, and now she could wind up pregnant. Why hadn't she run the other direction the moment she saw him coming, the way she had with every other man she'd ever met? Why him? A man with trouble stamped clearly across his forehead with a capital T?

A moment of hormonal weakness, and now she might be trapped. Pregnant with a mobster's baby. It sounded like a bad made-for-TV movie.

"Oh god." She plopped down hard on the edge of the mattress.

Cian crouched before her. "Please don't worry. I've been given every test under the sun and I'm all good."

He gazed up at her with such sincerity that she couldn't help but reach out and touch the side of his face. "Thank you. But I'm more worried about getting pregnant."

"You don't have to worry about that either." He wrapped his large fingers around her hand. "I promise."

"You can't promise something like that."

"I can." He moved to sit beside her on the bed.

The mattress dipped, bringing her body up against his, from their shoulders all the way to their knees. He opened his mouth, but rather than words, a long, heavy sigh seeped out of him.

In the quiet, she studied his profile, but he'd pulled a mask into place, shuttering his expression.

"I was sick."

His words hit her like a splash of ice-cold water. "Sick? Sick how...?"

"Cancer. I had Hodgkin's lymphoma." At her soft gasp, he squeezed her hand. "I'm better now, but the treatment was harsh, and there were side effects. The chemo killed more than the cancer. It's likely I'm sterile."

Her emotions swung from fear to despair so fast, her heart wanted to throw up. "Are you sure?"

"My doctor is pretty sure."

"What did they say?" she asked softly.

"He says a lot of fucking things." The sharp edge of his frustration made a crack in his mask. "You know how doctors are. Percentages and likelihoods and all that. My counts are low, fighting is a risk. All side effects of the chemo."

The surge of sorrow and affection she felt for him frightened her. "Are you…? Is that…? I mean, does it bother you?"

"I never really thought about having kids before, so I won't grieve something I wasn't even sure I wanted."

"Just because you can't have kids of your own, that doesn't mean…." Her words felt empty, so she trailed off.

"Aye, I know."

"There are a lot of kids out there who need a dad. If you ever decide you want that…." More words that somehow seemed meaningless.

"I know."

There was nothing she could say that would take away his personal pain. Still, she wanted to reassure him. She wanted him to understand he wasn't alone in his grief.

"After my mom died, I spent a couple of months in foster homes before I aged out." She watched his face for his reaction, worried what she would see.

But she glimpsed only a softness that touched her heart.

Their hands remained clasped, and she looked down at her fingers intertwined with his. "Any foster kid would be lucky to have someone like you to look out for them."

It surprised her to realize she wasn't lying. She believed what she'd said.

She believed he was a good man.

No matter what choices he'd made, or what he may have done. There's no way she would've slept with him if she didn't believe that way deep down.

Or else it was just the sex endorphins muddying her thinking.

He looked at her for a long moment. Then he leaned close and slipped his hand along her jawline. Gently, he tilted her chin up and kissed her.

On the other side of her bedroom door, a loud thump sounded.

She pulled back, but only far enough to break the contact between their lips, and listened.

A groan leaked from her. "My brother's home."

"Should I go?"

A pang pinched her chest. "We just have to be really super quiet."

He brushed his thumb across her cheek and kissed her again, letting his mouth linger over hers.

She opened for him, and his tongue swept inside.

Mutual moans escaped them to echo off the walls of her tiny bedroom.

They broke apart.

"Yeah, I should go," Cian said at the same time she told him, "You should go."

He dressed quickly while she draped a robe around her nakedness.

On his way to the window, he shrugged into his wool coat.

He slung one leg over the sill, but lingered there. "What are you doing next week?"

Her heart fluttered. "Uh, working and stuff. What about you?"

"Same. I have a lot going on this weekend, but after that, can I see you again?"

"Do you want to see me again?" The question leapt from her heart to her mouth with no input from her brain.

His eyes moved over her body. "Aye, I do."

Her smile was way too wide. "But... it was just this once, remember?"

"Things are different now."

"The reasons we made that deal aren't." Regret nicked at her heart, but she ignored the ache. "They're exactly the same."

"Right, so, virgin sex, broken condom. There're two reasons right there." He gave his head a slow shake. "No way am I disappearing after that."

A ripple of worry slipped through her. He might think he wanted more than a one-night stand now, but when he figured out who the real Avery was, he'd regret his sudden reversal. Soon enough, he'd realize she wasn't what he wanted. She wasn't a forever girl.

And when that fact dawned on him, she feared how much it would hurt.

She expelled a bored sigh. "Tell me you aren't going to do that whole possessive guy thing. I won't end up pregnant, and even if I did, I can take care of myself. There's no need for the hero act."

"Not an act, but nice try." He gripped the windowpane with one hand.

"What try?"

"You're trying to piss me off, so I'll leave." With his other hand, he gripped her nape and his mouth claimed hers in a kiss so hot and demanding, she was grasping fistfuls of his shirt by the time he pulled away. "I know you can take care of yourself, but I'll be here, anyway."

She opened her mouth to protest, but his hand on her neck squeezed gently and she forgot what she was going to say.

"What just happened between us wasn't a hookup, Avery. We both felt it. There's something between us, and it's possible it's a little stronger than either of us wants it to be, but those are the facts. Everything has changed." He dropped a kiss on her forehead, then stepped the rest of the way through her window. "I'll see you in a few days."

~

THE NEXT MORNING, she floated into the Daily Sun's offices on a cloud of lingering lust and dreamy memories minutes before she was due to meet with her boss and pitch him her story about Manny Moretti.

"What have you got for me, Bishop?" Charles barked when she entered his office.

Avery settled into the chair across from Charles and took a slow, steadying breath before she launched into her rehearsed spiel. She'd practiced it for days, making sure she hit all the most salacious details. That way, he couldn't say no.

But she'd only gotten as far as Moretti and his criminal empire when Charles stopped her. "We're a tabloid, Bishop, not the damned Chicago Tribune."

"I haven't gotten to the best part yet."

"Get there. Fast."

She rushed through the rest of her speech, glossing over the bits about the illegal gambling ring to hit the sex, drugs, and women for sale to wealthy celebrities and politicians hard.

"Celebrities *and* politicians?" A skeptical frown twisted his mouth. "Like who?"

"Congressman Vance."

One of Charles' dark eyebrows hitched upward. "Anyone else?"

"Loads more." She listed the names of the other public servants she'd seen at the party, plus the athletes on the city's professional football and hockey teams, including the fighter Cian had knocked out. Though she conveniently left Cian's name off her roster. "Believe me, this story will be juicier than a sirloin steak."

"Hmm...." His chair creaked when he leaned back and propped his feet on his desk. "You got proof?"

"I got proof." She leaned forward. "I was at one of Moretti's parties last weekend. It was *full* of important people. I saw them with my own eyes."

At that, both of Charles' eyebrows climbed. "And just how did you get invited to a party like that?"

"Well…" She lifted one shoulder. "I might've crashed it."

Laughter erupted from him, which he quickly snuffed out. "You're not getting reimbursed for your travel expenses."

She held up her hands. "I caught a free ride."

"Good girl." He smacked the desk with his palm. "Get something to me Monday morning and let me look at it. If I like it, it's a go."

It wasn't the glowing green light she'd been hoping for, but she'd just earned a chance to prove herself, so she hustled out of his office before he could change his mind.

When she reached the cubicle she shared with Simone, her friend spun around in her chair. "Why were you late this morning?"

"I had an appointment." Avery slid in behind her desk.

"You're a terrible liar." Simone studied her through narrowed eyes. Then she gasped. "OMG, you had sex."

Avery's mouth went slack. "How did you know that?"

Simone pointed at Avery's lap, where she clutched her bag. "No cupcake."

A wave of regret rolled through Avery. She could really use a cupcake right now.

"So, who is he?"

She could not tell Simone she'd hooked up with one of Moretti's men. "Just a guy I met at a party."

"What party? Why didn't you call me?"

"It was a last-minute thing. The party sucked, actually."

"And…?" Simone leaned close and dropped her voice. "How was it? I need details."

Delicious heat burned Avery's cheeks remembering the, uh, details. "It was better than cupcakes."

Simone tossed her head back and cackled. "I told you so."

Despite herself, Avery laughed with her friend.

Gasping for air, Simone slouched in her chair and crossed her hands over her stomach, as though it ached from her belly laughs. "You're gonna see him again, aren't you?"

Her heart stuttered. "I think so."

Simone gave Avery a sharp look. "You think so? Why don't you know so?"

"Well, we're both busy and…" And he's a mobster, and she's officially writing a story that'll expose his and his friends' criminal activities and… "I guess we'll see what happens."

"Ah, I get it now. You just wanted him for his body." Simone raised her palms to halt Avery's denials. "It's okay. No judgment. I'm just really glad you finally did it."

Avery was glad she finally did it, too. She'd never made a conscious decision to wait until she was twenty-four to have sex. It'd just happened that way. Mostly because she'd never met a guy that remotely interested her.

After waiting so long, the act of losing her virginity had become this huge, almost frightening thing in her mind. But the reality of it hadn't been frightening at all.

Far from it.

Was it because sex was great, as everyone had tried to convince her all those years she'd waited?

Or was it because sex *with Cian* was great?

She'd learned a long time ago that she always needed to be on guard for the next disaster—the next firing, the next eviction, the next night they'd spend without a place to sleep or enough food to eat. With her shields up so high all the time, she may have missed out on a few things. Like dating guys, or making lots of friends, or falling in love.

Maybe, possibly, it was time she let live a little.

If doing so meant she got to spend a few more nights with Cian, then she was all for trying it.

Butterflies alighted in her stomach just thinking about it.

Next to her, Simone's palm smacked the desk, and Avery jumped.

"O.M.G." Simone gaped at her. "You love him."

"What?" Avery pulled a face. "Don't be ridiculous."

Knowing brown eyes studied Avery for one long, drawn out moment. "I'm not. You're really into this guy."

The light fluttering in Avery's chest made it impossible to deny. It was tragic, but Simone was right. She was *way* into Cian.

"It doesn't matter if I am. We have no future."

With an impatient wave of her hand, Simone batted away Avery's words. "That's what they always say."

"He's not saying it. I am. And I mean it. The last thing I want is a man controlling me."

The tinkle of Simone's soft laughter ricocheted off the cubicle walls. "That's the thing about love. You don't control when or with whom it happens. *It* controls you. It'll make you do things you've never done before. You don't need to worry about a man running your life. It's your own damn heart you gotta watch out for."

Avery tipped her head to one side and considered her friend. "Have you ever been in love?"

"Of course. What girl hasn't?"

Avery stabbed a thumb at herself. "This girl."

"Oh. Right."

"So, what's it like?"

"What's what like?"

"Love. I mean, if I were in love, which I'm not, but if I were, how would I even know it?"

"It's like…," Simone searched for words in the space above her head. "It's like getting hit by a bus."

A burst of laughter poured out of Avery. "Ouch."

"You can't miss it. It's suddenly right there in front of you and *BAM*—" When Simone clapped her hands together, the crack of sound rent the air. "Runs you right over."

"Sounds painful," Avery deadpanned.

"Only a little." Simone's pretty face lit up brighter than a lightbulb. "But you're so happy to be alive, you can hardly feel the pain."

Avery switched on her computer and waited for the login screen to pop up.

"Hey," Simone said. "There's something I wanted to talk to you about."

Avery finished typing the last letter of her password, then hit Enter and turned to Simone. "What's up?"

"What would you think if I applied for the promotion?"

The words knocked into Avery, and she fell back in her chair. "What?"

Worry crowded Simone's features. "I know you wanted it, but you said you weren't applying, and then I found out Kasey applied. Can you believe that? If you can't have the job, I definitely don't want Kasey to get it."

"No, we don't want that." Avery's voice sounded weak, so she injected as much strength into it as she could muster. "You should go for it. You deserve the job."

"So do you."

No, Avery didn't deserve it. She hadn't earned it. Yet. "Actually, I'm twelve credits short of earning anything."

"Thanks, Babe. You're the best." Standing, Simone collected a notebook and pen from her desktop. "I gotta run down the hall before my meeting with Charles. I'll catch ya after lunch?"

"Okay, catch ya later."

Simone poked her head over the top of the cubicle. "Oh, and Ave?"

"Yeah?"

With a cheeky smile, Simone winked. "Watch out for those buses."

CHAPTER 24

*W*hen she returned home to her apartment that night, she let herself in through the front door and nearly crashed into Jamie, who was on his way out. Dressed in his black uniform, he was headed downtown to the building where he worked the night shift as a security guard.

"Where were you last night?" he asked, zipping his gray hoodie up to his chin.

In my bedroom having secret, mind-blowing sex.

"None of your business." She ignored his scowl. "Did you give Moretti the money?"

"I'm still alive, aren't I?"

"What did he say?"

"Relax, will ya?" He yanked the hood over his dark hair. "I took care of it."

"Seriously? You're gonna tell me to relax?" She gaped at him. "Manny Moretti is not someone you want to be involved with. Tell me you know that."

Jamie held out his hands as he backed through the door. "Can we do this later? I'm running late."

"Wait—"

He flung the door closed with a decisive bang.

Unsettled by Jamie's strange behavior, she dove back into her research on Moretti with a determination bordering on manic. For dinner, she microwaved a frozen meal and ate it while reading some old newspaper articles she'd found online about Manny.

Shortly after ten o'clock, her cell phone rang. She didn't recognize the number, so she accepted the call with a touch of wariness.

"Hey, it's Sasha."

"Oh, hey, Sasha." Avery's spine straightened with her surprise. "What's up?"

"So, uh, I hate to ask this…."

At Sasha's timid opening, Avery's heart pinched. She remembered well the sting to her pride when she needed to ask for a favor.

She jumped in. "You need a place to stay?"

"Would that be all right?" Sasha asked. "It'll just be this one time—"

"Of course." Avery closed her notebook. "And you can call anytime. It's not a problem. I swear."

Sasha's relieved sigh carried through the phone.

Avery gave her the building address and apartment number, and when they disconnected, she quickly cleaned up the papers and notebooks she'd spread around the living room while she'd worked.

She hunted up an extra pillow and blankets and was finishing the makeshift bed on the couch when Sasha arrived.

Avery showed Sasha the tiny kitchen and offered her something to eat, but Sasha said she was too tired to stay awake long enough. They talked for a few minutes about nothing in particular, and when an enormous yawn overcame Sasha, Avery moved toward her bedroom, which connected off the main living area.

"My brother is working tonight, so he'll probably wake you

up pretty early when he gets home." She stepped into her room and flipped on the light. "You can just ignore him, like I do."

Avery closed her bedroom door on Sasha's soft laughter.

The next morning, Avery rubbed her eyes as she padded into the living room from her bedroom. On the couch cushions, the blankets she left for Sasha were folded into a neat pile with the pillow stacked on top. Sasha was already gone.

Avery spent the day working on her story. So far, she'd gathered evidence of at least four different illegal schemes. On top of running the gambling ring that'd ensnared Jamie, Moretti operated as a high-level smuggler, trafficking guns, drugs, and even women. Anything that'd put money in his pocket.

The names of players involved in his criminal enterprise jumbled inside her head, so she flipped open her notebook to a blank page and drew a big circle with Moretti's name in the middle of it. Then she filled in the surrounding spaces with the details she'd learned.

By the time she'd finished crafting the intricate web of depravity, dinner time had come and gone.

She took a long, hot shower to clear her mind, then she settled at the small desk in her bedroom and started drafting an outline for the story she'd give Charles on Monday.

Sometime later, a soft bump interrupted her concentration, and she glanced over at the clock. It was nearly eleven. It seemed kind of late for her neighbor to be getting home from work.

Another thump sounded, louder this time, and she turned her head.

Her heart leapt in her throat to see the form of a man at her window. When the man lifted his hand, a kick of fear slammed inside her chest.

Her mind scrambled, pinpointing items she might use as weapons should he attempt to break in—

He rapped lightly on the glass.

What the—?

But her heart had already provided the answer.

Cian.

Under her, her feet moved rapidly, in time to the beat set by her sped up heart rate.

Only hours before, she'd tried to convince Simone, and herself, that what had happened between them was only sex. But the sad, troubling truth was, she wanted more than Cian's body.

As she approached the window where he waited, anticipation swelled in her chest with the memories of his softly spoken naughty words and quiet, sad eyes. He'd been through so much, and she wanted nothing more than to lay his head in her lap and rub the lines of anger and sorrow from his forehead.

At the window, she hauled it open, and a rush of cold air swept into the room.

"I'm sorry if I scared you," he said the moment she yanked the curtains out of the way.

"What are you doing out there?"

He sat on the window ledge. "I didn't know if I was allowed to use the door."

She stepped back. "Get in here. It's freezing out there."

When he swung his leg into the room, a sharp grimace contorted his features. Then he was standing in her tiny bedroom, big and beautiful and—

She gasped. "Omigod, what happened to you?"

"It's nothing." He staggered over to the bed and dropped down heavily on the edge of the mattress. "I was in a fight."

Sitting in the spray of soft light from the lamp on her bedside table, she could see a droplet of dried blood near one corner of his mouth and the dark bruise forming on his left cheek. He hunched over, as though his ribs ached.

"A fight with who?" She didn't wait for his answer but hurried into the kitchen and filled a Ziplock bag with ice. When she returned, she wrapped a towel around the bag and pressed it against his left cheek. "Were you mugged?"

"Thank you." He laid his hand over the towel. "It wasn't that kind of fight."

In the hall outside her bedroom door, she plucked a washcloth from a shelf in the linen closet. "What kind of fight was it?"

"A professional one."

She ducked into the bathroom and wet the washcloth with warm water in the sink.

When she rushed back into the bedroom, he'd closed his eyes, and by the way he sat, he appeared to carry the weight of the world on his broad shoulders.

She approached him quietly, but his eyes fluttered open.

He watched her closely as she moved to stand between his thighs, and his eyes never broke contact with hers when she knelt before him.

She reached out, and he jerked his head back.

"You're bleeding." With the washcloth, she gently dabbed at the blood on his lip.

"You don't have to—"

She shushed him. "I got it."

While she cleaned the blood and grime from his skin, his gaze remained fixed on her face.

Her heart jumped and fell into a rhythm that matched the intensity of his expression. "I thought you retired."

"I'm officially out of retirement." He winced when she brushed too hard.

"Sorry," she murmured, and gentled her strokes. "Didn't your doctor say it was too dangerous?"

"He said there were risks, aye."

The tender wrench of sorrow squeezed the back of her throat, and even though she had no right extracting any vows from him, she met his gaze, then said, "Promise me you'll be safe."

He slipped his hands under the hem of her T-shirt and took a leisurely journey upward. "I promise."

Warm hands cupped her bare breasts. His touch was both

gentle and commanding at once and she closed her eyes for a moment, reveling in the feel of his calloused palms against her sensitive skin.

"I wish I'd known you had a match tonight." She opened her eyes, and her gaze danced over his battered face. "I would've liked to have been there."

"Want to watch me get pummeled, do ya?" The smile he attempted pulled at the cut on his lip and he winced.

She dropped a whisper-soft kiss on the corner of his mouth. "I don't care if you lost."

A strange light came into his eyes then. "I didn't lose."

CHAPTER 25

"Oh. Well, that's good." A frown puckered her brow. "Isn't it?"

It was not good. Not at all. He was supposed to go down in the second round.

Instead, the fool they'd put him up against strutted around the ring like a damned peacock, shaking his feathers for the crowd rather than delivering the match-ending blow. In a last-ditch effort to make the fight appear legit, Cian took a half-assed swing at the prancing gobshite, who never saw the hit coming.

He'd dropped like a boulder to the bottom of a lake.

"You aren't happy."

With Avery's beautiful tits filling his hands, it was hard to be upset. But no, he wasn't happy. By not losing that fight, he'd lost Moretti a ton of money in gambling winnings. He had no idea how much exactly, but it had the potential to be a significant amount. And there was no telling how many other crooks and liars he'd just pissed off that'd trusted Moretti to rig the match.

He didn't know what would happen next. After the fight ended, he'd hightailed it out of the venue before Moretti could find him.

He'd made it halfway to Avery before he stopped to think about what he was doing. Need drove him the rest of the way to her.

But now, her pretty face was filled with questions. Questions he could not answer without dragging her deeper into Moretti's dark, dangerous world. If she had information Moretti wanted, she'd be in trouble. He had to keep as much of the truth from her as he could manage.

He shouldn't have come.

But he couldn't stay away.

"I had to see you." His voice grated with his emotion. "There's something I need to tell you."

Her big brown eyes filled with apprehension, and the pain in his body converged inside his chest.

Between his knees, she reached out and pressed the tip of her index finger against his lips, stopping him from saying more.

Slowly, she dipped her head, and when she replaced her finger with her mouth, they released a moan at their connection.

The kiss started slowly, but with the soft lick of her tongue, ignited into something urgent and desperate.

She reached for the hem of her T-shirt and whipped the material up over her head. The tips of her breasts puckered in the chill air, and he pulled the pebbled peak into his mouth. With a shudder, she slipped her arms around his head.

He feasted on her round, lovely breasts and dragged her pajama bottoms down over her generous hips. When he revealed the springy curls at the apex of her shapely thighs, lust swelled inside him, spilling and spreading everywhere.

She gathered fistfuls of his shirt and dragged it up his body. He lifted his arms.

Sudden pain sliced through his side, and he gasped.

She murmured tender apologies as she carefully helped him shuck his T-shirt. Her small hands delved beneath the waistband of his black joggers, and they worked together to free his straining erection.

Her lips parted as she gazed at him, and the punch of his arousal left him dazed.

She scrambled over to the nightstand and plucked a condom packet from the drawer. When she returned to him, she tore open the package and, as she eased the condom down the long length of his shaft, sensation pummeled him.

With the condom secured, she gently placed her hands on his shoulders, then pressed one knee onto the bed by his hip and straddled him. When her moist curls brushed his aching cock, his breath hissed between his teeth.

"I'm sorry." She started to pull away. "Does that hurt?"

He gripped her hips with both his hands. "God, no."

Need whipped through him, and he ground upward, straining toward her, only to experience another sharp pang in his side.

"Here, let me do it." She reached between their bodies, where he'd grown so aroused that she had to pull his shaft away from his stomach and guide him to her humid hollow.

A deep purr of pleasure vibrated in her throat when his hard length pushed along her slit. She moved her hips, but it was obvious she'd never taken a man like this before, and it took her a few clumsy, gloriously erotic moments to work out the logistics.

Nestled at her entrance, her pussy kissed the head of his cock, and a primal growl ripped from his chest. By the time she'd eased him fully inside her sweet, snug flesh, his entire body corded with tension and he clutched fistfuls of the bedsheets at his sides.

She moved her hips, working him slowly at first, then faster. While she rode his cock, she explored him with curious, inexpert hands. Soon, every nerve in his body prickled with the fire of his arousal. Sensual pleasure rolled through him in great waves.

Her warm wet depths sucked him, and the glorious torment was soon pulling words out of him. Endearments, pleas, dirty words, love words.

He didn't know what they're doing, but it didn't feel like fucking. It felt like something else. Something more. Something crazy. Emotions he couldn't name alighted in his veins like a searing fire.

Where at first his movements had been careful, cautious, need soon took over. Pain melted away, and he thrust his hips, pounding up into her. The long sweep of her dark eyelashes hid her eyes from him. Her skin flushed pink and her brow puckered as she bounced on his lap, taking everything he gave her.

A pang of tenderness pinched his chest, and the pain was greater than all the aches and bruises on his flesh.

He longed to stay suspended in this moment forever. He never wanted it to end.

Too soon, her body clamped tightly around him, and he closed his eyes, giving himself over to her squeezing, throbbing flesh. Damn, but he wished he had more strength to tease and pleasure her a little longer.

Her pulsing sex coaxed his climax from him in a shuddering surge that vibrated every nerve in his body.

When she collapsed onto the bed, he pushed to his feet.

The wince of pain he experienced only reminded why he was hurting. Fucking Moretti. His joggers had gathered around his ankles, and he gingerly bent down and dragged them over his hips. Every step he took over to the trash can delivered a fresh lance of pain. His aggravation grew.

Irritably, he wanted to demand they do it at his place next time. They needed a bathroom he could use without tripping over her damn brother, and he needed to fuck her good and hard, with no concern for all the sex sounds and noises he intended to wring from her.

But there couldn't be a next time. That much was now clear to him.

Two days ago, he'd convinced himself he could handle more than "just this once." But he'd been wrong. He shouldn't have come to her tonight, or any other night. Not when doing so would only put her in more danger.

Not when the pull between them grew tighter every time they were together.

Even if he kept all the ugly details about his business with Moretti hidden from her, if Moretti ever found out about her and how much Cian wanted her, he might try to use her to control Cian. The same way he'd used Brynn to control her father.

Cian could not let that happen. No matter what.

He needed to put an end to this now. Before it was too late.

When he turned around, she sat on the edge of the mattress, watching him with huge, round eyes. "It's okay. I know what you're going to say."

He experienced a sharp wrench inside his chest. "What do you think I'm going to say?"

"That it's over." Her throat worked when she swallowed. "That we can't see each other again."

His heavy sigh dropped like a lead balloon between them.

"Am I wrong?" A quiet hope echoed in her voice.

It was true he needed to break things off with her because of Moretti. He needed to stay focused and to keep her as far away from the mobster's crosshairs as possible.

But that wasn't the only reason he had to walk away.

If he stayed, he was afraid he might do something really stupid. Like fall in love with her.

That would be a fucking catastrophe. He'd survived cancer, but only because he'd conquered the fear. Fear of his own death, and of dying. If he loved someone, that fear would return. It would rule him, and he couldn't be ruled by fear. Not again.

"You're not wrong," he said quietly.

Her expression crumpled, but she ducked her chin, hiding her face from him.

He took a small step toward the bed, but then stopped. "I'm sorry."

"I said it's okay." She lifted her head, but she wouldn't meet his gaze. "This is what we agreed to."

His T-shirt lay in a heap on the floor at his feet and a low groan leaked from him when he bent down to pick it up.

"Will you be okay?" Her softly spoken question gutted him.

She was worried about *him*? She should be pissed at him, but here she was, caring about him anyway.

Now he struggled to meet her eyes. "I'll be fine."

He just needed to lie low for a while, until he talked to Kendrick and they figured out Moretti's next move.

In the silence, he pulled on his shirt, then his sweatshirt, and when there was nothing left to do except leave, his eyes finally found hers.

Their gazes collided and held. While the moment stretched out, neither of them looked away, knowing when they did, their connection would be lost. Severed forever.

Her lashes fluttered, and she turned her face away. "You should go."

As his feet carried him away from her, he hated himself more with every step.

It had to be this way. There was no other choice.

Only one thing mattered now. Destroying Manny Moretti once and for all.

CHAPTER 26

One perk of not dating was that she'd never been dumped by a guy before.

Though technically Cian hadn't dumped her. They'd agreed to one night, slipped in a second encounter, and then parted ways. It wasn't complicated.

And yet, she never wanted to experience anything remotely like splitting up ever again.

After Cian left, she spent the entire next day cycling through the five stages of grief—binge watching romcoms, online shopping, ice cream, wine, and finally, forgoing basic hygiene to stay in her pajamas all day.

By Sunday evening, when she caught herself partaking in all five stages at once, she switched off the TV, put away the ice cream, and delved back into her article.

It offered her the distraction she so desperately needed, and when she turned her pages into Charles on Monday morning, he liked them enough to give her the go-ahead to write more.

Avery spent the next two weeks digging and compiling information on the rat, Moretti. Eager to steer her thoughts away from Cian, she'd over-focused on the task, devoting nearly every waking moment to the getting the story.

Which is how she wound up crouched behind a dumpster in the alley behind a swanky hotel restaurant where one of Manny Moretti's "business meetings" had taken a bad turn.

The pungent stench of garbage filled her nostrils as she peaked her head around the side of the large metal container.

Light from the streetlamp illuminated the darkened corridor only enough for her to make out the silhouettes of three men. Manny, the brute Cian decked at the party, and a third man Avery didn't know, who suffered the misfortune of having provoked Moretti's ire.

Voices echoed down the alley, but the men were all talking at once and she could only make out snippets of their conversation. Something about money owed and pleas for more time….

She gulped down the terror rising in her throat and leaned a little farther out from behind the dumpster, tipping her body so that she could get a better view of the scene.

The men's voices grew louder and more agitated. Over the chorus, the brute pushed the pleading man to his knees.

Avery's heart lodged in her throat. She fumbled for her cell phone and started recording.

As she steadied the shot in her camera's lens, another man appeared at the mouth of the alleyway. It was too dark to see his face, but he walked toward them with a sure, graceful stride.

The hairs lifted on the back of her neck and arms.

"You don't want to do this here." The newcomer called out before he'd reached the others and spoke with an unmistakable Irish accent.

Avery's chest squeezed so tight the flow of air into her lungs ceased.

"I don't want to hear it from you." A sinister fury shadowed Manny's sharp tone. "I'm very unhappy with you right now."

"Please," the man on knees begged. "I have the money—"

Moretti's brute kicked the man in the stomach, silencing him.

"This neighborhood is crawling with cops." Cian sounded calm, as though this were nothing more than a day at the office. "That's the last thing we need right now."

Manny cursed and paced a few steps away. Abruptly, he jerked back around. "I want the money tomorrow," he told the man, who was still on his knees. "We'll leave you with a little reminder in case you forget."

With a nod to the brute, Moretti turned and carved a path toward the door.

Everything seemed to happen at once. With one hand, the brute grabbed the kneeling man's shoulder, then he raised his other arm high. In the faint lighting, she caught only a flash of the metal object clutched in his hand.

A knife.

The blood in her veins turned to ice.

"Please don't," the man on his knees cried out. "Please, no no no—"

The brute's arm slashed downward.

The world dropped out from under her feet, and her phone slipped between her fingers and rattled to the ground at the same time Cian caught the brute's slashing arm.

Avery gasped, and air flooded her lungs.

But she couldn't breathe because Cian and the brute had twisted toward her. Nearly at the door, Moretti stopped, and his head whipped in her direction.

For a moment, she stood frozen, afraid to move, while shock and terror spiraled through her, and the men stared right at her.

Mobsters.

Looking. Right. At. Her.

She snatched her phone off the ground and ran.

Her feet struck the pavement hard as she sprinted deeper down the alleyway. Behind her, shouts rang out and footsteps pounded the asphalt.

They were chasing after her. Hunting her.

Cian might be one of them.

She didn't dare look back.

A brick wall loomed ahead of her, a literal dead end. Spasms of fear and anguish choked her. Panic darkened her vision.

Then she spotted it. A door.

She threw her body at the barrier as she wrenched the handle, and when the door gave way, she stumbled into a desolate hallway. Glancing around, she realized she was inside the hotel next door to the restaurant where Moretti had been dining.

She slammed the door shut behind her and darted toward the end of the hall, praying she'd make it around the corner before her pursuers followed her through the door.

A crack of noise sounded when the door banged open moments before she rounded the corner.

Blindly, she ran, darting left, then right through the hotel's hallways.

The footsteps grew closer.

Her lungs ached, and even with the adrenaline charging through her body, she was tiring.

Soon, they would catch her.

What would they do when they did?

Stark horror propelled her down another hallway and around another corner. Her foot met an imperfection in the carpeting, and she faltered, crashing hard onto her knees. Pain jolted through her body and something that sounded suspiciously like a sob ripped from her throat.

Footsteps thundered, and she scrambled to her feet. But she'd lost so much ground.

Despair pressed down on her, and she whirled toward the footsteps rushing at her. At any moment, they would round the corner and spot her.

Just then, she noticed a plain white door tucked into the plain white wall. She lunged through it, then eased it quietly closed behind her.

In the darkness, she backed deep into the space, but her heel caught on something, and she stumbled. Her hand shot out to catch herself, but rather than finding purchase, she started a cascade of objects falling and clattering to the floor. In the pitch black, she never even saw the blunt, heavy thing before it smacked her temple.

She swallowed a cry of pain and covered her head with her arms as tears blurred her vision.

Footsteps thundered in the hall outside the door, so she bit her tongue and shrank away from the sound until her back pressed flat against the wall.

Air burned through her exhausted lungs as the footsteps drew closer.

Terror choked her, and she huddled on the floor.

These were the men she'd worried would hurt Jamie. The very men she'd tried to ask for more time to come up with the money he owed them. Exactly as the man in the alley had been doing.

Now they were coming for her.

Cian was one of them.

Her stomach heaved.

How could this be happening? He wasn't like the others. With his gentle hands and heart, he was different.

She'd thought he was different.

Her world was collapsing in on her, spinning out of control, and she dropped her forehead to her knees while images of him in her bed, between her legs, and the soft pleasure on his face when he slid inside her, played through her mind.

The storm of footsteps was upon her now.

Trapped. She was trapped. She couldn't breathe.

The thunder faded. She didn't dare move or even breathe while she listened.

Soon, all sound dwindled away.

Alone in the dark, her limbs trembled as the adrenaline leached from her body. How long should she wait here? Would they realize she was hiding and came back?

Even if she wanted to keep running, she couldn't move. The fear paralyzed and terrorized her. She might remain crouched on the floor in the hotel custodial closet for days before someone found her.

ust then, the door flung open, and light flooded her hideout.

She squinted up at Cian, who loomed in the doorway, a furious spring rain brimming in his eyes.

She shrank back.

He leaned back out into the hallway, and his head snapped to the right and the left. Then that fiery gaze found her face. "Come with me. Now."

The snap in his tone made her body jerk, but her feet refused to obey him.

When his arm came out, she flinched, but he only held out his hand to her. Green eyes compelled her.

Slowly, she reached for him.

He clamped his fingers around her wrist and yanked her out of the closet. She stumbled after him, nearly jogging to keep up with his long strides. The fog of her terror formed a haze around her, and she watched the floor pass under her feet as he led her through the hotel halls.

Suddenly, he changed direction and urged her ahead of him through a darkened doorway. Light from the hallway allowed her a glimpse of brocade wallpaper and gold accented décor before the door closed and plunged them into darkness.

She reared back, but his hand clasped the back of her neck, and he tugged her tight to his chest.

"Easy." His voice puffed next to her ear. "I won't hurt you."

Despite everything, she leaned into his embrace. "I thought they were going to kill me. I thought you were—"

His curse rent the air and his hand at the back of her head pulled her tighter against him. "Never—"

The trembling in her hands spread to the rest of her body and she turned her head, burying her face in the fabric of his wool coat. She squeezed her eyes shut, as if she might block out the dark, dangerous threat that existed on the other side of the door.

"That man—" Her throat constricted. "What's going to happen to him? What were they—you—doing to him?"

His heart thrashed loudly against her ear. "We have to get you out of here."

At his non-answer, her fear spiked. She tried to summon the strength to pull away from him, but she was too weak and sagged against him instead.

As if through a fog, she realized he was talking to her, but she couldn't make sense of his words.

"At the Carlisle," he was saying. "Meet me at the Chestnut Street entrance."

"I don't know where that is," she tried to tell him, but he was pulling her through the hallways again.

"We're on the way now." Cian shoved his cell phone into his coat pocket and clutched her hand inside his.

They hustled down long corridors, making several twists and turns that quickly left her disoriented. Unsure where they were inside the building, she tripped along behind him.

She could only hope he wasn't taking her to Moretti.

A blast of cold air slapped her in the face when they stepped outside the hotel and onto the city sidewalk. Cian slipped his arm around her shoulders and steered her toward a vehicle idling at the curb.

He yanked open the door to the backseat and motioned her inside, then placed his hand on top of her head to stop it from bumping into the car's roof. She winced when he touched the sore spot near her temple, but climbed the rest of the way in and slid to the far side to make room for him.

But he didn't follow her into the car.

Instead, he bent at the waist and peered into her face. Then he rattled off a string of four numbers. "I need you to remember these numbers." He repeated the series of digits. "Got it?"

She repeated the sequence back to him.

"That's the passcode to get into my apartment. This is Ben." He gestured to the man behind the steering wheel. "He's a good friend of mine and he's going to take you there now. Go inside, lock the door, and wait for me. I'll be there as soon as I can."

Then the car door slammed shut, and the vehicle eased out into traffic.

Cobwebs cluttered her brain and her head hurt too much to pick out her separate thoughts from the jumbled mess. Trying only exhausted her, so she spent the car ride repeating the numbers Cian had given her over and over again inside her head to make sure she didn't forget them.

By the time Ben pulled up in front of a soaring skyscraper and parked outside the entrance, she'd rehearsed the password enough times that it was all but tattooed on her brain.

Her car door opened, and Ben helped her climb from the vehicle. The cool wind lashed at her, and she ducked her chin inside the collar of her coat.

"Floor one-twelve." Ben searched her face with kind eyes. "You remember the passcode?"

Her mind was as blank as a field of freshly fallen snow, but she nodded.

Ben had a friendly smile. "Go on up then. Don't forget to lock the door behind you. I need to get back in case Cian needs me."

She entered the building through a set of gleaming glass doors, but as she made her way toward the bank of elevators, a little man in a silly uniform rushed over to her.

"Excuse me." He placed one of his tiny hands in her path. "This building is for residents only."

"I'm visiting a friend."

"Name, please? I'll just make sure you're on their list."

"Cian Nolan."

"And your name?"

She gave it to him, then watched his tiny fingers slide across his tiny tablet. Why was he so tiny?

"Sorry, but you're not on Mr. Nolan's list of approved visitors. Give me one moment and I'll call up to the residence."

"Oh, he's not there. He's on his way, though."

His regretful frown appeared more smug than sincere. "I'm sorry, but you'll have to come back when he's in the residence."

Velvet-covered sofas dotted the grand lobby, and the one closest to them called out to her. Why was she so sleepy all of a sudden? Was it an adrenaline crash after a near-death experience?

"I'll just wait for him over there." She shuffled toward the nearest sofa.

But she made it only a few steps before the tiny man stopped her. "The lobby is for residents and their guests only."

She rolled her eyes, which caused her head to scream with pain. She would've argued with the silly little man, except her head hurt too much to muster the venom. "Fine. I'll wait outside."

Ben was long gone when she stepped outdoors. She considered heading back to her apartment, but it was a long trek from this part of town, and she just wanted to rest for a bit before she began the long journey.

The cold chased her into a corner where the building blocked the biting wind and she hunkered down there, curling her body into a tight ball.

She'd only rest for a few minutes.

CHAPTER 27

Cian moved through the penthouse lobby with long strides. When the new doorman popped into his path, he barely constrained the snarling growl that'd been building in his chest.

"Th-there was a woman here to see you."

"Thank you." Cian couldn't help it. A snarl leaked out.

"She wanted me to let her into your residence, but of course I didn't."

Abruptly, Cian stopped. "Why not?"

"She wasn't on your list."

Cian rubbed an agitated hand over his short hair. The only reason he stayed in the penthouse, which Brynn technically owned, was because of the tight security. Working alongside someone like Manny Moretti, he needed layers of protection. But he would never get used to the strict protocols.

His gaze sliced across the lobby. "Where is she?"

"I instructed her to come back when you were here to take her call. I'll ring you the moment she returns."

His heart dropped to his stomach. "She *left*?"

"Yes, sir."

"Where the hell did she go?"

"I-I-I don't know," the doorman sputtered.

On a sharp curse, Cian filched his cell phone from his pocket. He dialed her number, but with each unanswered ring, fear unfolded in him like the slow-motion waves of an explosion.

When his call forwarded to her voicemail, he hung up and immediately redialed. Phone pressed to his ear, he retraced his steps to the front entrance and burst out into the frigid cold air.

She better not have gone back to her apartment. Frantic fear slid through him with the thought. It's possible Moretti already knew her identity. By now, he might know where she lived. He may even have sent someone to her place.

Ground-eating strides turned to running lunges as he darted toward the garage where his car was parked. When the ringing in his ear stopped, her voice instructed him to leave a message.

At the beep, his fear and rage erupted. "Avery, where the hell are you? I told you to wait for me. Wherever you are, it's not safe. Get your ass to my place *now*, or so help me—"

"I'm right here."

He skidded to a stop so suddenly his feet slipped on the concrete. Righting himself, he turned toward the sound of her voice.

"What the hell are you doing?" The sharp bite in his words caused her to flinch. With difficulty, he gentled his tone. "Why are you out here in the freezing cold?"

Didn't she know how fucking dangerous it was? Not only had the temperature dipped well below freezing, but Moretti's men were on the prowl.

Her teeth chattered. "They wouldn't let me inside."

He spit out a curse. "Why the hell not?"

A sardonic smile twisted her mouth. "I don't exactly fit in around here."

Confusion pummeled him, and he stared hard at her. "What are you talking about?"

She opened her arms, as if to say, "look at me." "It's obvious I don't belong here."

Another curse fell from his lips. "This is Lincoln Park, not Buckingham Palace," he muttered. "C'mon. we need to get you someplace warm."

She struggled to gain her feet, and he helped steady her.

Finally standing, she frowned at the ground a moment, then her knees buckled.

He caught her arm. Alarm shot through him.

She reached up to touch the side of her head, and he brushed her hand away. "Let me." He gingerly explored with his fingers. "Does this hurt?"

When he grazed the small goose egg near her temple, she sucked a hiss of air between her teeth. "Yeah. Ouch."

His heart thrashed inside his chest cavity.

Her entire body shivered with cold.

"Here. You're freezing." He shrugged out of his coat, but when he moved to hang it around her shoulders, she shrank away from him.

The gut punch nearly dropped him to his knees.

She was afraid.

Of him.

"What were you doing in that alley?" Her toffee brown eyes were huge in her pale face. "Wh-what's going to happen to that man?"

His stomach heaved to recall Moretti's fury with the foolish man who owed him money and the Baby Assassin's deranged enthusiasm to exact revenge. When Derek had struck out with his intent to maim the guy, Cian's instincts had taken over and he'd blocked the blow.

In a cruel twist of fortune, Avery had been detected at just that moment. After Ben removed her to safety, Cian found Moretti and convinced him he'd saved their asses tonight by thwarting the assault before they made the woman in the alley an eyewitness and let her capture the whole thing on her cell phone.

By then, the man had escaped, and while Moretti ranted at Derek about the debacle, Cian seized on the excuse to go search for the fool and slipped away. Then he'd contacted Kendrick, and the agency had already moved to protect the man from Moretti.

"He's okay. He's... with people that can help him now." After taking a step toward her, he stopped. "I'm sorry. I can't tell you more than that."

She inspected his face for several moments, which felt like an eternity. When she sighed and shuffled toward the building, his heart soared.

At the entrance, he pulled open the glass door and followed her inside.

Right away, Avery spotted the doorman, who was cutting a straight path in their direction.

She ducked her head as they walked toward the bank of elevators. "Watch out for that guy. He's mean."

The doorman obviously had a death wish because he skated into their path.

Anger burned through Cian like licks of fire searing bleak white paper and he glared at the smaller man, daring the little fecker to piss him off. He was itching to hit someone.

"Miss Bishop, welcome back."

"Uh, thank you."

"If there is anything we can do for you while you're staying with us, please don't hesitate—"

Cian kept them moving through the lobby. He wasn't interested in meaningless words just then.

At the elevator, he stabbed the keypad with his index finger, entering the passcode that'd take them to his apartment's private entrance. The doors slid shut behind them and the car climbed.

The mirrored walls inside the elevator seemed to magnify his fury. His reflection glared back at him because he couldn't bring himself to look at her. She was humiliated, wounded and afraid, and he hated it. He hated anything and anyone that would cause her harm because, dammit, he cared about her.

She was slowly carving her way into his heart, and it hurt.

His anger gnashed and gnarled as they rode past the lower floors to the penthouse suites perched atop the sleek skyscraper. With a soft ping, the doors pulled open, and they stepped into the penthouse.

Hesitantly, she hovered in the foyer and took in the sweeping, opulent space. "Nice place."

"Thanks." Moving deeper inside the suite, he slung his coat over the back of an armchair on his way to the fireplace in the main living area.

She took a few tentative steps forward. "You don't strike me as the penthouse kind of guy."

He plucked the remote off the mantle, and with the punch of one button, flames flickered to life in the hearth. "What kind of guy do I strike you as?"

"I don't know. Something less… grand."

His gaze mimicked hers, taking in the massive square footage, the million-dollar view, the sleek styling, and the highest of the high-end finishes available on the market. "Aye, tis grand, isn't it?"

She picked up one of Brynn's ancient-looking vases. "You like porcelain?"

"Is that porcelain?"

"Yes."

"Then, aye, I like porcelain."

She set the vase back down. "This isn't your place, is it?"

"My stepsister owns it. I'm just staying here." Heat from the flames warmed his back. "Come, stand by the fire. Get warm."

She complied, but her shoulders remained high and tight.

"I'm sorry about the mix-up with the doorman."

"Don't worry about it." The soft glow of the fire cast a honey glow over her skin as she stared into the blaze. "It's no big deal."

He wasn't sure who she was trying to convince, but he could see that it'd wounded her.

"I'll talk to management tomorrow."

She shot him a dark look. "Don't you dare."

When she'd turned her head, the firelight caught her temple where the shadow of a bruise was forming over the slight bump.

With some urging, he helped her out of her coat and hung a blanket around her shoulders. Then he dragged an armchair closer to the fireplace and motioned for her to sit. When she collapsed into the cushions, he crouched before her and set to work, unlacing her boots.

Clumps of snow froze the laces, making the task more difficult. But finally, he freed her feet from the wet shoes. Amidst her protests, he dragged off her damp socks, then tucked another blanket snug around her bare feet.

He left her thawing by the fire, and in the kitchen, started a pot of coffee brewing. From the freezer, he dug out an ice pack and wrapped it in a dish towel.

He returned to the living room and lowered his body onto the stone hearth beside her chair. With a short word of warning, he gently pressed the cold pack to her forehead.

She ground her teeth against the stinging cold, but she took the towel from him and held it to the sore spot on her head while he dimmed the lights low and retrieved a bottle of painkillers from the bathroom cabinet. He'd experienced enough concussions to recognize the symptoms and made plans to monitor her closely over the next several hours.

When the coffee finished percolating, he poured a cup, and when she accepted his offer of cream and sugar, added both. He delivered her the steaming mug, then fixed another for himself.

Out of tasks, he swung the other armchair around and sat

beside her before the fire. While they sipped their drinks, the flames danced.

After a time, he asked quietly, "What were you doing in that alley?"

She set her mug on the hearth, then snuggled deeper into her blanket. "Research."

"Research." Fear crackled, and he tamped it down. "Is that why you've been following Moretti all over town? For research?"

"Yes."

At her clipped, passionless response, his terror blazed to life. "Why? What are you hoping to find out?"

Her small shoulders hitched. "Everything."

He dragged the back of his hand over his mouth, trying to stop the flood of obscenities from pouring out. "And then what?"

She gripped the blanket tight beneath her chin and returned his steady gaze. "I'm going to write a story about him."

He erupted to his feet. "Dammit, Avery—"

"Do *you* want to tell *me* what you were doing in that alley?" Large doe eyes blinked at him.

He clenched his jaw so tight pain ricocheted around his skull.

"I didn't think so." There was no smugness in her voice, but only a sad disappointment.

He wanted to tell her everything. He wanted her to know he believed what she believed and wanted what she wanted. Moretti was a menace and the sooner he went down, the better off they'd all be.

But he couldn't tell her that. Not when doing so would put everything at risk.

They were so close. Moretti was piling up crimes faster than Cian could file reports with Kendrick. He just needed a little more time.

"You nearly—if I hadn't been there—" Fear choked off his words.

"I'm fine."

"Fine? *Fine?*" A chaotic cacophony of emotions rumbling around inside his chest. "You are not fine."

How could she say that? She'd nearly stumbled right into the middle of a mob hit and had been lucky to escape with only a lump on her forehead. Apparently, it'd knocked her senseless.

Well, if she was too confused or concussed to see the writing on the wall, he'd have to spell it out for her. "You cannot write this story. I won't allow it."

CHAPTER 28

"You won't allow it?" Icy water spilled through her, and she gaped at him. "You can't stop me."

His mouth thinned into a tight, grim line. "It's too dangerous."

Her heart thrummed a warning tune in her ears. "Dangerous for who?"

He flinched, but his gaze remained steady. "You think I'm protecting my friends?"

"Mobsters don't have friends." She swallowed the aching lump in her throat. "I think you're protecting yourself."

The light in his eyes flashed. "Moretti just saw your face back there in that alley. If there's a story about him with your name on the byline, how long do you think it'll take him to find you? And what do you think he'll do when he does?"

The ice in her veins pierced her heart.

"He'll come after you."

There was so much she hated about this day, but she loathed the quiet certainty in his voice the most.

He lowered his big body into the armchair. Sitting near the edge, he peered hard into her face. "Drop the story."

Against the slash of pain, she squeezed her eyes shut. Never in a million years had she expected him to support her in this. But she hadn't expected it to hurt so much when he opposed her.

His arguments were good ones. She'd known it would be dangerous to write a story like this one, and what she'd witnessed tonight only confirmed just how dangerous it could be to cross Manny Moretti.

But she *needed* to write this story.

She wanted to stop Moretti from hurting people and ruining lives. She'd witnessed up close entirely too much of the pain he caused, and she was tired of it. So damn tired.

A story about Moretti, *her* story about him, could be good enough to end him.

It could win her the academic scholarship, and with it, she could earn her degree and the world would stop viewing her as nothing more than poor white trash that needed to be kept out of swanky penthouses.

"I can't." Her heart thrashed beneath her breastbone. "Someone has to stop him."

He made an agitated noise. "You think one tabloid story is going to do that?"

"Maybe if I expose him…" Hearing how ridiculous that sounded, she trailed off.

Slowly, he reclined in his chair. Shadows danced across his face, obscuring his expression. "All you'll be doing is putting a target on your back."

Anguish squeezed her chest. "Is th-that a threat?"

"It's the truth."

To hide her heartache, she turned away and stared into the fiery flames. "I don't know how much Moretti is paying you, but he should give you a raise for all the work you're doing on his behalf today."

"I'm not speaking as Moretti's man."

An inelegant snort escaped her.

"I'm speaking as someone who cares about you."

She sucked in a sharp breath, and her startled gaze swung over to him.

"It's true." His granite hard tone softened. "Dammit."

She barely noticed the curse over the sound of her galloping heart.

"My brother and stepsister dared to go against Moretti, and they haven't known a moment of peace since. He's made their lives hell. Both of my brothers have suffered because of him. I don't want that for you." The leather chair groaned when he sat forward. "If you write that story, Moretti will find you. He'll find out where you live, where you work, and he'll threaten and harass you until to stop." A slight tremor stirred his voice. "He'll do whatever it takes to stop you."

"I know what he's capable of," she said quietly.

"You don't, or you wouldn't be fighting me on this." He implored her with glittering green eyes. "If you keep trying to expose him, he won't be understanding, or forgiving. He will hurt you."

"All he ever does is hurt people."

"Dammit, Avery—"

The truth bled from her as a near-whisper. "My dad worked for him."

Shock froze him in place.

"He wasn't a mobster, but a pawn. Just an employee at his company." Her voice darkened with the memories. "Then one day, Moretti took an interest in my mom. He propositioned her and when she refused him, he forced himself on her. When my dad found out, he confronted Moretti."

Cian sat unnaturally still, as if holding some raw, savage emotion in check. "What did Manny do?"

"He didn't kill my dad. Not right away. He fired him, of course, then forbid anyone else in town from hiring him. Eventually, we were evicted from our house. We moved into low-income housing, but Manny knew the guy that owned the housing complex and had us kicked out of there too.

"Over the next several years, we scraped by. Homeless. Hungry. Hiding." She gazed into the fire, remembering. "My dad committed suicide when I was fourteen."

When she glanced back, Cian peered hard at some point on the floor between them.

"My oldest brother tried to take his place, but it was too much for him. He started using, and Moretti's pushers were always there with more and harder drugs. Four years ago, he overdosed. Moretti didn't kill my dad or my brother, but he took their lives just the same."

"And your mom?" he croaked. "What happened to her?"

Avery's heart compressed inside her chest. "She got sick. One winter, she got pneumonia. She couldn't work and we didn't have health insurance and... we lost her. A few years after my dad."

"*A mhuirnín*, I'm so sorry. For everything you've been through." His voice sounded stretched, strained. "For all that you've lost."

Into the heavy silence, she whispered, "I can't let him get away with it anymore."

"I never said we were going to let him get away with it."

Her lips parted with her surprise. "We?"

Had she understood him correctly? Or was her tired mind playing tricks on her?

A brilliant bloom of hope unfurled in her chest. "Who are you?"

A terrible tension rode his shoulders. "I can't tell you that. But I don't plan to let Moretti get away with anything. And I need you to forget this conversation ever happened."

"Why?" Drunk on hope, she couldn't resist teasing him. "Are you Batman?"

His crooked smile appeared. "I do look good in black."

Hope and doubt tugged and tangled inside her. *Oh, god*—so much hope.

"Can I ask you something? I just need to know this one thing." The words poured out of her, desperate and urgent. "Just one truth."

His smile faded, taking with it a piece of her heart.

"If I weren't me—" She stopped, then started again. "If you didn't already know me, what would you have done when you found me in that closet?"

His level gaze held hers. "I wouldn't have given you my passcode. And I would've asked my friend to take you wherever you wanted to go."

"You're not a bad guy, are you?"

One corner of his mouth quirked. "It's complicated."

He might not wish to confirm or deny her questions, but she held onto the hope inside her heart. She couldn't let it go. No matter how dangerous it was.

Through the windows making up the outer wall around the penthouse, big, fluffy snowflakes fell, spinning lazily down. The dark sky split the world into two halves. On one side, the cityscape brimmed with twinkling lights, while on the other, the stark black void of Lake Michigan at night held up a halo of sparkling starlight.

"It's a great view," she said.

His gaze followed hers. "Aye. I never tire of it."

For a long while, she watched snow blanket the earth. How many times had she looked up at a skyscraper such as this and wondered how different her life might be if she lived inside one of them?

"When I was a teenager, I used to take the L up here and watch the people who lived in buildings like this." She tried on a smile with the memory, but it didn't stick. "At night, you can see right into their living rooms. I always thought the people who lived in places like this didn't have problems." When he remained silent, she slid him a questioning look. "I'm stereotyping you. Aren't you going to challenge me?"

A tender wrench of sorrow touched his features. "Is that what you want me to do? You want to fight?"

"No. I don't want to fight. Not with you."

He held out his hand, palm up.

No demand. No pressure. Just a strong, warm hand.

She clasped her fingers around his.

Hand in hand, they watched the snow fall.

"People here still have problems," he said. "But the view helps."

Exhaustion pulled at her, spurred on by the heat from the fire and the comfort of his touch. She yawned.

In the quiet, he asked, "Will you at least think about it?"

"I will." She stared at their clasped hands. "But what happens if I don't drop the story? Where will that leave us?"

Us.

The word hung in the space between them.

CHAPTER 29

"Us." He repeated.

The way he said it, softly and with a tender weightiness, the word instantly became her favorite.

Another yawn overcame her. Her limbs were impossibly heavy as he led her down the hallway to a bedroom that, though smaller than she expected for such a magnificent home, was as opulently decorated as the rest of the penthouse.

He helped her with the suddenly complicated fastenings on her clothing, and when she slid under the bedsheets, the luxurious fabric was soft against her skin and the mattress like a cloud of foam beneath her body.

Rich people had the best beds.

She couldn't ever recall feeling so tired, but as she drifted toward sleep, she shook off the veil of slumber and tried to sit. "Aren't I supposed to stay awake? In case I have a concussion…"

He sat on the edge of the bed and peered into her eyes.

"Are you checking my pupils?" She blinked her eyes open wide and sent up a silent prayer that he wouldn't suggest she go to the hospital.

As always, funds were tight and there was no way she could afford a trip to the emergency room right now.

One corner of his mouth twitched. "Rest now. I'll watch over you."

His words sloped through her like a healing balm, and she sank into the mattress.

He'd watch over her.

Because he cared about her.

He'd said he did. Just said the words. Without conditions or modifiers hooked onto the end of his statement.

Though her head ached, a smile bobbed inside her heart as she dropped into the heavy darkness.

She drifted in and out of sleep, and every time she gained consciousness, Cian was there. Sometimes, he laid in the bed beside her, while other times he sat in the midnight blue armchair near the window. Every time she slept, he visited her in her dreams.

The next time she woke, the throbbing inside her skull had eased. With a deep sigh, she stretched and relished the absence of pain.

From the armchair where he sat with his legs outstretched and a book opened in his hands, he looked up. "Hey."

"Hey." She glanced around the room, which had soaring ceilings, an enormous window with a view of the city, and yards and yards of plush fabrics from the draperies to the bedcovers. There was also a large object leaning against one wall with a white sheet thrown over it. "Is this your bedroom?"

"It is."

Outside, pink and lavender swirls painted the sky.

She rubbed both of her eyes with her knuckles. "What time is it?"

"It's almost dinnertime."

She'd slept all night and the entire next day?

Her fingers brushed the tender spot on her forehead. "You've been here the whole time?"

"Of course I have. I live here."

"Oh. *Oh.*" She bolted upright. "I'm so sorry." She tossed back the covers and bounded out of his bed, but when her feet hit the floor, a wave of dizziness swamped her, and she plopped down hard on the edge of the mattress.

In a flash, he was at her side. "Easy. Let's take it nice and easy."

She swallowed thickly.

He peered closely into her face. "Just breathe."

She closed her eyes and focused on taking deep, slow pulls of air into her lungs. When the wave of queasiness subsided, she opened her eyes and offered him a weak smile.

"That's better." Past his smile, concern crowded his handsome features, and his deep green eyes brimmed with worry.

Because he cared about her.

With his fingertips, he brushed a strand of hair away from her eyes. "How are you feeling now?"

She rubbed the back of her neck. "Like I've been hit by a bus."

"Let's get you back in bed."

She didn't argue with him, but collapsed into the pillows as he dragged the covers over her body.

When she woke sometime later, the bedroom was dark and quiet except for the faint sound of running water.

Just when she decided she felt well enough to leave his bed and return home to her apartment, the door to the ensuite bathroom opened.

Cian emerged on a cloud of steam with a towel wrapped around his lean waist. Tiny droplets of water skated along his bare torso and trailed invitingly down the flat plane of his stomach.

The soft fluttering in her heart dipped low into her belly.

When he saw she was awake, a smile touched his mouth. "How are you feeling?"

"Much better." She slipped out from under the covers and carefully pushed to her feet. When she experienced no signs of nausea or lightheadedness, she breathed a sigh of relief.

"I'm glad." His gaze swept over her body, as though taking his own assessment. "Is there anything I can get you? You must be starving."

She glanced longingly at the bathroom door. "Do you mind if I shower?"

He jerked a thumb toward the ensuite. "That, or there's an enormous tub."

The thought of soaking in a warm bath pulled a whimper from her.

With a quick smile, he retraced his steps, and she followed him into the ensuite.

They filled the large soaker tub until it was brimming with bubbles, and she slid into the hot, sudsy water with a groan that was part pleasure and part pain. Her skin protested the biting heat even as her aching muscles delighted in it.

While she soaked, he moved about the steam-filled space, fetching her dry towels and a packaged toothbrush. Her limbs became so relaxed that the actual task of bathing proved too much for her.

Without a word, he went to the head of the tub and gently massaged shampoo into her hair. The combination of his strong, kneading hands and warm water lulled her, and she closed her eyes.

The experience was sexy, sensuous, but also so much more. He took great care with her, anticipating and attending to her every need. With a jolt, she realized just how much she'd been missing out on.

It was such a lovely thing, knowing he was there to help her if she couldn't help herself. Knowing she would be taken care of, no matter what.

When the water grew tepid, he helped her climb out of the

deep basin and wrap a huge, fluffy towel around her body. As he used another towel to draw the excess moisture from her hair, some unfamiliar emotion squeezed her chest. It wrenched like sorrow but was far lighter. Not merely affection, but similar. Heavier.

He tossed the wet towel over the drying bar, and when he opened the bathroom door, chilly air rushed into their humid sanctuary. Wrapped in the towel, she followed him into the bedroom.

She paused in front of the large object swathed by the white sheet. "What is that?"

He looked up from the dresser where he'd been picking out clean clothes. "It's a mirror."

For a moment, he considered the veiled mystery, then he crossed over to it and gave the sheet a firm tug. The fabric fell away and revealed a massive mirror encased in an ornate gold frame.

Avery stared at her reflection in the eight-foot-tall piece of glass. "That's a big mirror."

With the sheet gone, the glass reflected the light from the windows and the room appeared instantly larger than it was.

"My stepsister is into antiques and things. I guess it's old."

She gazed into the looking glass. "I see why you're afraid of mirrors."

His smile was as fleeting as a ghost. "When I was sick, I lost my strength and my career. Everything I thought my life would be disappeared right before my eyes." He turned away from the glass. "I'm not a fan."

A soft anguish pierced her heart. She wondered how sick his treatments had made him, and if anyone had been there to help him, the way he'd helped her.

Such an illness would be terrible for anyone, but she imagined it was especially hard for a man like Cian, who'd been young and strong, and accustomed to hammering opponents and pushing his body to its physical limits.

A part of her wished she'd known him then. She wished she could've been a source of strength and comfort for him when everything sucked, and he was scared. The way he'd been for her.

She watched in the mirror as he retrieved a clean pair of joggers from the dresser and laid them on the bed behind her.

When he looked up, she caught his reflection in the glass.

His movements stilled. A lustful secret glittered in his eyes and the throbbing in her heart arrowed straight to her core.

Lightly, she toyed with the spot between her breasts where she'd tucked in the towel.

She wanted to make him forget what he saw when he looked in that mirror. She wanted him to see the man she saw.

Her heart pounded with her nervous pulse, but she ignored it.

And tugged.

With a soft *whoosh*, her towel dropped heavily to the floor.

In the mirror, his green eyes flashed and clamped onto her naked breasts. He moved to stand behind her, then slipped his arm around her waist and pressed the front of his body against the back of hers.

The delicate catch of his teeth against her earlobe sent a delicious shiver chasing down her spine.

"Avery." The low timbre of his voice grabbed her insides.

He grazed the underside of her breasts with the backs of his fingers, then cupped her fully with his large palms.

She arched into his touch and reached behind her, fumbling for the edge of the towel tucked around his waist.

"We should wait." He sounded out of breath. "Until you're feeling better."

"I don't want to wait." Gently, she yanked his towel away. She turned to face him, then curled her fingers around his hard length. "I feel good. Let me show you."

Slowly, she lowered to her knees before him.

CHAPTER 30

When she sucked him inside her hot mouth, a growl of want and need ripped from his chest.

In the mirror, her bare ass rested on her heels and his hands played through the silky strands of her hair while she took a long pull from him.

Desire slammed through him, and he watched the scene playing out before him with awe.

A goddess at his feet, the sick, defeated man he'd last seen in this mirror was long gone, replaced by someone else.

This new man far exceeded anything he'd ever dreamed of becoming. He was so much more than the smug punk that liked to pick fights and finish them.

This man, getting sucked off by this woman, was a god.

The first ripples of his release stirred, so he hauled her to her feet. In one rough motion, he clapped his hand on her nape and tugged her to him, swallowing her shocked gasp with his mouth.

His tongue licked and lashed with the violence in his heart. He tried to gentle the kiss, but she nipped his bottom lip and commanded his lust by gripping his hard length in one hand and squeezing his balls with the other.

She kept tempting him to taste life again, and he was becoming a glutton.

His hands shook when he cupped her face and devoured her mouth. Soon, he neared release once more. He backed her toward the bed.

But she wasn't done with him yet.

A soft smile curved the beautiful mouth that'd sucked him so good when she placed her hands on his shoulders and guided him to sit on the edge of the mattress. Then she faced the mirror.

He gripped the neat curve of her waist above the rounded globes of her lush ass as she lowered down onto his lap.

Perched on his thighs, she caught his gaze in the mirror. At the mischievous glint in her dark eyes, his cock jumped.

Slowly, she hooked her thighs over his knees, parting her legs wide.

A punch of lust knocked into him, and his gaze riveted to her sex.

When he dipped his fingers into her honeyed heat, her gasp of pleasure slid into a moan.

His erection strained while he worked her body with his fingers, whipping heat into her chest and cheeks.

Her head fell back onto his shoulder and her breaths came in short gasps. The swivel of her hips mesmerized him. Their increasingly frantic revolutions as she chased her arousal echoed inside his chest.

She was so beautiful. So strong. A fighter to the very end.

When her tight flesh started to clamp around his fingers, he pulled his hand away.

He stood so abruptly that she tumbled off his lap. Before she fell, he caught her with a firm arm around her waist and hauled her body to his. He dragged his mouth down the column of her throat, then he tossed her onto the bed.

Her heavy breasts swayed with the movement, and a punch of

need knocked the air from his lungs. He rescued a condom from the night table and sheathed his long length.

For a moment, he stood over her and gazed down at her naked beauty.

Need spilled through him like black ink over a white canvas. A dark stain of lust and greed throbbed in his chest. He needed her. He needed to fuck her. He needed to love her and never let her experience another moment of fear.

In that moment, when he hesitated, her knees fell open, and she showed him her glistening heart.

Need roared through his veins and overcame him.

He lowered his body onto the bed and brought their faces close. With their noses only inches apart, he nudged his hips between her legs.

He hovered above her, the tip of his cock teasing her entrance.

There, he lingered. "Avery, I need to know you're safe."

Beneath him, she wriggled, and her warm, wet pussy kissed the tip of his rigid shaft.

Blood rushed through him like fire, burning and singing every nerve in his body, and he gasped. "Avery, please—"

Big, beautiful eyes stared up at him. "I'm safe." She took his hand and laid his palm on her chest, over her heart. "I'm here and I'm safe."

He pressed his forehead against hers and squeezed his eyes shut, fighting the urge to plunge deep inside her.

She dragged his hand over her breast.

He cupped her, then rolled her nipple between his thumb and index finger.

Rising on one elbow, he trailed his fingertips between the lush mounds of her heavy breasts, and downward to her navel. With the backs of his fingers, he circled her belly button.

When his hand stilled above her dark curls, she lifted her knee, inviting him to explore further.

He stroked lightly along her slit. Her eyes fluttered shut, and she titled her hips.

He pulled his hand away.

With a gasp, her eyes flew open.

"I need a promise from you, Avery." Another brush of his fingers elicited another gasp of pleasure from her. "Promise me."

A ripple disturbed the soft pools of her brown eyes. She understood he was asking her to drop the story, and the request pained her.

His heart wrenched with a pang of regret.

"I want to make you happy, Cian." She pushed her fingers through the hair on his chest. "I want to please you."

"You please me very much, *a mhuirnin*." The Gaelic endearment rolled off his tongue. "But right now, I need your promise."

She stared into his eyes for several heartbeats, then she reached up and tugged his head down.

The kiss she gave him was so much more than a kiss. She fucked him with her mouth, taking slow, deep, dirty licks with her tongue. With bitten-off noises that broadcast her need, the damp slip of her mouth mimicked the way his body fucked her.

When she broke the kiss, he was trembling with need and frustrated desire.

Before he could regain his composure, she rolled onto her stomach and pushed up onto her hands and knees. With the first brush of her ass against his hard shaft, he nearly exploded.

But he wouldn't quit this fight so soon. It was too important.

She arched her back, and he parted her with his fingers. Her slick arousal sucked at him, and he replaced his fingers with the tip of his aching cock. When he nudged inside her, a dark, primal groan ripped from his chest.

He pushed deeper, then retreated.

She cried out with her unrealized pleasure.

"Please don't fight me on this, Avery." He teased and nudged, but resisted the urge to slide fully inside her.

"Cian!" She gasped his name as both a curse and a plea rolled into one.

Her body begged him.

He eased deeper and deeper still, then withdrew.

Her moan of pleasure morphed into frustration.

"Avery, you know what I need from you." His arousal grew painful, tightening his balls and making him harder than he'd ever been. "Please give it to me," he rasped. "Avery, please promise me."

"Cian, *please*. Please fuck me."

His control slipped. He plunged deep, burying himself for one brief, glorious moment.

Then he pulled out.

She clutched the bedsheets above her head and whimpered.

"I need you to promise me, Avery. I need you—"

His raspy plea was cut off when she tilted her hips higher, giving him her whole heart.

A guttural groan tore from his chest, and he thrust fully inside her, pulling an answering cry from her.

She won.

But he couldn't mourn his loss with her body clenched tight around him. He pumped his hips and nipped her shoulder with his teeth. Her breasts swayed as he rocked into her.

The mirror captured fragments of light and shadow and reflected the brutal beauty of their bodies moving together.

He rose onto his knees behind her, and she gasped with the new angle, but lifted her ass higher, granting him access to all of her.

She gave him everything.

He watched their reflection while he fucked her with increasingly urgent, desperate thrusts, his hips and his heart pounding in time with his need.

The tight muscles of her body spasmed around his cock and

drew his orgasm from him. Together, they came, their bodies feeding off each other as wave after wave of sensation rolled through them.

When she collapsed beneath him, he eased from her body with a shudder and shifted off her.

On shaky legs, he stumbled into the bathroom. After he discarded the condom and washed up, he returned to the bed.

Lying on her stomach, she looked over at him with soft, sad eyes. "I'm sorry. I can't give you what you want."

The hitch in her voice took a notch out of his heart.

"Don't be." He rolled onto his side and smoothed his palm down her back. "On the bright side, I don't think I'll be afraid of mirrors anymore."

Her soft laugh soothed the ache in his chest somewhat.

He dropped a kiss on her shoulder, then nuzzled the hollow beneath her ear. Her shuddering sigh echoed in his bones.

Though he needed more time before he'd be able to go again, he craved her. His desire for her was an ache with no remedy.

Grief crashed over him.

She must've felt it too, because she whispered his name and reached out her hand.

He laced his fingers through hers. The touch was still foreign to him, and he reveled at the miracle of her small, warm hand inside his.

His tender heart wrenched.

"What are we doing?" Her weighty whisper was tinged with panic.

He knew she wasn't asking him about the sex. She was asking him about the rest of it, about the ache, and the need, and the wild, reckless wanting.

Hell if he knew what burned between them. He only knew he wanted to lie in the dark and hold her hand and fuck her sweet pussy for as long as she'd let him.

For as long as the world would let them.
He never wanted it to end.
"I don't know," he murmured.
Six months ago, he was living just to breathe.
Now, he no longer merely existed.
Now he had Avery.

The elevator doors slid open, and Cian towered before her. Tall, dark, and so beautiful, she wanted to both curse and praise the gods for their amazing work.

Then the lopsided grin lifted one corner of his mouth, and her heart cracked open. From the chasm, a furious flutter arose.

"I thought you left." He tugged her inside and claimed her mouth with his in a soul-stealing kiss.

Her stomach flipped over with delighted somersaults, and her worries that he'd resent her for refusing to drop the story melted into a puddle at her feet. By the time he broke the kiss, her breaths were coming hard, and a dizzying cloud of desire engulfed her.

When she was certain she could stand on her own, she lifted the box in her hands. "I did leave. Long enough to get breakfast."

She could feel his eyes on her back, warming her neck and shoulders, as she moved into the kitchen and pulled down plates from the cupboard.

Heat from his notice spiraled through her while she arranged the plates on the kitchen island and popped open the box.

He moved to peer over her shoulder. "Cupcakes?" His voice was gravelly with sleep. "For breakfast?"

A shiver raced through her at his nearness. "As often as possible, yes."

"Ever try coffee?"

She bit into a sugary baked good and moaned.

With the coffeepot in one hand, he froze, and his eyes clamped onto her mouth.

A punch of pure lust slammed into her, and she gulped down the now tasteless sweet treat.

He returned to pouring his coffee, and she yearned for his hot gaze the way lungs craved oxygen, as though his eyes on her were necessary for her survival.

Fear took root inside her.

The desperate longing, the flutters, and somersaults… they all pointed to one thing.

She had fallen for him. She was head over heels, drop her panties and take him anytime, anywhere, into this guy.

Her body tensed as, with her whole being, she resisted the idea. *No!* It couldn't be true.

It was just the sex. At least, that's what she told herself. They were really good together, sexually. That's why her body reacted to him like he was a gourmet cupcake. The sex was really, *really* great. Fantastic. That's all it was.

But why was the sex so great? Was it just hormones? That chemical connection that drew them to each other? What was the reason she kept coming back for more—no, the reason she couldn't walk away?

She'd tried to leave him this morning, sneaking out while he still slept so that he wouldn't tempt her to stay. But after a quick stop at the delicious smelling bakery across the street, she wound up right back at his penthouse.

From beneath the sweep of her eyelashes, she stole glances at him, and though she should've gone home after the bakery, she wasn't upset with herself for caving. Because now she knew how he looked when he first woke up.

The hard set of his features had softened and the sharp sadness in his eyes had been replaced with a playful glint. It was like he was someone else. She liked this guy, too.

A lot.

So, what if it wasn't just the sex? What if the reason the sex was so great was because of him? What if the sex was so great because *he* was great?

Really, really great.

Across from her, he leaned against the counter and took a sip of his coffee. "The way you're eating that cupcake is doing things to me."

"Sorry." She swallowed thickly. "I really enjoy eating them."

"Sweet tooth?"

"Not really, no." With the tip of her finger, she swiped off some frosting, then licked her fingertip. "It's just the cupcakes that I like so much."

His pupils darkened. "What do you like about them?"

"What's not to like? They have pretty sprinkles, bright colors, silky frosting, and a luscious cake. They're over the top, totally impractical for the cost and labor, and have zero nutritional value."

"You like that?"

"They're pure decadence. Frivolous and fun." She hitched her shoulder. "They're everything I never had growing up."

Tenderness touched his expression. "To remind herself you're not that kid anymore," he said softly.

Heat warmed her cheeks. "I know it's silly."

"It's not silly at all." His gaze shifted to the box, and he pointed with his coffee mug. "There's one missing."

"I gave it to the Henry."

"Who's Henry?"

"The doorman." Her smile was a little devilish. "I'm gonna make him love me."

Something flared in his eyes, and his sudden, slightly wild look entranced her as he closed the distance between them, cupped her face in both of his hands, and took her mouth in a searing kiss.

With his tongue, he licked and ate, and a hum of pleasure vibrated in his chest. "You taste like frosting," he murmured.

"Ooh, cupcakes."

At the sound of the stranger's voice, they jerked apart.

"Rory." Cian let out a long, audible breath. "I didn't know you were here."

Rory shuffled by on his way to the refrigerator. "Where else would I be?"

"Avery, this is my brother."

In greeting, Rory tipped the beer bottle he'd pulled from the fridge at her. He wasn't as tall as Cian, but the brothers shared the same dark, almost black hair, striking, well-formed features, and a sharp jawline heavily shadowed with scruff.

She recognized him as the driver that picked them up from Moretti's party.

"Hi." Avery tipped the box toward him. "Cupcake?"

"Hell, yeah." Rory twisted the cap off his beer, then selected a cupcake from the box. "Thanks."

He settled on a barstool at the kitchen island. And she couldn't help but catalog the similarities and differences between the two men while they ate. While Cian's hair was clipped short, Rory's thick locks brushed his ears and neck. Their eyes were similar shades of green and fringed with black eyelashes, but Cian's irises were a touch brighter.

On one hand, Rory's fingers had an odd bend, and her gaze lingered for a moment as she wondered what had happened to cause the slight curvature.

Cian finished his coffee and rinsed his cup in the sink. "What are you doing today?" he asked as he returned to his spot leaning against the kitchen counter.

Even though it was Saturday, she'd missed work the day before and needed to catch up. Luckily, Charles didn't care what hours his staff kept, but only that the work got done.

"I have to work." Nervous dread crept up her spine and she held her breath.

Was he going to bring up the story again? She didn't want to fight with him anymore.

Instead, he held up his hands in a sign of surrender. "That's not what this is about. I have another story for you to write."

She swallowed a bite of cupcake. "Oh? What about?"

"Me."

Her gaze bounced to Rory, who glared at his brother with a scowl remarkably similar to one Cian often wore. "What about you?"

He shrugged his broad shoulders. "How about a comeback story?"

She wiped the stickiness off her fingers with a napkin. "You probably want a sportswriter for that."

"I don't want a sportswriter to write it." He held her gaze. "I want you to."

She stared at him, baffled. "Why?"

A muscle ticked along his jawline, betraying his dispassion. "Because it's not a sports story. I want it in the scandal pages."

Rory, who had just taken a swig of his beer, stilled.

Cian placed his palms on the counter's ledge behind him. "I need you to write about me and my brothers."

Rory's beer bottle hit the stone countertop with a loud thud.

Without acknowledging his brother, Cian pushed on. "I want you to write about the way I pushed my brother and stepsister out of their company."

"You did *what*?" Anger rolled off Rory in distressing waves.

"I conducted a hostile takeover while they were out of town.

On their honeymoon, no less. They've been cut out entirely of the business they built with their own blood, sweat, and tears." Cian rattled off the details as though he recited the grocery list. "They lost everything, stolen from them by someone they trusted."

"What in the hell are you doing?" Rory was on his feet. "Where is Aiden?"

For the first time, Cian's gaze slid over to his brother. "On a plane with Brynn to an unidentified location as far away from this city as possible."

"Did you really do all that?" A dull, aching dread spread through Avery. "Did you steal your brother's and sister's company?"

"Stepsister." Cian and Rory said together.

Jaw clenched, Cian captured her gaze with his. "Write it. Please."

$\mathcal{A}$very gaped at him. "But…why?"

His broad shoulders lifted in a shrug. "You're a writer, right? Say whatever you want. Make up something good. The more salacious the better." He jerked his thumb in Rory's direction. "Say they sided with this one when he cheated with my fiancée and I wanted revenge."

A curse shot from Rory. "It wasn't like that." He twisted toward Avery. "It wasn't like that."

"While I was fighting cancer, my girlfriend and my brother fell for each other," Cian said coolly. "Those are the facts."

"No one did any falling. Jesus." Rory paced the length of the island. "She never fell for me, and I sure as shit never fell for her." He dragged a hand through his ruffled hair. "You were sick, and it was hard on her. She was… confused and scared. We both were."

Cian made a noise in the back of his throat.

Rory stopped abruptly and aimed his solemn gaze at his brother. "Even if I had loved her, which I didn't, I wouldn't do that to you."

Cian carefully averted his eyes, and the hard set of his mouth told Avery he wasn't buying Rory's denials.

Her heart gave a gasping wrench for both men, and a sharp twinge for the woman that came between them. She could only imagine the heartbreak they must've experienced, from the moment of Cian's diagnosis, through his treatments, and as he became sicker. No doubt fear and grief had consumed them. She had no trouble picturing how feelings, or confusion about feelings, might develop.

She tipped her head when she looked at Cian. "You don't really want all this in the tabloids, do you?"

He rolled his shoulders. "You print this kind of stuff all the time, right?"

"Well… yes, but—"

"Print it." His tone brooked no debate. "All of it."

"Why are you doing this?" Pain glittered in Rory's eyes. "Is this about Moretti?"

Surprised zinged through Avery at that. What would Manny have to do with any of this?

Cian eyed the box of cupcakes. "He'll read it, if that's what you're asking."

"Oh, sure he will. Everyone knows any self-respecting crook consults the tabloids for their news. God, I feel gross just saying that." Rory cut a glance at her. "No offense."

"None taken," she said.

Was he right? Was Cian hoping Moretti would read the story? How would that help him?

"You know what? Do whatever you want." Rory returned to the fridge and retrieved two more beer bottles. He walked to the front door, where he pulled on a black parka and slipped the beers into the pockets. Then he tipped his head at her. "Catch ya later."

When the penthouse door closed behind him, a heavy quiet settled over the room.

Into the silence, Avery asked, "Are you sure about this?"

Cian leaned against the counter with his arms crossed in

front of him. "I don't want anyone to think my brothers are anything other than enemies to me." He glanced at the door. "Shouldn't be too hard."

"What about your other brothers? I think you said they're your half brothers?"

His eyes swung to her face, and she saw that the sadness had returned to his eyes. "Leave them out of this. Please. I'd rather you don't mention them at all."

For a long moment, she considered him, wondering why in the world he'd want the whole town to think he hates his brothers.

"You're trying to protect them." Sshe said softly. "Aren't you?"

Just like he was trying to protect her by demanding she drop her story about Moretti.

Somehow, he thought a public feud would help keep his family safe, though for the life of her she couldn't comprehend how he expected this plan to accomplish that.

Still, her heart softened. With slow steps, she moved to stand in front of him.

A sudden fiery hunger glinted in his eyes when he looked down into her face. The muscle in his jaw ticked. "Will you drop the story?"

"No." She hated to admit how much she didn't want to disappoint him. "I'm sorry."

With a sigh, he dropped his head and ran a hand over his scalp. "Don't apologize."

"I could lie to you, if that would make things easier?"

"Do not lie to me." A biting snap rode the edge of his words.

A strange, primitive resentment seeped in to haunt her. "Your ex… did she lie to you?"

"It doesn't matter."

But the creeping jealousy told Avery it did matter. It mattered to her. What was the woman he once loved like? Before things turned bad, he was going to marry her, and it mattered very much to Avery how things unfolded between them, and how the person he once was became the sad, hardened man standing before her now.

"You're right that it doesn't have to matter. I'm not her. And I won't lie to you." She inched closer, shrinking the space between their bodies. "If I do, you have permission to punish me."

"Oh, yeah?"

"Oh, yeah." She raised her fists. "But I grew up with brothers and I know how to fight. Consider yourself warned."

A scowl twisted his features. "Is that how you make a fist?"

She took a pretend swing at him, which he easily blocked by capturing her fist with his hand.

"Not like that." He was shaking his head. "Never choreograph your attack like that."

"Oh." She dropped both of her hands to her sides. "Okay. What am I supposed to do then?"

"Here, like this."

He showed her how to curl her fingers into her palm and tuck her thumb over her knuckles. For a long while, he went on about the positioning of her thumb, but she became distracted watching the lively animation on his face while he talked, and she missed most of what he said.

They practiced her form next, until things derailed when he put his hands on her hips to show her a proper stance and she wiggled her ass at him.

She was a dedicated student, however, and challenged him to a mock fight. He took a couple of soft swings at her face, then trailed his fingers down her cheek.

When she came at him again, he ducked and scooped her up off the ground. Bending her over his shoulder, he clamped one hand on her bottom.

She gasped and squealed his name.

"I thought you wanted to fight." With the pad of his thumb, he stroked the curve of her ass cheek.

"No," she breathed. "I don't want to fight anymore. I want to be conquered. Over and over again."

He set her upright, then snatched her to him and captured her mouth with his. When he slipped his tongue inside, her body melted against his.

She gripped his neck, pulling him closer, and inhaled his incredible scent into her senses. She wanted to breathe him, lick him, eat him, drink him. If she could, she would consume him, and take him inside her heart.

Hunger pounded through her veins until she feared her chest might explode. She never wanted anyone like this before. Ever.

"Damn you," she murmured against his mouth.

"I'm sorry." His breaths came in short, sharp pants.

"You don't even know what you did."

He pressed his forehead to hers. "Then tell me so I can fix it."

"You're making me doubt myself."

"How so?"

"Men. I thought you were like cupcakes. Cute and yummy, but unnecessary, and probably bad for me."

His expression softened. "And now you're not sure?"

Emotion piled in her throat, and she nodded.

He didn't feel frivolous or unnecessary, or bad for her. When she was with him, she felt like she'd found the elusive puzzle piece she'd been searching for all her life.

She felt whole.

With his fingertips, he toyed with her hair near her temples. "And that's a bad thing?"

"If you turn out to be like all the other guys, I'm gonna be so mad at you."

One corner of his mouth tilted upward. "And what if I'm different?"

"Then I'm in trouble."

CHAPTER 33

Avery's story about Cian dropped on Thursday and by Friday night, Moretti had read every word of the ridiculous tabloid tale and was having a blast ribbing Cian about it.

"Your brother stole your girlfriend?" A soulless and cruel man, his laughter also carried a soulless and cruel ring.

The others in the room joined in on the heckling, including the little punk from the mobster-in-training program, who was play-acting as security guard at the door tonight. Manny allowed only the most obedient soldiers into his private home.

"That's right." With a smirk, Cian shrugged. "So I stole the other one's business. Seemed like a fair trade."

From behind his oversized mahogany desk, Manny wagged a finger at Cian. "I knew I liked you."

The knot screwing Cian's shoulder blades into pretzels eased somewhat. The ploy was working. Moretti had decided Cian was too useful to him to let the mix-up with the fight get in the way, and now he'd let Cian into his inner circle.

He just had to keep at it a little longer. Soon, he'd get his chance to takedown Moretti. He could feel it.

Given Moretti's good mood, Cian took his shot at casting a

new net. "Now that I'm in charge of Hathaway Group, maybe we can discuss a future venture?"

The more crimes he lured Moretti into, the better chance they had of finding one that'd stick.

Manny watched Cian with eyes hooded like a hawk. "We'll see. First, I'm gonna need you to do me a favor."

Alarm skittered along Cian's spine. "Oh, yeah? What's that?"

"I need you to fight again." Manny flipped open the humidor perched on the corner of his desk. He paused with his hand over a cigar and pinned Cian with a dark stare. "But this time, you go down in the third."

Cian bristled with feigned offense. "I'm not the one you need to worry about. Talk to the other guy."

"That won't be a problem." A slimy smile ghosted Moretti's lips as he rolled a cigar between his thumb and forefinger. "You'll be facing Vasquez in Vegas next weekend."

"Vegas?" Surprise jostled the word out of Cian. "I didn't think you'd want me anywhere near the cage again, let alone in a marquee matchup."

Moretti struck a match and puffed on the Corona until the end caught fire. Then he waved his hand over Avery's tabloid. "Seems everyone loves a comeback kid."

This could be it. This could be the opportunity Cian was looking for to nail Moretti. Having talked to Kendrick before the last fight, Cian knew rigging matches wasn't going to put Moretti away for long, but it was possible the crime could carry a sentence of five years or more.

Still, unease dragged at him. If he listened to his doctor, he shouldn't be fighting. Though he hadn't asked if a fake fight counted.

He rolled his shoulders. "And if I already have plans next weekend?"

"Cancel them." A billow of smoke leaked out of Moretti. "You fight, or you'll be under the fucking bridge. Either way, you won't be making your date."

At Moretti's threat, Cian concealed a satisfied smile. He happened to know, when trying to convict a career criminal, threats of violence only helped the FBI strengthen their case.

Before Cian could leave, a knock sounded on Moretti's office door.

"Yeah?" Moretti coughed when he called out to the newcomer.

The door creaked open and a young woman with dark hair stepped into the room. "You wanted to see me?"

Manny's mood darkened, and with it, a frisson of tension passed around the room. Everyone here recognized this mood. Some small, seemingly insignificant upset might set him off, and that's when he was the most unpredictable. The most dangerous.

"Emerson." His chair groaned when he pushed to his feet. "Come here, let me see you."

The woman wore a white, form-fitting dress and moved with the stiffness of a mannequin as she crossed over to stand before him.

She was young, not more than nineteen or twenty years old, if Cian had to guess. She was familiar to him, though he didn't exactly know who she was.

Indeed, her identity was a bit of a mystery. Some said she was Moretti's illegitimate daughter, while others claimed she was his mistress.

"You missed dinner." Moretti took a deep inhale from his cigar. "Where have you been?"

"At the library s-studying for my final exams." The slight stammer was the only indication of Emerson's emotional state.

Manny questioned her on the topic, inquiring about the subjects she was studying at the university, her professors, and her grades. He seemed to take an immense interest in her education.

When he'd finished questioning her, he held out his hand to her.

She hesitated, but then she placed her hand in his.

It appeared to be a fatherly gesture until Manny lowered his cigar and pressed the fiery butt against the snowy white skin on the inside of her forearm.

A cry of pain erupted from Emerson and shattered the quiet in the room.

Chaos erupted inside Cian. He took two steps forward, but Moretti sliced him with a look that froze him in his tracks.

His eyes on Cian, Moretti applied more pressure on the fiery poker.

The smell of burnt flesh filled Cian's nostrils, but he couldn't move. It was another test. If he failed the test and interfered, Emerson would be punished for it.

Every man in the room faced the same test, and they endured it in various ways. Some, with shifting feet and gazes, could not watch. Others looked on dispassionately.

Emerson faced the hardest test of them all. Only once her screams dissolved and silent tears streamed down her cheeks did Moretti pull the cigar away from her skin and release her.

Cian felt ill.

This was Manny Moretti. This is what he was capable of. This is what he did to anyone he wished to control. To this poor woman, and so many others, including Brynn.

Cian gripped the back of his chair and stared hard at the horror before him. He needed to bear witness. He needed to remember why he'd given up a normal life to go after this monster.

Because fuck Manny Moretti.

Fuck the evil that lived inside him.

He didn't know whether something had happened to turn Moretti into the monster he was. But somehow, somewhere along the way, his heart or his soul had been destroyed. He'd lost his humanity. If it ever lived within him.

"Don't lose track of time again." With a tip of his chin, Manny sent Emerson scurrying for the door.

That's how he treated someone close to him. Someone he supposedly cared about.

There was no telling what he'd have done to a strange woman pleading for leniency for her brother.

Or one working to expose his crimes to the entire city.

"Bishop!" Avery jolted when Charles barked her name from his office doorway. "Where's my story?"

"Right here," she called over her shoulder even as she finished typing the sentence she was working on.

"You got five minutes." Charles slammed his door shut with an indisputable bang.

Avery's fingers flew over her keyboard, trying to squeak out the last few points she wanted to include in her exposé of Manny Moretti.

She'd stayed up late every night the past week trying to finish the story. If it was going to make a difference to her life or Moretti's, it needed to be perfect.

The previous night, she'd stayed at Cian's penthouse again, but she'd been so engrossed in her work, she hadn't noticed how late it was until he'd brought her a cup of coffee and dropped a kiss on her forehead, then shuffled off to bed alone.

Since that night over a week ago, he hadn't asked her again to drop the story, and although he knew what she was doing, he brought her coffee and snacks and gave her the space she needed to do her work.

Even though he didn't approve, he still supported her.

She hated she was doing something he didn't like. It was an

unfamiliar feeling, disappointing someone she wanted to please. She didn't like it much at all.

Avery hit Save on the document and opened her email. While she waited for the file attachment to upload, she flipped open her calendar to count how many days until her next assignment was due. She'd pushed everything aside to work on the story about Moretti, and now she was hopelessly behind.

She tapped her finger on each calendar square as she counted the days. When her finger landed on the tiny "p" she used to mark the date she expected her next period, she stopped counting. While she stared down at that little "p," her thoughts reeled.

The date was a week ago.

Her period was a week late.

Oh no.

It could be stress causing her to be late. That was the day she'd watched Moretti nearly maim another human being, and then she'd been concussed—

Oh god.

She'd thought the lingering queasiness was a symptom of her concussion. A week had passed and the low-level, nagging nausea persisted.

Oh shit.

Her hands shot to her breasts, and she squeezed.

They were sore.

Ohshitohshitohsit.

She sent the email to Charles, then shut down her computer, snatched her purse out of her desk drawer, and rushed out of the building.

Forty minutes later, she'd visited the corner drugstore on her way home and locked herself in the bathroom of her tiny apartment with a box of pregnancy tests.

After the first test, her vision blurred as she stared at the little pink plus sign.

She reread the instructions, then took another test, and consulted the instructions one more time.

The result screamed up at her in devastating black ink.

Pregnant.

P.r.e.g.n.a.n.t.

P. R. E. G. N. A. N. T.

PREGNANT!

She was pregnant with Cian Nolan's baby.

CHAPTER 34

He hadn't seen Avery in four days. That, combined with the shit Moretti had pulled with Emerson, he was more on edge than he could ever remember being.

The urge to pummel something, or someone, was overwhelming. Mouth-breathing, chest-heaving rage filled him. He wanted to strike and stomp, thrash and pound, until he was too exhausted to throw another punch.

But then, finally, Avery arrived at the penthouse, and just seeing her face helped settle the storm raging inside him.

When the elevator doors slid open, she took one look at him, and her eyes went wide a moment before he gripped her nape and dragged her to him for a deep, soul-calming kiss.

Her taste and scent, and the fact she was here, healthy and whole, soothed his raw nerves and went a long way to diluting the venom Moretti had injected into his veins.

Out of breath, he broke the kiss. But he refused to let her go just yet, so he held on tight and pressed his forehead against hers. And he breathed, finally.

Her soft smile had a playful tilt. "Paparazzi getting to you, are they?"

"What?" He frowned, then recalled the throng of *eejits* downstairs waiting to snap photos and lob questions at him. "Fuck, no."

"There's a big group of them outside—"

She stopped abruptly when he brushed a strand of hair off her forehead.

He peered into her dark eyes. "You okay? You look tired. Did you make your deadline?"

A guilty flush stained her cheeks. "Yes."

He studied her, curious about that blush. While he stared, the flush deepened and spread.

She ducked her chin and stepped around him, but he caught her arm before she brushed by him. With his hand clamped around her wrist, he discovered that her pulse throbbed.

When she lifted her gaze to his, a defiant light blazed in her eyes. "What will you do?"

"What do you mean?"

"Aren't you going to try to stop me from printing it?"

"Even if I was stupid enough to try, I doubt I could stop you." With a sardonic smile, he hitched his shoulders. "I guess I'll just keep worrying."

The pucker that formed between her eyebrows revealed her confusion. "You're not mad?"

"You're trying to do what you think is right. How can I be mad about that?" He slid the pad of his thumb back and forth over the fluttering spot on the inside of her wrist. "Is everything else all right? Are you feeling okay?"

The color leached from her face. "Y-yes. I'm fine."

Suspicion slithered through him. Something other than the story had disturbed her. Had Moretti contacted her? Had her brother found more trouble?

"Avery—"

She interrupted with a dramatic sigh. "Fine, you caught me."

With another huff, she marched to the refrigerator and

yanked open the freezer door. After some prolonged rummaging, she plunked a carton of ice cream on the counter. "I ate half of it by myself the other night while you were sleeping. And I don't even feel bad about it. Happy now?"

A reluctant smile tipped up one corner of his mouth while he considered whether he believed the ice cream was the only secret she was keeping from him.

Before he could decide, his cell phone vibrated in his pocket.

He retrieved the device and glanced at the number on the screen.

Kendrick.

The storm kicked up inside him once more. "I need to take this."

Her gaze bounced to his phone. "Of course."

"I won't be long."

She waved him away, a touch too eagerly. "Do what you gotta do."

He slid open the patio door and stepped out into the frigid night air. As he hauled the glass door closed behind him, he caught her watching him, a thoughtful frown on her pretty face.

It wasn't his first secret phone call, nor the first time she'd visibly contemplated his clandestine conversations.

If they were a normal couple, he'd expect her to probe him with questions about other women the moment he ended the call. He almost wished that was her fear, and not that he was sneaking off to take criminal orders from Manny Moretti.

As usual, he and Kendrick skipped the small talk.

"I want out." The words erupted from Cian before he'd fully formed the idea in his mind.

That scene at Moretti's had shaken him. He hadn't intended to have this conversation with Kendrick now, but with the words out of his mouth, there was no hauling them back. Besides, he didn't want to take them back. He needed to get out before something happened. Something irreversible. He was done being an informant for the FBI.

"Everything all right?" Kendrick asked, unfazed by the sudden outburst.

"I met someone." A rush of emotion infected Cian's voice. "I can't do this anymore."

"Congratulations," Kendrick said easily.

"If it were only me, that'd be one thing." Cian smoothed his palm over his over as the realization hit him. All his big plans to take down the mob had been fucked from that first moment he met her. "But it's more complicated now."

Through the patio doors, he heard the penthouse's intercom chime. He'd ordered takeout earlier and assumed it was the doorman calling for permission to send the delivery upstairs.

Still, his muscles tensed as Avery moved toward the door.

He feared her answering the fecking door. It wasn't right. She deserved better than this. They both did.

"What do you want to do?" Kendrick's calm voice ran counter to the terror and dread spiraling through Cian. "It won't be easy to walk away now. You might need to disappear for a while."

That'd suck, but he couldn't worry about that now. "Whatever it takes."

"Unless…?"

At the intercom system, Avery had accepted the call from downstairs and chatted with the doorman.

"Unless what?"

After a nearly imperceptible beat of hesitation, Kendrick said, "Do the fight in Vegas. Afterwards, we'll move on Moretti."

Cian had told Kendrick about Moretti's latest attempt to make him fight again.

"I thought you said rigging matches wouldn't put him away for long."

"That's true, but if we do it right, we could get him five years, maybe more. That'd buy us some time to come up with more from the other angles we're working."

"Do it right?" Inside, Avery counted the cash Cian had laid on the counter for their dinner. "What does that mean?"

"Do the fight in Vegas. We get him for illegal gambling and racketeering across state lines. Once he pays up after the fight, we'll move in to make the arrest."

Cian wavered as a fierce pull of longing gripped him. At one time, Vegas was his dream. It was the crowning achievement of a successful career.

He gave his head a hard shake. That dream had died long ago.

"One fight," Kendrick said in a low voice, "then it'll be game over."

Just then, Avery opened the penthouse door.

A colorful curse burst from Cian.

"What is it?" Alarm stole through Kendrick's voice.

"Nothing. I gotta go."

"Let me know when you decide about Vegas."

With another sharp curse, Cian bit out his answer. "Let's do it. One last fight. Let's end Manny Moretti."

He disconnected the call while, inside, the first man through the door pulled off his tweed flat cap and blasted Avery with a mouth full of bright white teeth. His eyes sparkled like the sun on a cloudless day and whipped color into her cheeks.

The others filed in behind him, carrying Cian's takeout order.

"Who was that?"

Cian jerked around at the sound of the voice behind him. He peered into the dark until Rory's form materialized. Stretched out on a patio recliner, a beer balanced on his chest.

"*Jeezus.*" Cian laid a hand over his pounding heart. "What the hell are you doing out here?"

"Eavesdropping. Was that Kendrick?"

"Never mind that. We got company."

"What?" Rory hauled his upper body to a sitting position. "Who?"

"See for yourself."

Rory climbed out of the lounge chair and peered through the patio doors. "Ah, feck."

When they stepped inside, Shea turned to them with that million-wattage smile. "Top o' the morning to ya."

Her cheeks still warm, Avery giggled. "Your brothers are here."

"What are all of you doing here?" Cian put an emphasis on "all" and spared a look at each of his five half brothers, every one of them, suddenly and without warning, now standing in his living room.

"We didn't get our holiday invitations out in time, so we thought we'd deliver them in person," Shea said in his thickly accented, gravelly voice.

"All of you came to deliver one message you could've texted or emailed?" Rory shuffled toward the couch. "That's not disturbing at all."

"What do you say?" Shea spread his arms out wide. "Christmas in Michigan in a few weeks?"

Cian pulled up with his surprise. "You guys were serious about that?"

"Of course." Leo plopped down beside Rory. "You weren't?"

"Nah." With the wave of his hand, Cian brushed off the idea. "I thought it was one of those things where you say, "we should get together," and I say, "yeah, we should," then no one ever follows up and it never happens."

A murmur of ohs and ahs spilled around the room.

When the ripple reached Jack, the towering NHL star leaning with one elbow on the kitchen island, he straightened. "Well, what do you say?"

"I say that's bollocks," Rory snapped. "What's this really about then?"

Gazes collided and diverted, then Noah emerged as the unspoken spokesman. "Things sound interesting around here. Thought we'd stop by and see for ourselves what's going on."

Cian forced up the corners of his mouth. "Read the tabloids, do ya?"

Luke snorted. "Who doesn't?"

"Some damn good stories in 'em," Jack agreed.

"Thank you."

The room's collective focus swung to Avery.

"Hi. I'm Avery. I work for the tabloid." She tipped her head in Cian's direction. "I wrote the story."

The Queen of England might as well have stumbled into their midst with all the praise and adoration Cian's half brothers heaped upon her. They milled around her, asking her questions, peppering her with adoration, and gifting her with flirtatious smiles as they made their own introductions.

While Cian scowled at the spectacle, Rory returned to his side. "What'd Kendrick say when you told him?"

"Kendrick?" Shea's head snapped around and his brow creased. "You still talk to him?"

Cian slipped into French when he muttered to Rory, "Keep them out of this. All of them."

It was a tactic they'd stumbled onto when they were young and wanted to hide something from their ma, which was all the time. After that, Cian and his brothers had become fluent in several languages just so they could have private conversations whenever they wanted.

"Too late. They know something's up," Rory replied in the same language, then took a pull from his beer.

Cian had learned how to curse in French too.

One by one, the others peeled away the bubble surrounding Avery and scattered into a wider circle around the room.

"All they have are suspicions right now." Out of practice,

Rory's French made him sound drunk. That, or else he was, in fact, drunk.

"Watch out for the one with the cross tattoo." Cian described Noah rather than tip him off by using his name. "He's sneaky."

"It's true we are a naturally suspicious bunch," Noah said in French. "Comes with the last name, I suppose."

The others snickered, apparently understanding French as well.

Growing impatient, Rory gave them his back. "We need to talk alone," he said in German. "Can you get rid of them?"

Cian folded his arms over his chest and slipped into German. "How do you propose I do that?"

"If you have something pressing to discuss, we don't mind," Leo said in German when he resettled on the couch and plunked his booted feet on the coffee table.

"Are you going to talk about the girlfriend he stole from you?" Jack chimed in, his German a little rusty but clear enough. "We'd like to hear more about that."

An easy smile lit up Luke's uncommonly handsome face when he twisted toward Avery and asked in German, "Is this her?"

Avery blinked at him, confused by their conversation, and yet faintly amused.

Frustration tainted Rory's tone when he asked Cian, "¿Crees que también hablan español?"

The round of soft chuckles provided the answer.

"Por supuesto," Luke said, shaking his head and laughing quietly.

"Don't bother with Gaelic," Cian warned Rory in Latin. "They speak it, too."

"We're here to help." Shea matched the language Cian had used. "We're family."

A bitter taste flooded Cian's mouth. "Right."

Fucking family.

CHAPTER 35

On a barstool at the kitchen island, Avery munched on a French fry and listened to the conversations swirling around her.

She felt his warmth a moment before his deep voice murmured next to her ear. "Sorry about this."

"Are you kidding?" She gulped down her bite. "Who doesn't love a huge, messy family get-together?"

"Is that a serious question?" He swiped a fry off her plate and leaned against the island. While he chewed, he surveyed the room and the noisy gathering. "It's big and messy, all right."

Avery watched with him, amused and amazed by the Nolan clan, minus one out of the eight brothers. "You really just found out about each other last year?"

"Aye."

She gestured toward the room. "So all this is still kind of new to you guys?"

A scowl shadowed his features. "I still get Noah and Luke mixed up."

"Right? It's like a blur of handsomeness and testosterone." She popped another fry into her mouth.

His scowl darkened, but he didn't disagree with her.

She chewed, then swallowed. "They seem nice."

He made a noise.

She dragged a fry through the ketchup on her plate. "I think it's really cool they came all this way to see you."

His scowl took on comical severity.

"Guess the story didn't work to drive everyone away, huh?" She tipped her head to one side, pondering. "Actually, I think it attracted them instead." Laughter bubbled up.

She'd never seen a scowl so dark and so rigid.

A pang squeezed her heart for him and whatever had kept him and his brothers apart most of their lives. But also for herself, and the bigger, messier family she once had.

Her throat tightened, so she rolled her eyes. "Oh geez, a big loving family that wants to be a part of your life. The horror."

Laughing, she moved to walk away.

He caught her arm and tugged her back to him. His mouth came down on hers and then, right there in front of his brothers, he kissed the smile from her lips. He gripped her upper arms, then dragged his hands down and laced his fingers with hers.

The party continued while he pulled her down the hallway and into his bedroom.

He closed the door and pinned her with her back against the solid wood, then his mouth took hers in a kiss so world-tilting that she clutched his shirt in her fists and clung to him.

When they separated, she expected to see on his face the same liquid desire sloping through her veins. Instead, she glimpsed something entirely different. Not yearning, but tension. Not desire, but pain.

"What is it?" she whispered.

Emotions, raw and aching, battled for supremacy over his features. "I have to go away for a couple of days."

"Okay," she said slowly. "When?"

"This weekend."

Only two days from now?

A knot twisted her stomach. "Where are you going?"

"Las Vegas."

The knot gave a wrench. "What's in Vegas? You don't gamble, do you?"

He pulled back so he could see her face. "I have another fight."

Fear seized her heart. "A fight? Did your doctor say it was okay?"

"He did not. I'll be fine." He rushed to get the words out ahead of her protests.

"You don't know that."

He dropped his forehead against hers. "I have to do this, but it's the last time."

Frustration screamed through her. She wanted to yell and demand to know why he thought he had to risk his life. For what? What could possibly be worth it? Was it money? Did it have anything to do with his work for Manny Moretti? *Why* must he do this?

She closed her eyes against the onslaught of emotion that assailed her. Her heart ached. She didn't want him to go. She wanted him to stay here, with her, where she knew he was safe, and she could kiss him and touch him, and love him.

A fresh surge of agony gripped her. She didn't know what this thing was between them, but she didn't want it to end. She wanted to tell him she was pregnant, and for him to assure her that everything would be all right. That a baby didn't have to ruin her life, and t a way to finish college and have the stable life she'd always dreamed of.

A sudden burst of collective laughter trickled down the hall.

At the sound, she jolted. "We should get back."

"They're fine." He brushed her cheek with the backs of his fingers. "There's something else bothering you."

Since the moment they'd met, he'd been able to detect her moods and her thoughts, sometimes before she'd even become aware of them. At times like this, when she didn't know what she felt or thought about anything, it was damn annoying. It's why she'd been avoiding him for the past four days.

The moment she found out she was pregnant, she knew, until she was ready to tell him, she couldn't see him.

Her heart gave a painful kick. "How do you do that?"

"Do what?"

"Read me so easily."

"It's not hard." Glimmers of light reflected in his eyes. "I spend all my time watching you, thinking about you, wanting you. I can see something has happened to upset you."

This was it. This was her chance to tell him.

She opened her mouth.

I'm pregnant.

She only had to say it.

But the words wouldn't come.

Another wave of sound from the living room reached them.

"We can talk later." She started to pull away.

He didn't move. "We can talk now."

The world rushed at her. Fear surged and strangled her voice. So much fear.

Fear that he'll be angry.

Fear that he'll want nothing to do with her or the baby.

Fear that he will.

Fear that he'll be unhappy. He believed this was impossible for him. Now that it's a reality, will he be disappointed she's the mother of his miracle baby? Will he resent being tethered to a poor orphan kid from Chicago for the next eighteen years? He might find her acceptable for a brief fling, but what about as the mother of his child?

The fear hardened into a ball in the pit of her stomach.

She was so afraid. If she told him the truth, he'd be forced to decide, right then and there, if he wanted her. If he wanted them.

Or not.

She feared she knew the answer.

He would reject her. Because honestly, anyone would. Everyone else had. The entire world had written her off as someone not worth their time or consideration. Not worthy of their love.

Though Cian had told her he cared about her, she was afraid he would never love her, because she wasn't someone worthy of his love.

She was afraid to tell him the truth and make all her fears come true.

Panic choked her, and she sucked down a greedy gulp of air.

She had time, she thought. At the moment, she couldn't be more than a few weeks along. There was time to figure out what she wanted to do, and how to tell him.

"It's nothing. I'm just…" She dragged air in through her nose. "I've had this nagging headache all day."

He went into the bathroom and returned with a couple of painkillers. "I wonder if your concussion is still healing. Maybe you should see a doctor."

Oh, god. She needed to see a doctor.

That's the first thing she should've done when she realized she was pregnant. How could she have forgotten about that?

She was going to be a horrible mother.

Seriously, what kind of life could she give this baby? Most months, she could barely afford her rent. How in the world was she going to provide a child with everything they needed?

She couldn't do it. She had lost everyone in the world she'd ever cared about. Only Jamie remained. What if she couldn't protect her baby, either?

It all seemed so impossible. So overwhelming.

A baby.

Her baby.

Her baby with Cian.

Was she really pregnant with a mobster's baby?

Her stomach pitched, and she pushed away the tumble of thoughts inside her head. She couldn't think about it right now. She couldn't bring herself to tell him. Not yet. First, she needed to take a break from the worry.

With a trembling hand, she rubbed her forehead. "I think I just need to lie down for a bit."

Cian helped her under the covers, then dropped a kiss on her forehead before returning to his brothers in the other room.

But rather than rest, she lay awake in the dark while worrying thoughts bombarded her. She swatted them away and squeezed her eyes shut, craving the escape of sleep. Finally, a calming thought popped out of the cluster of frantic ones.

When he returned from Las Vegas, she'd tell him she was pregnant.

She had time.

The idea released her into a light slumber.

Sometime later, she awoke when he slid into the bed beside her.

Instinctively, she burrowed into his strength and heat, and for a moment, before everything came rushing back to her, her heavy heart felt buoyant.

Despite it all, she was glad she met him, and that they broke their promise of only one night. She wished they could have many more nights together.

She wished they had forever.

But after Las Vegas, everything would change, and in case it marked the end for them, she wanted to cram as much togetherness as she could into whatever time they had left.

She reached for him and pushed her fingers through the dusting of dark hair that covered his chest. Then she trailed her fingers invitingly down the center of his stomach. When she slipped her hand under the waistband of his boxer briefs and gripped his hard length, he sucked in a sharp hiss of air.

She stroked him, and he teased her until her breaths came

hard and fast. He held her gaze as he slipped his long, thick fingers inside her. Her eyes fluttered shut, and she moaned, relishing the sensation.

Beneath his tender touch, the aching in her soul eased, then burned away completely by the fire he stoked.

He rolled on a condom, and when he moved over her, the heart-rending tenderness of his expression elicited a hot ache in the back of her throat and behind her eyes.

He nudged at her entrance and found her slick and ready for him. Indeed, her body begged for him, as did her heart.

The thick slide of his heavy cock tightened her belly. In and out, over and over, again and again, he pumped into her, until her core throbbed.

With each delicious stroke, her mind fractured, shattering into pieces of awareness—

—the exquisite glide of his thick shaft.

—her body's voracious hunger. For him. For all of him.

—the sway of her breasts as he pounded into her.

—the taste of his name on her lips as she pleaded for more.

—the tight clenching of his hard ass as he pumped his hips and gave her the world.

—need.

—want.

—secrets.

—lies.

—falling.

—spiraling.

Their bodies moved as one, straining and desperate for release, heedless to the world around them and all the reasons they should have never been together like this.

Fucking like this. Fucking like their whole lives depended on his body inserted inside hers. Fucking like their hearts would wither and die if he pulled his cock from her body.

She *needed* him.

When she cried out his name, her need burned her throat. She spread her legs wide for him and begged him to take whatever he wanted, even as he gave her everything.

He buried himself all the way inside her and she gripped him with her legs, holding him while her climax spasmed around him. The waves of her orgasm still crashed over her when he roared with his own release.

Afterwards, he pulled her into the crook of his body, tucking her curves neatly inside his own contours.

They lay together in the dark, not talking, and soon, the heavy cover of a deep, dreamless sleep drew over her.

When she next woke, the room was shrouded in darkness. She blinked open her eyes, then jerked fully awake and fumbled in the blackness for her ringing cell phone.

Jamie's number flashed on her screen, and her heart jumped into her throat.

"Ave, where are you?" Jamie gasped the moment she answered his call.

"I'm…at a friend's place. Why? What's wrong?"

"I need help."

Avery bolted upright in the bed. "What kind of help? Where are you?"

"At the apartment. Why aren't you here?" He sucked in a sharp breath and expelled it as a high-pitched curse. "Shit. Ave, I've been shot."

CHAPTER 36

Cian shook off the haze of sleep. On his stomach in the bed, he pressed his palms flat against the mattress and pushed up, craning his neck to follow Avery as she scrambled from the bed.

"Just hang on." She tried to whisper, but she was too upset to keep her voice low. "I'm going to hang up and call 9-1-1."

As though he'd been doused with a bucket of ice water, his drowsiness vanished. He bolted upright and flung back the covers.

"Jamie, calm down. I can't understand—"

When he flipped on the lamp on his nightstand and soft light flooded the room, Avery whirled toward him, and huge, panic-filled eyes punched him in the gut.

"I have to," she said into the phone.

He tugged on a pair of pants.

"What? Why not?" She stepped into the jeans she'd flung over the back of the armchair in the corner. "You're not making any sense."

He yanked a T-shirt over his head and stuck his arms through the holes.

"Fine. I'm on my way." She searched the room frantically. "Just hold on."

With panicked movements, she hunted for her shirt. "I-I have to go."

She moved to sidestep him, and he caught her arm.

When she looked up at him, her eyes were enormous in her pale face. "I can't lose him. He's the only family I have left."

He'd never heard that hitch of vulnerability in her voice before, and hearing it, his chest felt tight.

His hand slipped to her nape. "Listen to me. We're going to focus on getting to him. That's it. Block out all the rest right now and let's just get to him. Where is he?"

"My place."

He handed her the shirt she'd discarded on the floor earlier. "I'll drive."

But he struggled to follow his own advice. His body overly attuned to hers, he was acutely aware of the terror radiating from her as they moved swiftly through the complex to his car parked in the garage.

Her agitation became his as he navigated the city streets, and he gripped the steering wheel too tightly as his mind imagined what potential scenarios they might encounter when they reached her brother.

That fear chased him as he parked haphazardly on the street in front of her apartment building and rocketed out of the car. In his mind, he prepared for the worst as they charged up the three flights of stairs.

When they reached her door, he took the key from her, and while he worked the lock, he positioned his body so that he obstructed her view as much as possible, unsure what awaited them on the other side.

The door swung open.

Like snap shots in a comic book, he collected images of the scene. Unconscious man lying prone on the couch. Trail of blood ending in a pool on the floor. Handgun forgotten on the coffee table.

Cian moved forward. First, they needed to stop the bleeding. The blood originated from the leg, and Cian swept his gaze upward, searching for other wounds.

When he reached Jamie's face, he froze.

Even though his eyes were closed, Cian knew their color.

Brown.

Like Avery's.

The gears of his mind ground as he stared into the face of Moretti's mobster-in-training. The little punk who'd delivered word to Cian that he'd have to fight in Derek's place.

This injured man is Moretti's man.

What was Moretti's goon doing inside Avery's apartment?

Where was her brother?

Icy shock stole through his veins. Was he…?

Time slowed, and he watched in horror as Avery slipped by him and knelt on the floor beside Moretti's little punk.

"Jamie?" She brushed his forehead, and he stirred, then startled. "It's okay. It's just me."

Alarms screamed inside Cian's skull.

Moretti's man is Avery's brother.

Avery's brother is Moretti's man.

Jamie's eyelids fluttered, then finally opened. Glassy with pain, his gaze darted from Avery to Cian.

Recognition flared.

Fear rushed in and Jamie thrashed upright, "What the—?" But a cry of pain tore from him, and he collapsed back onto the couch cushions.

Avery glanced at Cian over her shoulder, then faced her brother once more. "It's okay. He's with me. We're going to help you."

She doesn't know. She isn't aware her little brother is working for the man she hates most in the world.

Jamie eyed Cian warily. The little shit was afraid. Terrified. As he should be.

At least he's not a complete idiot.

Avery cradled her cell phone in her hand. "Jamie, I have to call 9-1-1."

"No." His gaze slid to Cian. "No cops."

"I'm calling an ambulance. We need to get you to the hospital."

"I can't go to the hospital."

"What? Jamie, why not? You're badly injured. You're losing blood."

She was right. Jamie's lips were white, and if they didn't stop the bleeding, he had little time. But if he showed up at a hospital with a bullet in his leg, they would ask questions, and no matter what answers he gave, the emergency room staff would be obligated to contact the police, who would have even more questions.

Cian bet Jamie couldn't answer any of them without implicating himself, or Moretti, or both, in something illegal.

Focus.

He had to focus.

Just like in a fight, he needed to block out the noise from the crowd and the tension coiling through his veins to concentrate solely on his opponent. When he was locked in, he could anticipate his opponent's next move, sometimes even before the first muscle twitched.

He needed to be locked in now.

Not for his sake, or even for the little prick's sake. He needed to focus for Avery.

With a mental curse, he kneeled beside Avery and moved his hands over Jamie's body until he found the source of the blood.

A gunshot wound in the upper thigh. On the outer side of his right leg. Jamie was lucky the bullet hadn't hit an artery, or he'd already be dead.

"We need to stop the bleeding," Cian heard himself say. "Can you get some rags?"

Avery hustled into the other room, and Cian continued his assessment of Jamie's physical state.

Awake. Alert. Alive, thank God.

Cian was going to kill him.

"What in the hell are you doing here?" Jamie hissed. "Did Moretti send you? Why are you with my sister?"

"I'm here to help *her*." Cian added a punch of emphasis on the last word.

He only cared about Avery. Nothing and no one else mattered to him.

With a sharp tug, Cian ripped the hole in Jamie's pant leg wider to reveal the site of the wound. The movement jostled Jamie, and he cried out in pain.

Even though he was clammy and pale-stricken, Cian could see the likeness to his sister. Without direct knowledge of their kinship, he hadn't picked up on the resemblance, but there it was. Plain to see.

"How do you know her?" Jamie struggled to speak through the pain. "Are you using her to get to me?"

"There's no time for that now. What happened? Who shot you?"

"I don't know."

Cian clenched his fists, then clamped down on his teeth to keep from swinging.

"I don't know," Jamie repeated. "We were delivering the lot to Sanchez when something went wrong."

The curse burst from Cian. He was involved in Moretti's drug deals?

"There was a disagreement. Things got out of hand. I don't know who shot first, or whose bullet caught me. You can't tell Avery. She'll kill me."

It'd kill her.

Moretti had taken so much from her already. Now Jamie too? This might be the thing that finally broke her.

Fuck.

How could Jamie do this to her? The need to beat the hell out of someone, something, nearly overwhelmed Cian. He wanted to pound them all into the ground. Jamie, Moretti, anyone that would hurt Avery.

Avery returned with a pile of rags and dropped them beside Cian.

He filched a cloth from the pile and cinched a tourniquet tight around Jamie's leg, eliciting a groan from him. His coloring continued to lighten as Cian used the other rags to pack the wound as tightly as he could and slow down the bleeding.

Once done, he turned to Avery. Her bleak expression struck him in the solar plexus. "He's lost a lot of blood."

She blinked several times, fighting to overcome her shock. "We have to get him to an ER."

"No hospital," Jamie moaned.

Cian snapped. "At least you'd be alive."

"We don't have a choice." Avery pleaded with her brother.

Jamie's gaze shifted to Cian, and brown eyes, so like Avery's, pleaded silently with him.

If they took Jamie to the hospital, Avery would learn the truth about amie. If they didn't, Jamie could die. Either way, Avery's world was about to be changed forever.

It wasn't fair to her. She deserved so much better than this. Jamie didn't deserve her.

A droplet of doubt diluted the force of his fury. How long would it be before Cian dragged her into a nightmare such as this one? Even if Kendrick got him out, what kind of life would she have if she stayed with him? In witness protection. On the run. Always looking over their shoulders. Living in constant fear.

He couldn't do that to her.

Focus.

He hated to involve anyone else in this mess, but he couldn't bear the look on Avery's face. Jamie needed help, or she'd lose him. It was as simple as that.

Cian snatched his phone from his pocket. "Get him up," he said, his fingers moving swiftly over the keypad with the number he'd memorized long ago.

CHAPTER 37

Memories of the night Logan died flashed through her mind. Her breaths came fast, too fast, but she couldn't slow down the too-rapid inhalations. The worst day of her life was repeating itself.

She coaxed Jamie to sit, but he struggled to even lift his head off the couch, so she slipped an arm behind him and hauled him upright.

With his phone pressed to his ear, Cian walked the few steps over to the tiny kitchen. "Hey. I'm sorry to wake you."

She'd never heard him speak with such softness in his voice.

"I need your help," he said, then after a beat, "Not me. A friend... of a friend... he was at a nightclub when a fight broke out. Caught a bullet in the thigh."

She struggled against Jamie's weight, shoving her shoulder into his armpit, and straightening her spine.

"I can't meet you at the ER." Cian moved to prop up Jamie's other side. "He's... here illegally and is afraid to go to the hospital. Can I bring him to you? I know it's asking a lot..."

The trio seemed to hold a collective breath.

"We'll come to you. Be there in twenty minutes." Cian wrenched the phone away and slipped it inside his pocket.

His hands now free, Cian shifted Jamie's heft off Avery. She hustled ahead of them, opening and closing doors to ease their hazardous journey down the flights of stairs and over the slippery sidewalks to Cian's car.

When Jamie was stretched out in the backseat, she climbed in and tucked her coat under his leg to stop the blood from smearing Cian's seats.

The vehicle sped through the dark city streets. Every bump in the road jostled Jamie, pulling soft gasps and moans from him, which landed like daggers in Avery's heart.

She was drowning in fear.

If she lost Jamie, she'd be completely alone. She couldn't lose him, too.

When the panic started to choke her, she grasped and grabbed for something to latch onto. Instinct told her not to ask Jamie who shot him, or what he was doing when it happened. Instead, she concentrated on the scenery through the car window, watching as it changed from rundown buildings and graffitied walls to cozy houses with postage-stamp sized yards.

Cian parked in front of a small bungalow with a misshapen snowman keeping watch over the front yard. A woman stood on the porch, and the light from the house behind her silhouetted her petite frame.

In plaid pajama pants and a white T-shirt, she scurried down the steps and strode up the sidewalk toward them.

"Where is he?" she asked as Avery climbed out of the backseat.

"Here." Avery held open the car door.

She caught a whiff of the woman's flowery scent before she ducked inside as Cian came around the hood of the car to stand with Avery on the sidewalk.

Muffled voices sounded in the backseat, then Jamie's sharp curse rang out in the late night quiet.

The woman popped out of the car. "Bring him inside. Put him on the dining room table." Already halfway to the front porch, she never broke stride as she delivered her clipped orders.

With their two big bodies in the cramped space, Cian struggled to haul Jamie out of the car. When they finally emerged, Avery shuffled over to Jamie's left side, and they staggered up the front walk and into the house.

In the dining room, bright light from the overhead chandelier rained down on the table that'd been cleared off except for a cookie sheet filled with an assortment of tweezers, knives, and other kitchen utensils.

Her heart dropped to her stomach. While Cian helped Jamie onto the table, she backed away until she bumped into a chair heaped with white rags that'd been dragged against the wall and out of the way.

"Get his leg under the light," the woman instructed from the kitchen where she stood at the sink, ferociously scrubbing her hands and forearms beneath the stream of steaming hot water.

Beneath the glaring light, Jamie's skin appeared sallow. Beads of sweat dotted his brow, and the corners of his mouth were pinched with pain.

Panic climbed up Avery's throat and squeezed.

The woman swept into the room and moved to Jamie's side. The light caught the varied strands of her chestnut and auburn hair when she plucked a pair of scissors off the cookie sheet and sliced a long cut down the middle of Jamie's pant leg to the hem. Then she made another cut toward his hip.

She glanced at Cian. "Bring me the pot of water off the stove."

Cian moved away with long, purposeful strides.

"And a pair of tongs," she called over her shoulder as she dropped a heavy hank of blood-soaked fabric into a trash bag on the floor under the table.

Cian found the tongs in the first drawer he opened and delivered them to the table with the large cooking pot full of steaming hot water.

The woman hacked off another chunk of Jamie's bloody pants and dropped the soiled cloth into the garbage bag.

With Jamie's leg and the spot of the wound exposed, she held out her hand to Avery. "Will you hand me a rag?"

Avery plucked a clean towel off the pile and placed it in the woman's outstretched palm.

Using the tongs, the woman dunked the cloth into the steamy pot of water. When she could handle the wet rag, she used it to wipe away the blood staining Jamie's skin. Once, the rag swiped close to the wound and Jamie hissed in pain.

The woman ignored him. "Keep them coming," she said to Avery as she dropped the soiled rag into the trash bag.

Avery quickly handed over a fresh cloth, and soon, a heap of red-soaked garments had formed.

When Jamie's leg was cleaned, the woman picked a pair of long tweezers off the tray. She flicked on a lighter and held the metal in the flame. Then she bent over Jamie's leg and peered closely at the wound.

"Wh-what are you doing?" Alarm raised Jamie's voice an octave.

"I have to get the bullet out, and any fragments." She gave Cian a look, and though she didn't say a word, Cian seemed to understand her instructions.

He laid both of his hands on Jamie's shoulders.

From across the table, Cian's gaze captured Avery's, and he stared hard, as though trying to pass his strength over to her. Strength she didn't have, but desperately needed.

The woman lowered the tweezers and when the tip disappeared inside Jamie's leg, Avery squeezed her eyes shut.

Jamie bellowed. "*Fuck.*"

Avery's eyes flew open.

Jamie's body jerked and Cian flung his arms across her brother's shoulders and held him down while Avery gripped his leg with both hands to keep him from thrashing.

Helpless rage contorted Jamie's features. "That fucking hurts," he spat through clenched teeth.

"You didn't expect it to tickle, did you?" The woman, unperturbed, dug deep.

Jamie gasped and gripped Cian's shoulders. "Don't you have something you can give me?"

"If you wanted pain meds, you should've gone to the hospital." The woman gestured for another rag, and Avery thrust a clean one at her.

She used the cloth to catch the fresh trickles of blood streaming across Jamie's thigh, then resumed digging.

Jamie's entire body became tense and rigid. Sweat slithered down his forehead and dampened his dark hair. Avery watched with horror, recalling the convulsions that racked Logan's body moments before he died.

Her vision blurred, and she blindly handed rags to the woman she did not know. It was obvious she was medically trained, and her sure, commanding competence soothed the wild fear that thrashed and kicked inside Avery.

When Jamie's head lolled to one side and he ent still, the woman expelled a soft breath. "Thank goodness. I'm going to try to get the bullet out while he's unconscious. It's probably best this way. He won't tense up every time I touch him."

Avery tried to borrow some of the woman's calm confidence, but all she could do was stare at Jamie and pray he didn't wake up as long as the woman continued to dig and root around inside the wound.

With every tug of flesh, the tumult inside Avery intensified. She glanced at Cian, desperate for some of his steadying strength, but just then, the woman straightened.

"Ah-ha!" She held up the tweezers to show the oval-shaped hunk of metal pinched between the prongs. "Got it."

The bullet pinged when she dropped it onto the cookie sheet.

She instructed Cian to start another pot of water boiling, then followed him into the kitchen. While he went to the cabinet and retrieved a clean pot, she returned to the sink and scrubbed her hands and forearms in the same furious manner as she'd done earlier.

As Cian filled the pot with water from the dispenser on the refrigerator door, they chatted, their voices low and friendly. Familiar. Unable to hear what they were saying, Avery wondered who the woman was and how Cian knew her.

Her hands freshly washed, the woman returned to the dining room and selected a needle and a long strand of white thread from the cookie sheet.

Avery turned her head away when the woman pierced Jamie's skin with the needle.

Jamie roused, and his soft whimper punctured Avery's heart. His eyes fluttered open, and he lifted his head, but when the woman dragged the thread through his flesh, he went limp again. He moaned, and his face turned a pale shade of green.

"Cian, grab a Tupperware bowl and bring it here, would ya?"

Cian did as the woman asked, again knowing the exact cabinet where he could find the dish.

"Just put it by his head," she said when Cian appeared with the bowl. "In case he gets sick."

From there, things progressed quickly. She finished stitching Jamie's wound, then washed the area with clean water and rags. Under her careful direction, Cian and Avery moved Jamie down the hall to a spare bedroom.

"He can stay here tonight. I'm off tomorrow, so I'll monitor him for fever and pain." The woman pulled the bedcovers up to Jamie's chest, then faced them. "If he shows any signs of infection, I'm calling an ambulance."

"Thank you." Avery wanted to throw her arms around the woman and weep, but the events of the evening seemed to crash over her all at once and she could only stand there, mute and exhausted.

The woman turned soft gray eyes on her, and a sympathetic smile touched her lips. "He's going to be okay."

The crashing of fear and relief stole Avery's voice.

"We'll need to watch him for a couple of days, but it was a clean wound, and I expect him to make a full recovery." The woman squeezed Avery's arm. "You're welcome to stay with him. I'll bring you a blanket."

The back of Avery's throat closed, and she nodded.

The woman slipped from the room, and Avery took a breath for the first time since her cell phone had chimed with Jamie's call.

She wanted to talk to Cian, or maybe just sit with him since she was too tired to talk, and it always relaxed her to be close to him, but he followed the woman through the bedroom door.

His voice drifted in from the hallway. "Thanks, Corinne. I appreciate your help."

Corinne.

Though Cian had never said the name to Avery before, she knew the pretty, competent, take-no-bullshit trauma specialist must be Cian's ex. What else would explain the somber longing on both their faces when they looked at each other?

No wonder he was so bitter about their breakup. It would have devastated Avery too, losing someone like her. Smart, competent, professional, not to mention pretty and generous. She saved lives every day and could afford a house all on her own. Small, pretty, and fierce—she was exactly the type of woman Avery imagined Cian with.

The woman was everything Avery wished she could be, but wasn't.

Instead, she was a girl who could barely afford the rent for her crappy apartment, with a brother who got himself shot doing God knows what but something so untoward that he couldn't alert the authorities by seeking legitimate medical help. Oh, and she was pregnant by a man she had no future with.

"I'm sorry about all this." The shame in Cian's voice whipped heat into Avery's cheeks.

"It's okay." Corinne sounded sincere.

Guilt swamped Avery. She didn't know what Jamie was mixed up in. Had they made Corinne unsafe, bringing him to her cute little house in her quaint little neighborhood?

"It's good to see you." Corinne's voice softened with intimacy. "Really good."

"It's good to see you, too." Quiet sorrow latched onto Cian's tone.

They moved further down the hall and their voices faded away.

Avery's heart folded in on itself for several beats while she grappled with this new information, and the question in her mind slowly shifted from whether Corinne was the woman Cian once loved, or the woman he loved still?

CHAPTER 38

Cian tried to focus on what Corinne was saying, but all he could think about was Avery. How was she doing? Was she okay?

How long was he going to have to lie to her about her brother?

He hated lying to her.

With the furor of a thousand dying suns, he wanted all this bullshit to go away so they could just be together. No Moretti. No brothers. No secrets. No lies. He was beyond desperate to bring it all to an end.

"How are you doing?" A soft curve touched Corinne's lips. "You look good."

"I feel good."

"Good. That's good."

A taut silence dropped between them, then stretched tighter.

Until she looked up at him with earnest gray eyes. "I'm sorry. About everything. I didn't mean for any of it to happen." Moisture clung to her eyelashes. "I hurt you and I'll never forgive myself."

Surprise stole his voice for a moment, and the memories rushed in.

"It's okay," he said, and amazingly, it was true.

He hadn't seen or spoken to her in months, and here he was, suddenly right next to her, and none of the gut-gnawing anger or churning angst he'd experienced every time he thought about her over the past year disturbed him now.

All he felt was… grief. Grief for what he'd thought they were back then. Grief for what he'd hoped they would be. Before cancer derailed all their plans.

It was so very fucking sad.

"But it's not okay. I didn't love Rory." Her hand shook when she rubbed her forehead. "I was scared and lonely and… confused."

Cian recalled those months he wished he could forget. During the darkest days of his treatments, he'd withdrawn. He was sick all the time, and terrified, and he'd started pulling away from this world.

She was scared, too, and her fear had troubled him the most.

"Thankfully, Rory understood I wasn't thinking clearly and set me straight." The corners of her mouth pulled down into a grimace. "As humiliating as it was."

"Set you straight?" Confused thoughts tumbled through his mind. "How's that?"

A blush crept into her cheeks. "I'm sure he told you…"

"We've never talked about it."

"That's probably because nothing happened." Her flush deepened to crimson. "It was all in my head. I thought I'd developed feelings for him, but I just didn't want to be alone anymore. He knew that and refused me. It was humiliating. I can almost laugh about it now. Except for the part where I hurt you."

Regret tangled with his grief. If he were honest with himself, he'd have to accept the part he'd played in the whole affair. The fear had overtaken him, and he'd retreated from everyone, even Corinne, his fiancée and future wife.

Of course, she'd turned to Rory. One of only a few others who understood what she was going through, and who carried a likeness to Cian in both appearance and personality except with the additional benefit of being hale and healthy, and not dying.

As Cian stared down into Corinne's pretty face, he expected to feel something. Like the old days.

But he experienced only a soft affection. Not unlike the way he felt about his kid sister, Brie, or Brynn. He loved them both, and a part of him still loved Corinne. But Corinne didn't make him burn the way one glance at Avery did.

Corinne was nice.

Avery was *necessary*.

The realization unfolded inside him like grief. He didn't want it to be true.

But his wanting the thing not to be true wouldn't make it so.

Just as nothing Corinne had told him would change the way he felt about them as a couple. Too much had happened, and they were different people now. They no longer made sense.

And he'd known it long before this moment.

He'd known it since he'd first set eyes on Avery in that shady gambling hall. That was all it'd taken to convince him there was no one else for him.

It was the most natural thing in the world to open his arms, and for Corinne to step into his embrace. They'd been through hell and back together, and they'd survived. For the rest of their lives, they would be comrades.

A soft gasp sounded behind them, and they pulled apart. When they turned, Avery watched them with enormous eyes.

"I'm so sorry. I didn't mean to interrupt." Misery stole into her expression. "I was just going to use the bathroom."

The warmth in Corinne's smile echoed in her voice. "How's he doing?"

"He's still sleeping." Some of the color had returned to Avery's cheeks, but tinges of fear and exhaustion still hung in her eyes.

"Good," Corinne said. "I'll check on him soon."

"Thank you." Avery twisted her hands together in front of her. "I'm so sorry."

Corinne dismissed her apology with a smile. "Get some rest."

Corinne moved down the hall and, in her absence, an awkward chasm of silence opened between Cian and Avery. He was suddenly tongue tied. How did he tell her about Jamie? What words were there that wouldn't break her heart? That wouldn't destroy her?

No such words existed. None that he could come up with, anyway. He couldn't do it. He couldn't destroy her.

"She's the one, isn't she?"

His brain in tumult, he frowned distractedly. "The one what?"

"The woman from the tabloid story you asked me to write?" There was a hitch in her voice. "That's her? That's your ex?"

Dammit, he shouldn't have to be the one to break Avery's heart. She should hear the truth from her brother. Jamie did this, and how Avery grappled with it would impact him the most. He should be the one to tell her.

"Did you love her?"

He blinked stupidly, her question throwing a wrench into the gears of his thoughts. What were they talking about?

"Cian, I'm not mad. I'm jealous, of course, but I get it. You have a past relationship. There's nothing wrong with that." She gestured toward the end of the hallway, where Corinne had disappeared. "And I mean, she's kind of amazing. I see why you love her. I just met her and I'm already halfway in love with her myself."

Dumbfounded, he stared. Corinne. She was talking about Corinne.

He didn't want to talk about Corinne. He didn't want to talk at all because every moment he spent with Avery where he didn't tell her the truth about Jamie felt like a lie, and he didn't want to lie to her.

He'd gone round and round in his head about Jamie's betrayal. Was there any chance the little shit hadn't joined Moretti's side voluntarily? Moretti was scum, and he'd blackmail, bribe, extort, threaten, anything he had to do, to force someone into his service. But was that the case this time?

Cian's gut told him no. There's no way Jamie was working for the good guys or else he'd have gone to the emergency room like any normal, law-abiding citizen who'd been shot would have.

Ultimately, it didn't matter why Jamie was working for Moretti. The result was the same—the danger to Avery had increased a thousand-fold.

Sudden fury lit his temper. "Look, you should get some sleep. In case he needs you."

With the hurt that slashed across her expression, her smile fell. "Yeah, okay."

He wanted to say the words that would erase her wounded ook, but nothing that wasn't a lie or would only cause her more pain came to his mind. His chest ached with frustration and grief.

Soft, sincere eyes gripped his insides. "Thank you for helping Jamie. I don't know what I would've done...."

His fury swelled. Jamie had been a pain in Cian's ass for weeks now, and who knows how many countless others he'd harassed on Moretti's behalf. But among his many crimes, the worry and pain he'd caused his sister enraged Cian the most.

"He doesn't deserve you."

At the snap in his tone, she bristled. "He's my brother."

"He doesn't give you half the loyalty you give him."

Her lips parted with a gasp of pain, and he hated himself for it.

"Maybe not." Her dark, lucid eyes gleamed in her pale face. "But he's all I have left in this world."

"He's not all you have." Emotion made his voice ragged, raspy. "He's not even the one who needs you the most."

Before he could say more cruel words, he turned and walked away.

CHAPTER 39

The next day, he avoided Corinne's house. He couldn't bring himself to look Avery in the eyes, knowing the truth about her brother and not being able to tell her.

So he focused on Moretti and the weekend ahead. He talked to Kendrick, and they went over the plan again.

With Cian's help, the Feds had collected evidence of Moretti's illegal gambling racket. They knew which back rooms at which bars and restaurants Moretti used as cover to hide his illegal operation. They had proof Moretti had employed threats of violence against Cian if he failed to take part in the illicit scheme, and after Cian lost the fight in Vegas, going down in the third round as Moretti had instructed him to do, they'd watch in real time as Moretti sent Cian his cut for throwing the match.

Though the scheme accounted for only a fraction of the crimes Moretti had perpetrated, taken altogether, the Feds could soon charge and arrest him for illegal gambling and racketeering, and this nightmare would be over.

He needed to end this. He needed to end Moretti.

For Avery.

Damn, but he missed her. The ache was throbbing and raw.

He stood before the penthouse's wall of windows and stared toward Corinne's house. The urge to charge over there, snatch Avery and bring her home, nearly overwhelmed him.

But she wasn't about to leave her brother's side, and he knew her well enough by now to know that barring bodily harm, she wouldn't go anywhere she didn't want to or do anything she didn't want to do.

Despite everything, a reluctant smile touched his lips. She was a fighter.

Still, he should be there with her. In case she needed him.

His chest squeezed, and he turned away from the window just as the penthouse doors slid open and Rory stepped into the foyer.

When he caught sight of Cian, his expression changed, then closed completely.

If Cian's chest squeezed any tighter, he'd need to schedule an appointment with Dr. Hoffman for a workup.

With a quick head bob, Rory headed for the hallway.

"I talked to Corinne," Cian said, stopping Rory in his tracks. "She told me what happened between you two."

A flicker of alarm flashed across Rory's face. "Nothing happened between us."

"That's not exactly true." Cian pushed his hands into the pockets of his joggers. "She told me she fell for you, and that you turned her down."

Unease clung to Rory's shoulders, and he shuffled his feet. "She didn't know what she wanted."

"I know. She explained." Cian experienced no sorrow with the memories. "I get it now."

Shock froze Rory in place.

"Thanks for looking out for her." A smile tugged up one corner of Cian's mouth. "Thanks for looking out for me, too."

Still stunned, Rory shoved a hand through his thick, dark hair.

With a shrug, Cian said, "If you want to be with her, I won't make it weird."

"I don't want to be with Corinne." Sounding exasperated, Rory gaped at Cian. "I want my brother back."

Pain slashed through Cian's chest cavity. Straightening, he caught Rory's gaze and held it steady. "You got it."

After a beat of shocked silence, Rory nodded. "Okay then."

"All right." Cian dragged a deep breath into his lungs.

Rory gestured with one hand. "And if you two want to get back together, don't let me stop you."

The idea swept over Cian like a soft, insignificant breeze. He'd traveled a long, hellish road in the past year and a half, and he'd lost a lot along the way. It'd been an excruciating journey, one he never wanted to retake. But somehow, it'd led him here.

To Avery.

Right where he needed to be.

The realization struck him like a thunderbolt, jolting his body with a current of shock and pain. He'd found the woman he wanted to be with for the rest of his life.

Forever.

His heart slammed against his sternum.

For a guy with a limited number of tomorrows, *forever* echoed in him like a threat. However long that'd be, it wasn't enough.

"Corinne and I are good," he heard himself say over the roar of his frantic heartbeat. "We'll always be friends. But we're not right for each other."

He tried to relax the tension coiling through his body by sharing a beer with his brother. They sat at the dining table, drinking and practicing their language skills, and talking like they used to before his diagnosis. Eventually, things devolved into a competition to see who could come up with the most colorful curse words in the various languages they spoke.

It did a lot to ease the tightness in his chest.

But the next morning, he woke up feeling anxious and agitated.

In a few hours, he'd board a flight to Las Vegas, and he had no idea what was going to happen. Things might go sideways, and he'd need to be whisked away into witness protection after the fight. Or his heart could stop, or collapse, or do whatever Dr. Hoffman had warned him it could do if he pushed his body too hard.

With the roll of the dice, anything could happen, and before he left, he wanted to see Avery's face one more time. Just in case.

A fresh layer of snow had fallen, and his boots crunched on the crisp powder as he strode up the front walkway.

Corinne let him indoors, and as he moved down the hallway toward the spare bedroom, Avery came through the door.

Seeing her, his pulse kicked, and his breath snagged in his lungs.

Her eyes grew wary. "Hey."

"Hey." He hated that guarded look. "How's he doing?"

"We had a scare last night, but Corinne thinks he's turned the corner."

His fingers twitched with the urge to haul her to him. "Has he said anything? About what happened?"

She shook her head, and a sigh carrying the weight of the world leaked from her. "No."

Damn. So he hadn't told her. She still didn't know her brother worked for Moretti.

"I was just going to make him some lunch." Biting her lip, she risked a peek at his face. "Afterwards, maybe we can talk?"

"I've got to catch a flight."

A shadow haunted her features. "To Vegas?"

He inclined his head. "Can we talk when I get back?"

"Sure. When you get back."

His throat ached with all the words left unspoken. There was so much he wanted to tell her. So much he needed to hear her say.

Not now. But soon.

He jerked his head toward the kitchen. "Go ahead. I'll sit with him."

Avery slipped down the hall. When she turned the corner, he slipped inside the bedroom and eased the door shut. Slowly, he walked over to the bed.

Jamie slept, and even lying unconscious, he appeared exhausted. His skin had taken on a pallid hue, and his breaths were shallow. He looked young. He was just a kid.

Cian pulled back his foot and kicked the bedpost hard. The bedframe rattled and a crack of sound ripped through the quiet room.

Jamie jerked awake, and the movement tore a howl of pain from him.

Cian waited until Jamie's gaze fixed on him, and the disorientation of sleep had faded from his eyes.

"I won't lie to her."

Jamie's throat worked when he gulped. "You're going to tell her?"

"I'm not. You are."

"But... I wa shot."

"Then you better hurry and do it before you die." Cian barely restrained the fury thrashing inside his chest. "Wouldn't want a lie like that weighing on your eternal soul when you meet your maker."

He watched the emotions chase across Jamie's face. Anger and denial, fear, and then finally, his mouth pulled into a thin, tight line. Acceptance.

"I'll give you until tomorrow."

"Gee, thanks," Jamie muttered.

"After that, you have a choice. Your sister, or your life of crime. You can't have both."

"Who the fuck are you to decide that?"

"You can only pick one," Cian said softly. "When the time comes, you better know which one you choose."

"What about you?" Jamie's dark eyes glittered. "Does she know you work for Moretti, too?"

Cian refused to provide an answer.

Jamie rolled his head to one side, turning his face away. "You're not good enough for her, either."

The words landed like a knockout punch.

She deserved better than what he could give her.

A crater of grief opened at Cian's feet. "I know."

But he had one shot to change all that.

CHAPTER 40

When Avery returned to the bedroom, Cian was gone and Corinne bent over Jamie, inspecting his wound.

Jamie hissed through his teeth. "Ouch."

"If you relaxed, it wouldn't hurt so much." Corinne eased the sheet back over his body.

When Corinne tucked the quilt over his chest, Jamie closed his eyes and inhaled deeply. "I think the bullet hurt less," he grouched.

Corinne's pleasant smile was at odds with the challenge in her voice. "I'd be happy to shoot you again if you'd like to find out." Just then, she spotted Avery and her spine snapped straight. "Ah, here's your lunch."

Jamie slitted open his eyes. "More soup?"

"Yes." Two pink stains colored Corinne's cheeks when she lifted the food tray out of Avery's hands and placed it on the nightstand beside the bed. "And you'd better eat it all today, or I'll put in a feeding tube."

With that, Corinne breezed from the room.

Watching her leave, a shadow of a smile haunted Jamie's mouth.

Avery ate her own smile as she approached the bed. "Where did Cian go? Did he leave?"

That chased the lingering light from Jamie's face. "Yeah. He said he had to go."

A pang squeezed her heart. He'd left without saying goodbye? Was he mad at her for staying to help Jamie? Or was there some other reason for his sudden departure?

Jamie waited for his lunch, so she arranged her features into a careful mask and moved to the bedside.

When she held out the spoon for him to take, a scowl marred his face.

"Everything okay? Is your leg hurting too much to eat right now?"

He shook his head. "Do you have a minute?" The column of his throat worked when he swallowed. "There's something I need to tell you."

Unease slithered up her spine. "Of course."

"Will you close the door?" An awful dread that crept into his eyes.

Her stomach twisted into a knot, but she moved to the door and eased it shut. Slowly, she turned to face him. It was as though her body understood her heart's need to delay whatever he was about to tell her.

While she waited for him to speak, time stretched out, then spiraled as the words emerged from his lips. "I've done something and you're not going to like it."

"What is it?" To her own ears, her voice sounded weird, calm when she felt chaotic. "What have you done?"

"I've been working for Manny Moretti."

The floor dropped out from under her feet, and she sagged against the door. "What do you mean?" She grasped the doorknob at her back. "Working for him, how? Did you take a job at one of his businesses?"

Jamie's impassive expression was unnerving. "No."

With that simple denial, a pit of darkness unfolded beneath her. "You've been… helping him? How could you do that? After everything he's done…" The black hole tried to swallow her. "After I risked my neck to get you that money. After what he did to mom and dad—"

"I don't have a choice."

She latched onto the steadying notion. "He's forcing you?"

"Yes. Sort of. I—" He licked his lips nervously. "I could work for him, or I could keep working three jobs and getting nowhere. He offered me a way out. What was I supposed to say?"

"You were supposed to say hell no." Hysteria claimed her voice.

"It's not that easy. You don't say no to a man like him." A desperate edge rode his tone. "Ave, you gotta understand."

She understood everything. She'd been a fool, fighting to protect Jamie when he wouldn't protect himself. Risking her life to save her family when all she'd been doing was permitting her brother to make poor decisions. Believing he was the only person who cared about her when all he really cared about was himself.

Her hand on the doorknob, she gave it a wrench and hauled open the door.

"Where are you going?" He tried to sit, but a slice of pain stopped him.

"I need to get away from you."

"Avery, c'mon—"

She whirled on him. "Don't you dare. I've put my neck on the line for you. Over and over again, I tried to help keep you safe from that man, and instead of learning from your fuck ups and doing better, you just walk right into his evil lair and start working for him?"

His body was rigid with tension, but he offered her no answers.

"How many people have you hurt for him? How many lives have you ruined?" She was yelling now. "Why? Because you don't want to be poor anymore? God, Jamie, do you even hear yourself?"

"Look—"

"Stop talking." Her arm shot out, and she held up her hand. "I don't want to hear your excuses. I know how hard it's been for you. I've been right there beside you this whole time. Nothing you can say will justify what you've done."

The first flicker of fear flared in his eyes. "So, what do you want me to do? Quit? Turn in my two weeks' notice?" With a sneer, he shook his head. "C'mon Ave, it doesn't work like that."

She gaped at her little brother and wondered what the hell had happened to him? She remembered him when they were little, before Moretti ripped their lives apart, and he'd been fun, and funny, and full of curiosity.

How had he become the jerk before her now? When had the transformation happened?

Memories assailed her, and she realized the change in him had been gradual, occurring slowly. But it'd begun with Moretti.

When he'd ruined her parents' lives and the family became hard up, their entire world changed. Even the way the world viewed Avery and her brothers changed. When they weren't invisible to their teachers and peers, they were looked down on. Like they were less.

Unworthy.

But she and her brothers had never looked at each other that way. Or so she'd thought.

It was clear now Jamie didn't think all that highly of her. He was disdainful and mean, treating her like she was stupid. And she was.

Or she had been.

But no more.

"I don't really care what you do, Jamie." The cold penetrating her heart reached her voice. "You're on your own."

She turned away from him.

He stopped her with a panicked plea. "Avery, you can't tell anyone about this."

She blinked, confused by his words. Who would she tell? What was he worried about?

Understanding snaked through her as a dark, slithering shadow. He feared she would go to the police. Even now, he was more concerned with saving his own ass than anything else.

Her heart shattered inside her chest cavity. "I don't owe you anything. Cian was right. You don't deserve my loyalty."

"Cian? Seriously?" Derision curled his upper lip. "You know he works for Moretti too, right?"

At his question, her mind seized. Of course, she knew Cian worked for Moretti, too.

But…

She faced Jamie fully. "You two met? Before you got shot, you knew him? H-he knew you?"

An uneasy stiffness crowded Jamie's shoulders. "Yeah."

The truth screamed through her in stages.

Cian knew Jamie.

He knew Jamie worked for Moretti.

He knew Jamie worked for Moretti, and he didn't tell her.

Turning blindly, she staggered through the door.

"Avery, wait—"

But she ignored Jamie's call.

When she fled Corinne's home, the frigid cold smacked her in the face. A blustery wind hounded her heels as she ran, her feet pounding the sidewalk. She didn't know where she was going until she reached Cian's penthouse.

She had no idea why she'd come. She should be angry with

him for not telling her about Jamie. How long had he known? Days? Weeks?

With trembling fingers, she stabbed his passcode into the elevator's keypad and the car swept her up.

At his floor, the doors opened, and suddenly he loomed before her, tall and strong, his expression filled with concern. But rather than pepper him with questions, she just stood there, unable to speak or move or even breathe.

Why, when her world had bottomed out, did she run to him?

The truth assailed her. Because despite everything, he was the one she trusted. The only one. Only he could hold together all the pieces of her shattered heart.

The trembling in her hands spread to the rest of her body.

Tenderness slashed across his features, and without uttering a word, he tugged her to his chest.

"You knew." His T-shirt muffled her voice. "You knew Jamie was working for Moretti and you didn't tell me?"

"I did."

The pain knocked her back a step. "How long?"

His Adam's apple bobbed. "I recognized him the night he was shot."

Her anguish spilled over into her words. "Why didn't you tell me?"

"I gave him the choice to tell you himself. Either he could tell you today, or I would."

She clenched her fists at her sides, trying to stop their shaking. "Is that why you left without saying goodbye?"

He bent his head. "It is."

"Is that why you didn't call or text me yesterday?" Unspoken fears rose and snarled inside her. "Or are you in love with Corinne?"

His head snapped up. *"What?"*

"Are you?"

A savage light burned in his eyes when he captured her gaze.

"I am not in love with Corinne."

His tone left no room for debate, and the knot wringing her stomach eased a little. "But then...why?"

Agony twisted his expression. "I didn't want to lie to you, so I stayed away. I didn't tell you because...because I didn't want to hurt you."

She grasped at her anger, clawing and clutching for something to hold on to against the flood of her anguish. "You thought you were protecting me? Is that it?"

"Aye."

With his raspy whisper, her heart cleaved and cracked open. He tried, imperfectly and maybe a bit heavy-handedly, to stop, or at least slow, the pain from reaching her. So he'd lied.

She'd lied to him, too. But not to protect him. Like Jamie, she'd thought only to protect herself.

Shame heated her cheeks even as the merciful touch of understanding brushed her heart. When Moretti destroyed her family, her world had fallen apart, and instantly became a darker, scarier, far less kind place. She'd thrown up walls to protect herself from it.

At first, she did it to protect herself from the very real dangers and predators like Moretti. But soon, it became more than that.

She didn't date or sleep with men, and other than Simone, who she only met through work and because they were randomly assigned to the same cubicle, she had very few friends.

Her wall was well constructed. No one got through. Because she believed what she'd seen reflected on the faces of those who looked down on her. She believed those who thought she was less. Less deserving. Less worthy. Less worthwhile. Less lovable.

And because she believed them, she'd kept herself hidden and locked away. She couldn't risk anyone seeing her. The real Avery. Because if they did, then they'd realize she wasn't worthy.

Her wall had been impenetrable. Until she met Cian.

He'd once asked her why him, and finally, she knew the

answer. Since the night they met, she wanted him. She wanted him more than she feared he'd never want her.

But the fear had haunted her. It's why she wanted to pretend to be someone else the night they were together for the first time. She didn't want to be Avery, who was unworthy of affection. She wanted to be someone he might want.

And it's why she hadn't yet told him she was pregnant. Because she feared he couldn't possibly want her.

But fear wasn't a good enough excuse. It didn't justify her lies.

He may never love her, or fi her a worthy mother for his child, but none of that changed the fact she needed to be honest with him. He deserved to know the truth.

The knot in her stomach wrenched. She dragged in a shuddering breath and released it slowly. Then she opened her mouth to tell him the truth.

But before she could form the words on her tongue, she realized he wasn't listening to her. Instead, he'd turned his head and was watching the TV playing in the living room.

Avery followed the line of his sight and saw that the afternoon news program played. She read the chyron splashed across the local newsman's chest.

Explosive accusations about area businessman Manny Moretti

Her world tilted.

Images of a Daily Sun tabloid appeared in a window next to the reporter's head with the salacious headline about Moretti and Avery's name plastered in the byline.

Her shock slid into a dark satisfaction as the reporter summarized the article she'd written. All her hard work detailing Moretti's criminal schemes was now out there for the entire world to see. She'd exposed him, finally.

But her satisfaction was short-lived as an icy terror gripped her.

She'd exposed him, and he'd know she had done it.

CHAPTER 41

*A*very Bishop—her name was right there on the TV—had just poked the sociopathic bear that was Manny Moretti.

Air wheezed through her suddenly tight chest cavity.

As she stood staring at the television, her mouth was filling with sand and dread, Rory emerged from the hallway and sauntered by on his way to the kitchen.

He cut a glance at the TV, then halted his steps.

Wordlessly, all three of them watched until the segment ended.

When the program broke for a commercial, Cian's head snapped around, and vivid panic glittered in his eyes when he looked at his brother. "I need your help."

Wary alarm stole over Rory's features. "What do you want me to do?"

"I have to leave or I'm going to miss my flight." His gaze flickered over to her, then away. "Do not let her leave the penthouse."

Air flooded her lungs when she gasped. "Oh, no, I—"

"Don't let her out of your sight." He raised his voice to drown out her protests. "Not for one second. Not until I get back."

Rory's jaw hung slack. "You can't be serious."

"I am."

A flash of fear streaked across Rory's features. "Did you forget everything that happened with Brynn? Tell me you haven't forgotten that." His panic growing, he gave his head a hard shake. "I'm no bodyguard."

Misery tightened the knot in Avery's stomach. "Cian, he isn't comfortable—"

Piercing green eyes slammed into her. "Do not fight me on this."

"No, she's right." Rory's face took on a queasy pallor. "You can't leave her with me."

With a scowl as hard as granite, Cian pondered his brother for a moment. "I know you think you failed to protect Brynn, but you're wrong. She's alive, and she's well, and you had a lot to do with that. I trust you with my life." His voice dropped with the gravity in his tone. "Take care of her."

She stood helplessly by as Cian quickly collected his bag and personal items, then with long, harried strides, moved to the doors where Avery remained frozen, caught by the tangle of shock and fear and guilt coursing through her.

He stood close enough that she could feel his warmth. "I should be back in two days."

"Should be?" Ripples of panic chased up her spine. "You don't know?"

Instead of an answer, he swooped down and claimed her mouth in a fierce, desperate kiss that left her lips burning.

"I'll explain everything when I get back." His gaze shifted to Rory, and they shared a look that conveyed an entire conversation without either uttering a single word.

Then he was gone.

She brushed her fingertips over her lips, as though she might caress the memory of his kiss.

Into the silence, she asked, "What are we going to do?"

Rory plopped onto the couch and scooped the video game controller off the coffee table. "There's beer in the fridge, or maybe some food. Take whatever you want."

Soon, sound effects from the video game filled the suite.

Annoyance skittered along her rapidly fraying nerves. "You can't seriously think you're going to hold me hostage for the next forty-eight hours."

"Gosh, no. But I couldn't tell him that." He plunked his bare feet onto the coffee table. "Between you and me, you're on your own."

"Oh." Doubt stabbed at her. It was obvious Rory wanted nothing to do with any of this, and the obvious terror any talk of Moretti brought to his eyes riddled her with guilt. "So...should I leave?"

His attention riveted to the TV. "Where are you gonna go?"

The thought of departing the safety of the penthouse sent a fresh wave of fear rushing through her. If Moretti wanted to find her, she had no doubt he could do so, and quickly. What would he do to her? Threaten her to scare her off writing any more stories?

Or something worse? Something not designed to stop her from investigating him further, but to punish her for the trouble she'd already caused him?

Her wildest imaginings couldn't frighten her more than the panic and fear she saw in Cian's eyes. They'd found themselves in some dangerous spots the past few weeks and she'd never seen him so afraid.

She recalled the man in the alley who'd aroused Moretti's ire and what would've happened to him if she hadn't panicked and dropped her cell phone.

Helplessness lashed at her. "I don't know, but are we really just supposed to sit here and wait? Or should we do *something*?"

"Sit here." With his thumb, he executed a series of sharp jabs against the controller. "We should definitely sit here."

She flung her body into an armchair. "There has to be something we can do to help Cian," she muttered.

His gaze swung to her, sudden and exacting. "You just called out Manny Moretti to the entire city. He is by far the most vindictive, sadistic son of a bitch I've ever met, and he knows your name. Just what do you think you can do in this moment to improve your situation?" When she provided no answer, he nodded. "Exactly." He resumed his game. "Hide. If you really want to help my brother, sit tight until he comes home."

She hated that answer. But more than that, she hated to admit he was right.

Beeps and bleeps from the TV were the only sounds inside the penthouse as he clutched the game controller with his stiff, crooked fingers.

With a sigh of resignation, she pushed up from the chair and joined him on the couch. "Do you have another controller?"

THE FLIGHT ATTENDANT delivered a fresh drink to Cian's tray.

Since the outcome of the fight was rigged, he had zero incentive to stay sober, or even pretend to prep for the match. It didn't matter if he hydrated, or meditated, or did his visualizations. What food he ate leading up to the bout would have no impact on the outcome of this fight.

Before the attendant walked away, he'd already tossed back the whiskey. The liquid burned a path from his throat to his chest, but it did nothing to calm the storm whipping through him.

Moretti knew her name. He knew she'd been hunting him.

She was in danger, and Cian couldn't be there to protect her.

He'd gotten Kendrick on the phone and demanded protection for her, but then he'd boarded his flight and had no clue if they'd had time to put any safeguards into place.

He told himself he had no choice. That fastest way to stop Moretti was to carry out the plan and let the FBI arrest him before he could do anything to hurt Avery.

By the time his plane touched down, he was well and truly drunk. Which didn't make journeying to his hotel easy.

The world of Las Vegas assaulted him. Glaring sunlight burned his eyes, and he shoved on a pair of sunglasses. Heat radiated off the pavement until a slick sheen of moisture covered his skin. Traffic, noise, the crowded hotel lobby, and the adjacent casino's slot machines pummeled his senses.

He kept his sunglasses on as he rode the elevator up to his room, and when he stepped inside the quiet suite, he closed the door behind him, leaned against it, and shut his eyes.

The sharp rap on the door startled him. He yanked off his sunglasses and spun around to peer through the peephole.

A man dressed in the hotel's uniform wearing a name tag that said "Sam" rocked back and forth lightly on his heels.

When Cian opened the door, a wide smile split the man's face. "Mr. Nolan?"

"What do you want?" Wariness infected his tone.

Sam handed over a plain brown package. "This arrived for you earlier today. Sorry we missed you at check in."

Slowly, Cian reached out and took the envelope.

"Have a pleasant stay," Sam said, then retreated down the hall.

Cian shoved the door shut and dragged the swing bar into place. He ripped open the package and dumped the contents onto the bed. For a moment, he stared down at the small black cell phone on the hotel's pristine white comforter. Then it started to vibrate.

With a soul-weary sigh, he accepted the call.

"Cian." Kendrick's gruff voice crackled over the line. "Ah, good. You're in Vegas."

Cian pinched the bridge of his nose with two fingers. "I'm here."

"Let's go over what happens tomorrow."

Cian made a noise in his throat, which Kendrick took for his agreement.

"You go down in the third, collect payment from Moretti afterwards, and that's when we'll move in and make the arrests. They'll have to bring you in as well, but I'll get you out as soon as I can. You ready?"

Though he'd been waiting, wishing for this moment for months, a kick of nervous tension moved his feet under him, and he paced the hotel room. "More than ready. This time, keep him behind bars, will ya?"

A snort escaped Kendrick. "That's the plan."

"And if it doesn't work? Again?"

The silence on the other end of the line was deafening.

"If this doesn't work, what's the plan?" Panic grabbed him by the throat. "How will you stop Moretti before he goes after Avery?"

"We can protect her, and you." After a beat, Kendrick added, "But you'll need to be vigilant."

Abruptly, Cian stopped pacing. "You mean we'll be looking over our shoulders for the rest of our lives?"

"Possibly."

It wasn't anything Cian didn't already know. Still, hearing it from Kendrick brought the gravity of their situation screaming home. His feet grew roots in the carpet.

"Look, I won't sugarcoat things," Kendrick said. "You know what we're dealing with here. But you've given us a ton to work with, and we just picked up another informant, so I like our chances this time."

"Another informant?" Surprise cleared a sweeping path through Cian's frantic thoughts. "When did this happen?"

"This morning. One of Moretti's soldiers walked into our offices, ready to talk. With the work you've done and this guy's information, I feel confident we'll get him."

Cian rubbed a hand over his head. "Do I know him?"

"I don't know. Some kid named Jamie. He's only been working with Moretti a short time, but he has information we can definitely use."

Well, holy damn. The little punk did the right thing. For once.

"You've done good work, Nolan. If you decide to stick around—"

"I won't. After tomorrow, I'm done." Cian shuffled over to the hotel minibar.

"I understand."

With shaking hands, he cracked open a miniature bottle of whiskey. "Just get the bastard this time."

"We'll do everything we can."

Cian arrived drunk to the weigh in, and during the press conference that followed, he refused to speak, pretending he was too focused on the fight to engage in chitchat, and not completely bollocksed.

At one time, a Las Vegas matchup was his dream. Only the biggest brawls with the best fighters happened in Vegas. Before cancer, he'd been on track to earn the honors.

Now, the whole thing tasted like a bitter swill in his mouth. He took no joy in it and rather than relish the spectacle, resentment slithered through him.

Back in his hotel room, he experienced a fleeting thought that maybe he should sober up before the morning, so he ordered room service.

But when they delivered his dinner, they'd included a complimentary dessert.

A chocolate cupcake.

The sight of it slammed into his chest and he stumbled back, away from the food tray, until he bumped up against the bed and plopped down hard on the mattress.

He stared at the frosted sweet treat while his heart gasped

inside his chest. Not with grief, but something else. Something soft and sweet, and completely overwhelming to his senses.

Love.

The realization washed over him.

He loved her.

It hurt like hell, but there it was. The truth.

He loved Avery.

And he had for…ever.

Like a true warrior, he'd fought it until the very end, telling himself he couldn't love her because of Moretti, and because of the danger she'd be in, and because of cancer. Because… because….

Because he didn't want to love her.

He didn't want to love and lose. Or be lost. He couldn't love someone and watch them mourn his inevitable death. Not again.

So he'd resisted.

Why?

Because love is so very much like grief, and he couldn't take it anymore. He wasn't strong enough.

He wanted to hear her voice, but he wasn't strong or sober enough for that either. How was he supposed to bear it when she was scared and he couldn't be there for her?

But he needed to know she was okay, so he fumbled for his phone, and with clumsy hands typed a text to her. *How are you?*

Her response came immediately. *I'm with Rory. I'm safe. How are you?*

He was awful. Terrible. He was in love, for God's sake.

I miss you. Through the turbulence and chaos of his mind, that truth emerged.

I miss you too, came her reply.

He left his meal untouched and emptied the mini bar instead.

But his last thought before he passed out was a hopeful one. At least he didn't have to throw the match. He'd lose it the honest way—by sucking and getting his ass kicked.

Should be fun.

CHAPTER 42

Video games provided enough distraction to get her through the next several hours. Near midnight, her cell phone chimed.

Her heart squeezed to find a text from Cian waiting for her, and the vice only clamped harder when he told her he missed her. She struggled to remain impassive in front of Rory when she replied she missed him, too.

No more texts came after that, and soon, she and Rory headed down the hallway.

While Rory disappeared into his bedroom, shutting the door behind him, she slipped inside Cian's room. She shucked her clothes and crawled into his empty bed. The ghost of his scent lived in the crisp sheets, and she inhaled deeply.

She dozed when the soft vibration of her cell phone woke her.

In the dark, she fumbled for the device on the nightstand and squinted at the display screen. Surprise at the number burned away her drowsiness.

"Sorry it's so late." Sasha's voice sounded strained on the other end of the connection. "But can I crash at your place tonight? I don't have anywhere else to go."

Even through the hazy of her tiredness, Avery picked up on the edge in Sasha's words. "Is everything okay?"

"Yeah, everything's fine." A beat of hesitation followed, and then, "There's this creep that won't leave me alone. He's kind of freaking me out. But if it's not okay—"

"No, no. Sorry. It's just..." Avery smoothed the flat of her palm across her forehead, trying to clear the cobwebs of slumber. "I'm not at my place right now. I'm staying with a friend tonight."

"Oh, okay then—"

"No, wait, don't hang up." Clunky thoughts tumbled through Avery's brain.

She couldn't leave the penthouse to return home and let Sasha into her apartment. It was too dangerous. But neither could she let Sasha freeze outside alone all night. She remembered, not so long ago, the anxiety she felt on those nights when she had no safe place to stay.

What harm could there be in letting her crash on Cian's couch?

"Why don't you come here?" Avery said. "Let me give you the address."

Sasha's relieved sigh rattled through the phone's speaker. "Thanks."

Avery gave Sasha the address to Cian's penthouse. "Text me when you get here, and I'll come downstairs to meet you."

They disconnected, and Avery lazed in bed a few minutes before reluctantly leaving the warm cocoon to get dressed. She tugged on her jeans, and after an internal debate, put on her bra in case she encountered the gatekeeper, Henry, in the lobby.

She curled up on the bed to wait, and her cell phone vibrated sometime later, pulling her from a light slumber.

I'm here, Sasha's text read.

Avery climbed out from under the covers and padded quietly down the hallway. She tugged on her boots, then rode the elevator downstairs to the lobby. When the doors slid open, she poked her head out to signal to Sasha.

But Sasha wasn't within view of the elevators.

With a stab of uneasiness, Avery stepped out of the elevator, holding the door with her hand while she searched the lobby for Sasha. But there was no sign of her.

Apprehension rushed through her when she left the elevator behind and crept further into the lobby. Where was she?

At his post behind the front desk, Henry chatted on the phone. Had he barred Sasha from entering the building, too?

Avery walked to the windows across the front of the building and peered outside into the darkness. She pushed open the door and stuck her head out into the chilly air.

At one end of the building's covered driveway, a luxury sedan idled at the curb.

The backseat window lowered, and Sasha's face appeared.

Taking a small step outside, Avery waved at her. But her arm froze midair.

Sasha's face appeared white with fear.

Avery's heart stuttered.

"Look out—!" Sasha yelled.

From inside the car, a hand clamped over her mouth.

Avery twisted around to dash back inside the building, but just then, a large man shot from the shadows.

A scream piled in her throat, but she never made a sound before his meaty fist crashed into her jaw.

Pain exploded inside her skull, and the world went dark.

CIAN CRACKED open one eye and groaned when a hammer of pain pounded against his skull. When he crawled from the bed, his weak muscles ached and his gut churned with nausea. A hot shower did little to ease the pain or settle his queasy stomach.

He regretted all his choices.

For the rest of the day, he consumed fluids and worked at eating some food that he could keep down at the hotel restaurant, and when he arrived at the arena late that afternoon, he'd recovered enough that he felt somewhat certain he wouldn't vomit during the match.

He didn't bother going through his pre-fight routine, but he'd left his phone at the hotel and had nothing to occupy his mind, so he sat on a hard bench in the locker room with a towel draped over his head, trying to focus on the task ahead.

When the staff came to let him know it was time for the match to begin, he hoisted his exhausted body off the bench and made his way on heavy legs through the long hallway. Noise from the sizeable crowd gathered in the arena started as a soft drone and intensified as he neared the mouth of the tunnel.

Security held him up there to coordinate the timing of his entrance with the production team.

While he waited, the crowd's energy pumped through the facility and seeped into his bones. He bounced on his feet as a jolt of adrenaline surged through him.

Damn, but he used to love this. This moment, right before every fight, lit up his body and blood with anticipation. With energy. With the chance to take his best shot at his opponent and receive the other man's best in return.

But just then, he detected a movement out of the corner of his eye, and Moretti slithered up beside him.

Adrenaline morphed into fury.

A loud voice boomed over the arena's PA system, announcing the start of the fight.

Moretti surveyed the arena's massive crowd. "Good turnout. You better not mess this up."

With his jaw clenched, Cian stared straight ahead as the announcer introduced his opponent.

He felt Moretti's eyes on him, watching, assessing. "In case you need a little help this time, I brought along a reminder for you."

Alarm screamed through Cian, and he whipped his head around. "What are you talking about?"

Moretti made a sweeping gesture with his hand, and Cian's gaze traveled in the direction he motioned.

Over the packed crowd, the arena lights pulsed and swirled in time to the thumping music. Cian peered through the commotion and there, standing in the front row, he spotted the goddamned Baby Assassin grinning back at him.

At the signal from Moretti, Derek said something to the woman seated next to him. She pushed to her feet, and he yanked off her baseball hat, revealing her chin length dark brown hair.

Cian's gut clenched. *No. Please, no.*

Slowly, the woman turned, bringing her face into the light.

Avery stared at him with huge, fear-filled eyes. Her lips moved. *I'm sorry.*

Cian reared back, then made a vicious lunge at Moretti. He drew up at the last moment. "You lay one hand on her and you're a dead man," he rasped, his voice shaking slightly.

Triumph gleamed in Moretti's eyes. Finally, he'd found it—Cian's weakness.

Chuckling, Moretti held up both hands. "You have nothing to worry about. As long as you play by the rules, nothing will happen to her."

The music switched from a gritty rap tune to the driving beat of a rollicking Irish rock song, and the security guards led Cian from the tunnel.

Memories of Brynn's haunted eyes and Rory's mangled hand stalked Cian as the guards ushered him down the aisle toward the main stage and into the cage.

He raised his arm against the glare of the bright lights and peered into the crowd, desperate to find her. When he located her in the front row, she was now positioned between Moretti and Derek.

He'd never seen her so scared.

Fear and adrenaline obliterated his fatigue and illness.

When the referee pulled him and the other fighter into the center of the cage, Cian looked his opponent in the eyes when they knocked gloves, then the ref sent them to opposite corners. While his opponent danced around, Cian closed his eyes and envisioned the only thing that mattered.

Avery. Safe.

The ref asked the fighters if they were ready and when they'd both answered that they were, he clapped his hands together and the fight began.

The men circled each other, then took turns probing and retreating. The crowd lit up with every flash of movement they made, and the first round erupted into a series of sharp strikes and desperate dodges.

The moment the round ended, Cian peered through the crowd, chest heaving, until his gaze landed on Avery. She looked pale as her gaze bounced between Moretti and Derek, who appeared locked in a heated exchange.

The farce of a fight resumed, and both fighters did their part in the second round to make the battle appear legit, delivering hard blows and standing in to take their hits.

When the referee separated them, Cian's body ached from the kicks and punches he'd taken. He sucked down water, then found and held Avery's frightened gaze, willing her to hold on a little longer.

On either side of her, the disagreement between Moretti and the Baby Assassin escalated when Moretti made a comment that Derek visibly reacted to. His spine straightened, and he shifted in his seat to shout something in response.

Time to end this.

The third and final round began, and the other fighter moved in with a choreographed series of moves that Cian could've easily dodged. Instead, he let his opponent's driving fist slip through his gloves and stood there like a fool when the punch connected with his jaw.

Rather than stumble and try to remain on his feet, he crashed to the mat with a dramatic nosedive.

All he had to do was stay down and wait for the ref to call the count.

But he slitted open one eye.

Derek rove to his feet. He loomed over Avery as he shouted at Moretti.

Cian's body tensed and he lifted his head a fraction, unable to control the instinct.

An eternity passed while the ref counted off the seconds.

Every muscle in Cian's body coiled. Then the Baby Assassin's arm shot out and, though he may have been aiming for Moretti, his fist caught the side of Avery's head.

Cian exploded off the mat.

The ref stopped his count with three seconds left to go. With no thought of the consequences, Cian charged at the cage door.

In his path, his opponent's victory smile collapsed. "What are you doing?"

The man remained in his way, so Cian hauled his arm back and laid the other fighter out with one vicious strike.

The man dropped like a brick, landing hard on the mat, his mouth slack.

Cheering and chaos erupted, but Cian bounded over the man's prone body and plunged into the crowd.

He didn't care that Moretti would be out for his blood after this. Or that he compromised the mission. Or that Moretti would likely skate free again.

The only thing that mattered was Avery.

CHAPTER 43

Avery hit the floor with a jarring thud. Her head ached from the man's powerful fist, and she gave it a slow shake.

She pushed up onto her hands and knees. Beneath her, the concrete floor grew slick with—she blinked—was that blood? Droplets of bright red blood fell like raindrops in front of her.

Her kidnapper had threatened her with a knife he'd hidden in his clothing. Had he stabbed her? Adrenaline must have stopped her from feeling the wound. Where was the blood coming from? Was the baby all right? A protective instinct she h she possessed screamed inside her.

Mayhem erupted in the building. The crowd's thunderous roar throbbed in her ears. Feet pounded the concrete all around her.

On her hands and knees, she crawled toward the cage, wishing to get away from Moretti and the knife-wielding man. The screams and shouts around her seemed to swell.

Then two hands clamped down on her shoulders and her world tilted. With a dizzying swoop, she landed on her feet.

Cian, tall, dark, and fierce, filled her vision.

With a cry, she threw her whole body into him, and his solid arms clamped around her. She clutched him tight, plastering herself against his bare chest while the chaos and noise whipped around them.

Over his shoulder, her kidnapper fled up the aisle. Bodies pushed and shoved them as panic spread through the crowd.

When a surging mass of fleeing spectators rammed into them, they pitched forward, and she stumbled over someone lying on the floor. Fearing the fallen person would be trampled by the crowd, she reached down to help them stand.

And looked right into the face of Manny Moretti.

Blood leaked from his neck, soaking his crisp white dress shirt in crimson red. He stared up at her with a cold, blank expression.

Lifeless.

The crowd heaved around her while she stared down at Manny's dead body.

Blindly, she reached for Cian, and he steadied her. Then he was pulling her away from Moretti.

They joined the mass exodus of spectators now clogging the arena aisles. The sound of the crowd's growing fear echoed in the rafters. Trapped amidst the panicking hordes, icy terror gripped Avery's chest.

Then, over the chaos and noise, a strange, melodic whistle pricked her ears.

Cian wrenched his head in the sound's direction.

"What was that?" she asked.

"The family whistle." He grasped her hand inside his large palm. "This way."

With her hand clasped firmly inside his, he pushed through the crowd, and they scurried across a long row of seats. Ahead of them, a man in a black hoodie made the same cut through to the other side of the arena, and they followed him into the tunnel where Cian had entered before the fight.

With room to run, they charged down the tunnel and burst into the wide corridor.

Abruptly, Cian stopped, tugging her to a halt with him. "Where are you hurt?" His voice filled with terror as he tore off his gloves and tossed them aside. His shaking hands moved frantically over her body. "Are you hurt? Do you feel pain anywhere?"

"I'm okay." She caught his questing hands. "I'm not hurt."

A fresh shockwave crashed over Avery and the image of Moretti lying motionless on the arena floor flashed through her mind.

Cian peered closely into her face. Then he tugged her against his chest and clutched her tight to him, as though she might drift away if he let go.

"What happened?" His breaths came in sharp puffs of air that rustled through her hair. "How did Moretti get to you? What did they do to you?"

"Th-they tricked me." Memories from the past several hours pummeled her.

The man snatching her off the sidewalk in front of the penthouse, waking to discover he'd taken her to Moretti, Manny threatening to slit Sasha's throat if she uttered a word to anyone, then kicking her out of the moving vehicle, the flight on a chartered plane, and their arrival at the arena. The fear, the terror, the rage. All of it crashed over her now.

Cian pulled back and cupped her face with both of his hands. "Avery, did they hurt you?" His voice rasped with emotion.

She shook her head. "Nothing that won't heal."

His eyes searched hers, frantic with his desperate need to know she was safe.

"The big guy, he h-hit me, but Moretti stopped him." Her voice shook with the memory of those terrifying moments. "He said after the fight, he could do whatever he wanted, but he had to wait."

Cian closed his eyes and sucked in a deep breath.

"He was using me to control you. After that…," she swallowed with difficulty. "I don't know what would've happened."

Pain contorted his features, and she trailed her fingers down the sides of his precious face.

When he opened his eyes, fierce green pierced her. "You're okay now?"

Her throat squeezed. "I'm okay."

"You promise me?"

"I promise."

His shoulders sagged, and the tension seemed to drain from him in a rush.

Emotions suddenly swamped her, and an odd noise squeaked through her throat's narrowing passageway.

"Hey," he said softly. "It's gonna be okay now. It's over."

She covered her face with one hand, and a sob escaped. "It's not okay. I never cry."

He dropped his head, and his mouth brushed the side of her neck. "I think I might cry too. We'll do it together."

Her watery laugh bubbled up, and she pulled her hand away from her face. "God, I hate Vegas. Only Vegas could make me cry."

Another whistle split the air, and they turned their heads. Standing at the end of the long corridor, the man in the black hoodie twisted around and pushed deeper into the arena's interior.

They followed him, running to keep up with the pace he set. Though her breaths came hard, they raced to catch up to him.

When the crowd noise had faded, he slowed up a little.

"Well, that didn't go as planned." Rory craned his neck to glance back at them.

She stumbled with the jolt of her surprise. "What are you doing here?"

"I woke up, and you were gone." Panting, he jerked his thumb at her, and then at Cian. "And when you wouldn't answer your phone, I had no other way to warn you something might be wrong. But holy shit—what the hell happened back there? Is Moretti…?"

"He's dead." Astonishment roped around Cian's words.

A colorful curse burst out of Rory. "How?"

"DeMarco had a knife." Cian's mouth pulled into a grim line. "Went right at him."

Avery shuddered with the disjointed memories. "He was mad at Moretti, and they were arguing, and the next thing I knew, he… lunged."

"That is so messed up." The hood of Rory's sweatshirt slipped off his head when he made a sudden turn and yanked open a metal door.

They scrambled across the arena's loading dock landing and banged through another door.

The cool night air proclaimed their freedom. They scurried along the massive building's exterior wall, then rounded the corner and sprinted toward the adjacent parking structure.

People were streaming out of the arena and pouring into the streets surrounding the facility and they snaked between them, through the garage, and down a long row of cars before Rory slowed and drew up at a black sedan.

Her lungs aching, Avery placed her hands on his knees and sucked in gulps of oxygen.

"The cops gotta be swarming the place by now." Rory glanced around as he fished in his pockets for the car keys. "They probably want to talk to both of you. They might stop us if we try to drive out of here."

"Let's see if anyone stops us." Cian's bare chest heaved with his breathing. "I'll call Agent Kendrick as soon as we get to the hotel."

Avery's spine snapped straight. "*Agent* Kendrick? Who is that?"

Cian stiffened, but then his shoulders relaxed. "He's an FBI agent."

"And you know him how? Are you…?" Her jaw dropped.

He showed her his palms. "I am not law enforcement."

"Then what the hell are you?" she demanded.

He lifted his shoulders in a semi-shrug. "For the past few months—" He looked at Rory. "—has it been a year?"

"Not quite a year."

He turned back to her. "I've been working with the FBI, telling them whatever I learned about Moretti and his criminal activities."

Shock hit her full force. "You're an informant?"

"*Was*," Cian corrected. "I *was* an informant."

Several heartbeats passed while her mind fit together all the puzzle pieces laid out before her since she'd met him. Suddenly, it all made sense.

Her heart crowed with delight. "I *knew* it! I knew you weren't a bad guy." She smacked his arm. "Why didn't you tell me?"

He captured her hand and tugged her to him. "I couldn't put you in even more danger by telling you." His lips brushed her forehead. "I'm sorry."

The car lights blinked when Rory unlocked the doors.

He pulled open the driver's side door, then his gaze swept over Cian's bare torso and bright blue shorts. "This car doesn't have tinted windows. If you don't want to be seen, you'll have to duck in the backseat or something."

A slow smile tipped up one corner of Cian's mouth. "I have a better idea."

Cian walked around to the car trunk and, arching one eyebrow at her, popped the lid.

Her laughter still rang in her heart when she kissed him, then climbed inside the trunk.

God, how she loved this man.

Rory appeared at the end of the vehicle and peered down at her. "What the hell is this?"

"Never mind." Cian slipped into the trunk behind her. Reaching up, he grasped the lid. "Just get us out of here."

Then he yanked the trunk lid closed, locking them in darkness.

This time, she rolled to her side, facing him. He slung his arm around her and dropped a kiss near her temple.

In her chest, her heart ached with joy at his nearness. But the nagging fear poked holes in the bliss-filled bubble encircling her.

After the relief of surviving Moretti's diabolical schemes had passed, and once she told him about the baby, how would his feelings change?

She buried her face in his neck.

He hugged her close. "I don't know what I would've done if anything had happened to you."

She inhaled deeply, taking in his manly scent as she braced for what would come next. In the cover of darkness, she opened her mouth.

"I'm pregnant." She burst out with the truth at the exact moment he said, "I love you."

"Wait, what?" they said together.

"Did you say *pregnant?*" Shock filled his voice.

"I wanted to tell you sooner, but then everything happened with Jamie and Vegas and…. I'm sorry. I should've told you when I first found out. But I was scared, and…"

"Pregnant? Are you sure?" Shock slid into disbelief.

"I took three tests. You can see for yourself."

"I believe you, it's just…"

"No, really, I'm gonna need you to look at those tests. Maybe I did something wrong?"

"How could you mess it up?"

"What if I misread the instructions? I think I should take another test. In case the others were false positives."

"All three of them?"

"It's possible, isn't it?" She pulled her bottom lip between her teeth.

"I doubt it." He smoothed his hand down, then back up her spine. "But…how?"

She hitched her shoulder. "I guess you're not sterile."

In retrospect, she shouldn't have told him in the dark when she couldn't see his face or read his expression. Beneath her palm, his heart slammed against his breastbone.

He inhaled and expelled a shuddering breath. "Are you sure it's mine?"

"I should be pissed you asked me that."

"I'm sorry. It's just…" His voice rasped with emotion. "I thought it wasn't possible for me."

"It's okay. I get it. Yes, it's yours. There hasn't been anyone else. Ever." The thunderous walloping of his heart seemed to ricochet up her arm. "I guess the doctors were wrong."

He bit off a sharp curse. "How can they be wrong about something like that?"

"If I were you, I'd ask some questions."

The beat of his stunned silence stretched out.

She curled her fingers into her fist. "I don't need anything from you. I just thought you'd want to know."

He clamped his arm tight around her, pulling her close against his chest, and his rusty, wondrous laugh rumbled in her ear. "You might not need anything from me, but you're about to get all you can handle."

"Cian, it's okay." She tipped her head back. "I realize I'm not someone you would've chosen to be tied to forever."

"Are you serious?" He took her face in both his hands and the pads of his thumbs brushed over her cheeks, her mouth, her eyes, as though feeling her expression. "You're everything I've ever wanted and more. If I'd ordered up a woman to tie myself to forever, she wouldn't be half what you are because I never could've imagined someone so perfect for me. Didn't you hear what I said? I love you, Avery."

Her heart leapt to her throat. Oh, how she wanted to believe it was true. But… "Why?"

"There are a thousand reasons." Warm tenderness caressed his words. "You're gorgeous and smart. Loyal, and so fucking relentless. You're not just a fighter. You're a warrior."

A small, tentative smile touched her lips. "There's a difference?"

"Oh, aye, there is. Fighters are strong. They throw punches and can take a hit. But they fight because there's a battle that needs to be fought." He toyed with the silky strands of hair at her temple. "Warriors fight for a cause."

"What cause?" she whispered. "Justice?"

"Nah. Warriors fight for love."

"Love?" She reached up and smoothed her hand over his clipped hair. "Are you okay? Did you get hit on the head?"

"Things are finally making sense." He tucked her hair behind one ear, then explored the curvature of her bone and earlobe with his fingertips. "Love is the reason a warrior fights. It's why we breathe and bleed. We do it for the people and the places we love. Because we must." His mouth found hers in the dark. "Because without them, we're nothing. Love is the most important thing. It's the only thing." His voice dropped to a husky whisper. "It is everything."

His lips touched hers in the dark and years of doubt and insecurity melted like cotton candy in the rain, dissolved by the warmth and sureness of his kiss and the steady, rapid beating of his heart. The past no longer mattered, and her heart filled with the possibility of a bright, beautiful future where Cian saw her and loved her exactly as she was.

She trailed her fingers down the side of his face and murmured against his mouth. "That's so romantic."

"It's not romantic. Love is hell. Why do you think I've been avoiding it for so long?"

"You've been avoiding love?"

He stole another kiss from her lips. "I've been avoiding loving you."

"I didn't know that…" More ridiculous tears trembled on her eyelashes. "I might be in love with you, too."

"Might be?" Beneath her fingertips, his smile spread, growing to match hers.

"Can neither confirm nor deny," they said at the same time.

"I tried to fight it," she whispered.

"Me too."

"But it's too strong."

He pressed his forehead against hers. "Brutal."

"You feel it too?"

"I feel it too." He nudged his nose against hers. "And I've been feeling it ever since the last time we were locked in a car trunk together. I didn't know what it was. Ever notice how much love feels like grief?"

"OMG, yes. It *hurts.*"

"Damn straight, I wanted to avoid that kind of pain. I'm a warrior, not a moron."

After all they'd been through the past week, she had no clue how her heart could be so light.

"Holy shit, we're having a baby." Suddenly, he let out a loud *whoo!* and jabbed the trunk lid with his fist. "Rory needs to let us out of here. We've got work to do."

"Work?" she asked, laughing.

"Tomorrow we'll probably be busy giving statements to the FBI, then we need to get back to Chicago so you can enroll for next semester, and we need to find a place to live and get ready for the baby." He nuzzled her ear. "And start planning the wedding."

"Wedding?" Her breath caught in her throat. "What wedding?"

"What's that tone? You don't want to marry me?"

The stab of age-old self-doubt pierced her heart. "I knew when you found out I was pregnant, you'd think you had to propose. I love you, but I won't be a burden to you. My answer is no."

"You think I'm asking out of some warped sense of obligation?"

"Aren't you?"

"Have you forgotten five fucking minutes ago when I told you I loved you *before* you told me you were pregnant?" He shook his head. "Damn, we gotta work on your attitude."

"You took on the freaking mob out of some strange sense of obligation to protect your family."

"No. I did it because I'm a warrior. I did it for love." He dipped his head, bringing his mouth wa mere whisper from her lips. "The same reason I want to marry you."

Her heart heaved. "I'm sorry. It's going to take some time to get used to all this."

"It's okay. I've got the rest of my life to convince you." A sudden gravity weighed down his words. "I don't know how many minutes or days or years I have left, but I want to spend every one of them loving you."

Then he kissed her, lingering, savoring, tantalizing her with the promise of a delicious, decadent future spent together.

"Say yes," he murmured against her mouth.

She released a dreamy sigh. "Eighty percent of marriages based on lies end in divorce within the first two years."

"Did you look it up?"

"Not yet. But I'm sure it must be a crazy high percentage."

"What lie? I didn't lie about Jamie, and you didn't lie about being pregnant. We were only waiting for the right moment to tell each other."

Though useless in the darkened trunk, she scowled at him. "You let me believe you were a mobster."

"I am sorry, *mo mhuirnín*. I couldn't tell you the truth." He brushed the pad of his thumb across her cheek. When he dropped a mollifying kiss on her lips, she felt the slow, smug smile that hooked up one corner of his mouth. "But you fell in love with me, anyway."

"What can I say? You're like a cupcake." She nibbled a small taste of his lips. "I can't resist you."

"Is that a yes?"

"Yes," she breathed. "I will marry you, Cian."

He smoothed his palm across her cheek and dropped a slow, shivery kiss on her mouth.

Curled up together in the darkness, his lips moved against hers when he murmured, "Now *this* is a fucking family."

EPILOGUE

A week before the Nolan family Christmas get-together, Christmas in Michigan shifted to Chicago and doubled as a homecoming celebration for Aiden and Brynn. After a year of living in fear and hiding from Moretti, they were now finally free to come home.

On the porch, Cian glanced through the large picture window of Aiden and Brynn's spacious Greystone, which appeared cramped with seven of the eight brothers, their wives, and a handful of rug rats running around the place.

Watching the utter chaos that awaited them, Cian's chest filled.

Avery ran a hand down the front of the dress and released a shaky breath.

"What's that then?" The kick of his fear landed squarely in the sternum. "Are you feeling okay?"

Her hand hovered over her abdomen. "Just a little nervous. You have a really big family."

"They're going to love you. Like I do." He pressed a kiss against her temple. "And they're not just my family. They're yours, too."

"Aw, that's so sweet."

"It's not sweet." He stabbed a finger at the picture window. "It's DNA."

She peered through the glass, and the moment her gaze found him, her pretty face brightened. "Jamie's here? But how?"

"I invited him."

Her surprise slid into a soft tenderness, then she rose on her tiptoes and dropped a kiss on his cheek. "Thank you."

He inhaled her sweet scent and laid his palm flat over her stomach. "Now that we told them about the wedding, should we tell them about this?"

"It's a little early. What if something goes wrong?"

"Nothing is going to go wrong."

She pulled her bottom lip between her teeth to hide her smile, then she nodded. "If it comes up, we can tell them."

Love squeezed his chest when he slipped his hand inside his coat and pulled out a thin box.

He pushed the front door open wide and swept inside. "Hey, everyone," he shouted over the din of noise and lifted the box of cigars above his head. "We're having a baby."

A loud cheer went up, and a sea of love and smiling faces rushed forward to engulf them. Cian handed every one of them a cigar before he turned to Avery.

Her cheeks flushed pink when she sagged against him. "I cannot believe you did that."

He pulled her close. "Sorry, it slipped out."

"You are such a liar," she said, a flicker of tender amusement in her voice.

"Maybe I am." He tugged her earlobe between his teeth. "Are you mad?"

"Mad? At you? That's impossible."

Led by Brynn, a bevy of women swallowed Avery inside their circle of excited chatter.

Jamie stepped forward to shake his hand. "You work fast."

With a wide grin, Cian balanced a cigar between his lips. "Took me twice as long to convince her to marry me."

A smirk touched one corner of Jamie's mouth. "Why am I not surprised?"

"She practically made me beg."

"She's a stubborn one." Jamie clapped him on the back. "Good luck with that."

Cian's smile widened as he gazed over at Avery. "She is stubborn, isn't she?"

Jamie rolled his eyes. "You two were made for each other, all right. Have fun driving yourselves crazy."

"That's the plan," Cian called after Jamie as he returned to his position between Leo and Jack in front of the TV where a football game played.

"Stubborn, huh?" Aiden arched one dark eyebrow at Cian. "Who else do I know like that?"

Cian hauled Aiden into a bear hug.

"Congratulations, man." Aiden pounded him on the back. "I didn't think it was possible there could be a woman out there willing to put up with you. Sounds like she's perfect for you."

"She's the toughest fighter I've ever gone up against." When Cian held out a cigar for Aiden, he winked. "It's sexy as hell."

"That is so messed up," Aiden muttered as he took the cigar.

A soft chuckle trickled out of Cian. "Aye, it is."

With a slight crinkle between his eyebrows, Aiden pondered Cian for a moment. "She makes you laugh."

Avery not only made him laugh, and she made him feel all kinds of things he thought he'd never feel again. He was dead when he met her, but she wouldn't let him rest. She fought like hell and damn if she didn't pull off the impossible and bring him back to life.

When the party had worn on for some time, Cian slipped up behind her. "You ready?"

She tipped her head to one side so that he could nuzzle the

hollow beneath her ear. "Are you sure you want to take a walk right now? It's freezing outside."

He took her hand and laced his fingers with hers. "There's something I want to show you."

Snowflakes floated lazily to earth as they set off down the quiet street.

"How far is it?" A puff of white air appeared with her words.

"Not far."

For several blocks, they enjoyed the homes decked out in bright lights and with Christmas trees illuminating their front windows.

When they turned onto a tranquil, tree-lined street, she squeezed his hand. "Oh, I know this neighborhood. There's a house I love on this street."

"Is there?" He injected a hitch of surprise into his voice. "Will you show it to me?"

They passed three more houses, and at the fourth, she pointed. "Here it is."

He stared up at the old, abandoned home with broken out windows, a crumbling roof, and a jungle of overgrown shrubbery hiding countless other horrors.

"You love *this* house?"

She laid her head on his shoulder. "It was so grand once."

He rested his cheek against her soft hair. "Maybe a long time ago. But not now."

A dreamy sigh escaped her. "I know. I still love it."

"I know you do." Her smile warmed his heart. "Did you know it's for sale?"

"I thought it was abandoned."

"The city owns it. There's a developer who wants to tear it down and put up an apartment building."

"Oh, that's too bad." She lifted her head.

"C'mon, let's get a closer look." Without waiting for her reply, he tugged her up the home's uneven walkway.

On the front porch, he gripped the doorknob and gave it a twist.

"What are you doing?" She shot a nervous glance over her shoulder. "Isn't this trespassing?"

When the door's lock barred them, he pulled a key from his pocket.

"What are you…?" She trailed off as he inserted the key in the lock and turned it.

A smile playing on his lips, he watched her face when he gave the door a shove and it swung open to reveal the decrepit, rundown two-story Victorian's interior, empty except for the Christmas tree propped up in the foyer and sparkling with warm gold twinkle lights.

"Oh, my…" She stared, her mouth hanging open. "Cian, what is happening?"

He handed her a paper roll tied with a bright red bow.

With difficulty, she pulled her gaze away from the Christmas tree. "What's this?"

"Open it."

She tugged on the bow, then unrolled the paper. As she read her name on the deed to the house, her hand shot to her mouth. Then her eyes flew to his face.

"Merry Christmas," he said softly.

"You bought me a house?" Her shock faded into wonder. "Cian, I…" Her gaze swept across the once-grand foyer, then clamped onto his face. "I got you a wallet."

With the pad of his thumb, he brushed the rounded curve of her cheek. "You gave me my life back."

"I can't beli." Tears shimmered in her dark eyes. "Thank you."

"You're welcome," he said, and sent up his own thanks to the Gods for allowing him to live this moment. "We won't be able to move in for a while yet. The place needs a little work."

"A little?" Turning in a slow circle, she smiled through her tears.

"I've already sent Brynn the home's plans, and she's working on some designs for us."

"There's no way I can afford to hire Brynn."

A pang of tenderness wrenched inside his chest. "She would never take your money."

"But she doesn't even know me. Why would she help me?" Sincere confusion puckered her brow.

"Because we're family." He had so much to teach her. "Besides, she needs this as much as we do. She's dying to work on an old house like this, and she, Aiden, and Noah's wife—do you remember Mina? She does this type of work too—anyway, they're striking out with their own company and need to establish a portfolio."

Shaking her head, Avery swiped away a tear that leaked from the corner of one eye. "This is… you are…," she sniffled, "…so incredible." Then her hand found his nape, and she pulled his head down to hers. "You, Cian Nolan, have made every one of my dreams come true."

Then, in the glow of the Christmas tree, she kissed him.

She tasted like cupcake frosting with sprinkles, and he couldn't wait to spend the rest of his life feasting on her. A satisfied hum vibrated in her throat.

Their kiss heated, and just when they'd gotten to the good part, she gasped, and they broke apart.

"*Omigosh*," she squealed. "I can't believe we have a house."

Like a child on Christmas morning, her joy showed on her face as she explored her present, inspecting the main floor and all four bedrooms on the second story. They talked and dreamed about what they wanted to do with the space until they could no longer bear the cold.

But before they left their home, she threw herself into his arms once again. "I love it. I love you. And I promise, we won't bring a single calendar or mirror into our home. Not ever."

"Oh, there's gonna be mirrors." He nuzzled her ear. "Lots and lots of mirrors."

When they returned to the family Christmas party, Rory came through the front door just as they climbed the porch steps.

"I forgot something in my car." Rory lifted his coat collar against the cold. "I'll be right back."

After giving him a quick hug, Avery slipped inside the warm house.

"You have a car?" Cian turned with Rory as he bounded off the porch.

"It's new," Rory called over his shoulder. "Want to see it?"

"Hell, yeah, I do."

Cian caught up with him a few steps before he pressed the button on his key fob and the lights flashed on the sleek red sports car parked on the street.

He let out a low whistle. "Nice ride."

"Thanks. You bought it for me."

Cian lifted one eyebrow. "How's that?"

"I placed a bet on your fight." Rory's grin was wider and brighter than anything Cian had seen on his brother's face in over a year. "Won a fortune."

"You knew I was supposed to lose that fight, didn't you?"

Rory's smile widened. "Of course."

After a beat of surprise, Cian's bark of laughter echoed through the quiet night. "Well, all right then. Nicely done."

Slowly, Rory's grin faded, and a shadow fell across his face. "I, uh, picked up something else while I was in Vegas."

"Oh, yeah? What's that?" Cian asked, ripples of his laughter lingering.

"A wife."

It was the absolute last thing he expected Rory to say.

He sucked in a breath and twisted toward his brother. "Are you serious?"

Rory held his gaze steady. "I am."

Tendrils of shock and disbelief lashed at Cian. "Do I know her?"

"I suspect you do."

"Who is she?"

With one hand, Rory gestured toward the house. Cian turned, and through the large picture window, he quickly picked out the dark-haired woman from his family.

Shock flew through him, and he whipped his head in Rory's direction. "You married her? Are you sure about this?"

The edges of Rory's expression hardened. "I'm sure."

Cian gaped at his little brother. "I didn't realize you two even knew each other."

"We don't. Or, we didn't."

Finally, Cian's baffled exasperation spilled over. "Do you know who she is?"

"I know." A hint of warning infected Rory's tone.

Undeterred, Cian pressed on. "Why in the fuck did you marry Moretti's daughter?"

Thank you so much for reading WARRIOR!

Next up in the Nolan Bastards series is Rory's story, KING. Sign up to hear when KING is available.

Want to read more now? Check out Aiden and Brynn's complete story in HER WICKED STEPBROTHER and SAINT. Or snag both books together in the Nolan Bastards Duet.

ALSO BY AMY OLLE

THE NOLAN BROTHERS

Beautiful Ruin

Sweetest Mistake

Dirty Play

Mad Love

Last Heartbreak

THE NOLAN BASTARDS

Her Wicked Stepbrother

Saint

Warrior

COLLECTIONS

A Nolan Bastards Duet

ABOUT THE AUTHOR

Amy Olle is a USA Today bestselling author of contemporary and new adult romance novels. She enjoys putting her psychology degrees to good use writing emotional, redemptive love stories filled with beautifully flawed characters, cozy settings, and delicious sexiness.

Amy is living happily ever after in Michigan with her college sweetheart, their brilliant son, and a turtle named George.

When she's not busy burning up the pages in her next novel, she loves to hear from her readers. You can email her at amy@ amyolle.com or contact her on social media.